In Pursuit of Perfect Timing

By

Erica Longdon

In Pursuit of Perfect Timing

First Edition (paperback)

ISBN 978-0-9928041-0-7

First published in Great Britain

Copyright © Erica Longdon 2015

The right of Erica Longdon to be identified as the author of this work has been asserted in accordance with the Copyright Designs and Patents Act 1988.

All the characters in this book are fictitious and any resemblance to actual persons, living or dead, is purely coincidental.

All rights reserved.
This book is sold subject to the condition that it shall not be, by way of trade or otherwise, be lent, re-sold, hired out or otherwise circulated without the publisher's prior consent in any form of binding or cover other than that in which it is published and without a similar condition including this condition being imposed on the subsequent purchase.

Printed by CreateSpace

Cover Design by
Leonie Bunch

ABOUT ERICA

Erica Longdon began working in television and radio in the 1970s heralding a career which spanned three decades. A major car crash in the eighties started her on an alternative path to holistic healing and energy work, and awakened her gifts as a healer and psychic. She now works and teaches as a psychic advisor on 12Listen.com, broadcasts her weekly radio show: Breakfast With Erica on 12Radio.com; has her own healing practice in Kent, England; and is the author of Starscopes, her monthly horoscopes, which are published internationally online via 12Listen and Xperience magazine, and also in Kent's *Verve* Magazine.

In Pursuit Of Perfect Timing is her début novel.

More about Erica
www.Angelhandsheal.com
www.facebook.com/AngelHandsHeal
www.twitter.com/Angelhandsheal

Her blog
www.angelhandsheal.blogspot.co.uk

To my daughter Leonie.
Believe in your unique talent and the
world will see you shine.

PREFACE

There is no *right or wrong* way to live. There is only love. Love is the ultimate four-letter word. So much can be sacrificed in its name. Often what we mistake as love is fear manifesting as jealousy, control, insecurity, infatuation, lack of self-fulfilment, or neediness.

As you follow Cheryl's journey, you may wish to jot down your thoughts about relationships, past and present. I have left a blank section at the back of the book for your notes.

Sometimes it is better to walk alone until we have learned our lessons and the timing is right. Time alone, learning to accept and love yourself, is time well spent which strengthens self and soul.

Love is you, not about you.

'Between what is said and not meant,
And what is meant and not said,
Most of love is lost.'

Kahlil Gibran

CHAPTER ONE

That damn girl! Cheryl James swatted the image to the back of her mind. It ricochet right back to continue taunting her all through the shift. Her usual easy-going nature bristled with irritation. The microphone pop shield in front of her stank of smoke: in fact, even worse, it reeked of stale smoker's breath. Bad enough on any day, today her tolerance levels at zero, it provoked lip-curling resentment. *Disgusting!* She leaned back to breathe in what slightly fresher air was available in the cramped confines of Channel 9's continuity announcer's booth with its grey carpet walls, thankful that two years before, in 2007, smoking in public places had been made illegal. She recalled her early days in broadcasting, back in the nineties, when it was commonplace to find a fag-end-filled ashtray on the narrow script bench and the circular foam pop shield a-drip with tar and stinking of nicotine. *Who the hell still smokes? None of the regulars. Must have been the freelance.*

'Standby, Cheryl, coming to you in fifteen.' The presentation director's alert into her headphones prompted her to gaze through the double-skinned soundproof glass to transmission, where Robin sat poised to take control of the next transition from commercials to programme. Cheryl straightened up, nodded her compliance and focused her concentration on the four lines of script in front of her. Just fourteen seconds of prime time to promote tomorrow's film and introduce tonight's. Her jaw tightened slightly. She consciously released it. This was no time to dwell on the row with Ross. She wasn't even sure if there had been anything between him and *that girl on the doorstep.*

'It's nothing', he'd said, 'a silly girl with a crush.' Could she believe him?

'In five,' said Robin's voice.

Inhale; release; focus; the red light flooded the booth, live to the nation on Saturday night prime time. For fourteen seconds everything must be excluded except those words in front of her. She felt her lips moving around her teeth, her eyes scanning slightly ahead of the words issuing from her mouth. The countdown clock on the computer in front of her was relentless; it would cut her off half a second before the end of the link. Breath still supporting her voice – pause for the comma – emphasize the title – and finish. Done. Perfect, and an hour and a half before the next announcement. Her own drama replayed.

*

Yesterday had been a bright crisp day in late October, her day of leisure before a demanding weekend of long night shifts. Despite two showers, the vapour of chlorine had been faintly about her skin from swimming with her oldest friend. Sheila was her ally and confidant from the days when both were new to the world of television, and before either of them committed to marriage and parenthood. Over coffee Sheila had attempted to persuade her to share in an hour of tarot-card reading. Someone Sheila knew was learning and wanted test cases. Cheryl had hedged, it wasn't her thing: Sheila was into all that. It might be fun, who knew? 'Maybe,' she'd said pushing the blueberry muffins in Sheila's direction.

*

'Do you fancy a cup of tea?' Robin enquired through her headphones.
'Oh, yes, great. I'll go and put the kettle on.'
The bright strip light in the tiny kitchen assaulted her eyes after the dimness of the booth. It reflected back off the chrome of the kettle giving no respite even when she looked down. A spotlight everywhere and no escape – was that a metaphor for yesterday? Perhaps she had tried to look the other way, to ignore what was obvious.

*

Yesterday had been so routine, so normal. When she had turned the key to enter the Victorian villa, her home with husband Ross, her twins Zoë and Tom, and their two cats, her mood had been buoyant. Uplifted by the exercise of swimming, good company, and the promise of her monthly lunch with her other dear friend Joanna on the horizon, Cheryl had flung her gym bag into the cupboard, her washing in the machine, and hummed her way into the large open kitchen in the garden extension, where Ross stood reading at the breakfast bar.
'Sorry I'm a bit late – Sheila and I got talking.'
His brief touch on her shoulder had felt welcoming: 'No problem, darling – hardly noticed the time – I've been going through next week's schedule.'

'I'll get dinner started. Are the twins doing homework?'

Allegedly they had been – although Cheryl suspected social media held more allure.

*

Now she poured the boiling water for Robin's tea, the steam rising just as it had from Ross's cup last night, the finale to a pleasant dinner. As she reached for the milk a vestige of steam caught her arm, bringing the hairs to attention.

*

Ross had seemed tense, despite his superficial affability. Perhaps he was worried about next week's shoot? The downside to being an award-winning director was the pressure to better that accolade. Whatever the matter, he was not prepared to reveal it and, after eighteen years of marriage, Cheryl knew that prying would elicit an irritable temper. She had busied herself with the laundry leaving him to cogitate in the lounge.

The doorbell had rung just after eight, and Cheryl had allowed Ross to answer it. He had pulled the solid oak door open just as she emerged from the utility room carrying an armful of freshly laundered white towels. She arrived behind him in the hall on her way to the bottom of the stairs – whatever they were selling, Ross could deal with it. She would not have halted her ascent of the stairs had she not heard the enquiry through the open door.

In Pursuit of Perfect Timing

'Is Rossman coming out to play tonight?'

Cheryl leaned back to see around the door. Young, skinny-jeaned and blonde (which looked like off-the-shelf tint and not the subtly blended mix Cheryl's hairdresser charged her dearly for), the girl squirmed seductively on the doorstep. *Cheap little tart* Cheryl's judgment screamed.

And then it happened. Ross replied as if he knew her. Cheryl distinctly heard him stammer. He was a confident speaker and rarely tripped up, never mind stammered. Time had frozen, and her heart with it. She recalled the snapshot; that instant suspended in a tableau.

*

Now in the Channel 9 kitchen, eyes closed, looking back as if detached from her body, watching a scene on TV, she reflected that no betting man would have given good odds on who looked most shocked: the girl on the doorstep when she saw Cheryl appear in the background; Cheryl, when she saw the girl and instantly and intuitively picked up the inference of the invitation on offer; or Ross, who uncharacteristically stammered his response that he was not available. The scene played back in slow motion.

*

'Oh, fine! I see.' Miss Skinny Jeans sounded both offended and disappointed. Her face was petulant until she noticed Cheryl leaning back to appear behind Ross.

Her expression changed as realization dawned. Now she looked furious.

In the seconds the girl stood there, Cheryl had continued to take in her appearance. The brittle blonde hair was scrunched and twisted up into a windswept knot. Her fashionably distressed jeans complemented the shabby and skin-tight T-shirt under her jacket. She was tiny, with the figure of a young teenager. Momentarily Cheryl had thought perhaps she was a friend of Zoë or Tom. One look at the girl's face, however, told a different story. Skinny Jeans and Cheryl locked eyes in mutual appraisal. This girl was tough; she showed none of the awkward body language of a teenager. Cheryl felt the animosity of that pair of steely blue eyes glaring their ice-shard hostility straight back at her. The shocking-pink glossy lips morphed from pout into a thin sour line, before the girl turned on her high heels and stomped back along the drive to a mini parked in the road.

Ross had stood with the door open long enough for Cheryl to hear the mini's engine revved unnecessarily hard and the squeal of tyres as it drove away. Time had resumed, catapulting forward into the moment. She recalled her heart pumping furiously as if to catch up with the beats it had missed. Her skin was clammy against the fluffy pile of towels in her arms. She could feel the diaphragm-constricted shortness of breath.

*

Recalling her discomfort she squashed the teabag against Robin's cup with unusual force and venom before flinging it into the waste bin.

*

'Who was that?' Cheryl had asked, staring straight into Ross's face as he turned from closing the door. Why wasn't he meeting her eyes as he brushed past into the living room? Was he buying himself time before he inevitably had to come up with an answer? To compound his seeming culpability it was the first and only time Cheryl had ever seen him blush – and he made up for the previous absence of such an outbreak by going puce. The colour was still evident in his cheeks when Cheryl, still carrying the armful of towels, rounded on him in the living room.

'Who was that?' she repeated. 'And what did she want?'

Somewhere deep down Cheryl knew what the girl had expected. She had assumed Ross would be alone. *Surely not? How could she be so brazen as to turn up on the doorstep? She must have known Ross was married. Unless ... unless he hadn't told her. No, not possible, he wears a ring. It can't be. But why else would she turn up like that?* Clutching the towels to her chest, a large part of Cheryl hadn't wanted to hear the answer. She scanned his face from eye to eye accusingly, waiting, hoping for some reasonable explanation that would dispel the sickening shock in her stomach. He had given her nothing, no visible sign.

'Oh her! She's just the sister of someone at work. I think she's got a bit of a crush on me. She's becoming a bit of a pest actually.' Ross waved his arm dismissively. 'Don't worry about her darling, it's nothing.'

Part of Cheryl's psyche was relieved to hear this. She released the towels a little. Oh, thank goodness. Yes, that's it. She's just a silly girl who fancies him. The other part of her wasn't fooled. *But why was he so embarrassed? And the girl had used a pet name for him: 'Is "Rossman" coming out to play, tonight?' By implication there had been other nights. And he blushed –, he actually blushed! Why would he do that if she was just a girl from work?*

*

Lingering in the Channel 9 kitchen, her body relived the sensations.

Her mouth went dry: her tongue seemed unable to detach from the roof of her mouth. The same sensation that last night had prevented her from being able to swallow, let alone speak.

*

For a brief terrifying moment she had thought she might asphyxiate. A sharp intake of breath through her nose somewhat loosened the noose. Shocked into inertia she stood in the middle of the status quo, the comfortable, stylish family home that was her life, unable to utter. Thoughts had risen up as spectres and vanished before they could be brought into articulate focus. Ross had further emphasized his disinterest in the whole event by sitting down and picking up the newspaper. She was being brushed off, excluded. Cheryl's instincts told her he was being evasive, *but without any further evidence what can I say?* Intuitively, she knew this had been an epiphany, a gateway: one of those moments in life where stark reality rises up and slaps you in the face to force uncomfortable recognition. If ever she was going to confront the truth, now was the time. But the only thing more unthinkable than not facing the truth was facing it, and all that this might entail for their marriage and for the stability of their children's lives. Ross was intently reading the newspaper. Cheryl could either pick a fight, without any evidence to back herself up other than her feeling he was covering something up, or she could drop it. *A fling on location, out of sight, was one thing. On the doorstep! How dare she! How dare he! And what if I'm completely wrong and he's telling the truth?* Still shaken and feeling tears prickle, Cheryl had marched upstairs to immerse herself in whatever household task had occupied her before this revelation. Routine was comforting. Open airing cupboard door. Stack towels. Run a smoothing hand over the top. Neat, tidy, orderly. Nothing amiss. Familiar actions diverting the neurons and synapses towards the physical, away from the unbearable. Distraction therapy. She thought of the wartime slogan 'Keep Calm and Carry On' – that's what her grandmother, her aunts, her mother had always done. Come rain, come shine; come war, come peace; come love, come desertion. The women of the family had always kept going, holding it together. And so must she!

*

Cheryl's mind came back from her reverie. *Yes! Keep Calm and Carry On!* She forsook the glare of Channel

9's neon-lit kitchen, carefully placed Robin's tea down to his right, and took her own brew back to the booth together with her uncertainties.

CHAPTER TWO

The luminous green clock on her car dashboard showed it was ten minutes past one in the morning. The south London suburbs were empty. Fatigue hung on her shoulders; her thoughts waved for attention they were not likely to receive. After a ten-hour shift, Cheryl only selected those processes best suited to conducting her safely home. Nevertheless, as the destination neared, offering the comfort of rest and secure familiarity, her shoulders rounded creating a concave chest, a withdrawing, recoiling from that place of succour. *I don't want to go in. Ridiculous. Of course I do. I'm just tired, that's all.* Her flickering responses tuned to the indicator light, foreshadowing the final turn into her home street. *This has to be sorted out. I have to sort this out. Not now, too tired.*

A darkness-chilled wind blew as her house key turned, swirling with her into the wide terracotta-and-black-tiled hall. A single Tiffany lamp on the mahogany table cast soft light. Would Ross still be up? He was often in his den in front of the computer into the small night hours. Cheryl had long given up waiting for him to join her upstairs on such occasions. She knew interruptions, even to wish him goodnight, would be unwelcome when he was working. A slit of light glowed under his door at the far right end of the hall. She padded upstairs to the empty bed, alone.

Deep sleep came, and if dreams were part of that night, Cheryl had no recollection of them on groggily awakening. In the thin dawn light, Cheryl's half-lidded sight caught the glint of the ceremonial scabbard and ornamental hilt of the sword bequeathed by her late father. It hung on the wall; a star of memory was reborn. *Daddy.* The first man to break her heart. *I was only six on the evening when Daddy came to say goodnight. I used to love those goodnight hugs. But it wasn't the same as usual.* Instinctively, she had known something was different – wrong.

A glint of the morning light still refracting down from his sword refreshed the memory. *I was looking up at him, and he crouched down to my bedside to hug me. 'Good night my precious little angel.'*

'Night, Daddy.'

'I love you, darling.' His hand caressed my hair and he cradled my head for a moment.

Adjusting her position slightly in the marital bed, she brushed up against Ross, still snuffling in deep slumber. She had slept through his arrival at whatever hour he had left his den. There was an uncomfortable chill across her left shoulder where the duvet was missing. She was an only child; she hadn't grown up having to share. She'd had to learn. Why was he taking up so much room? She tugged at the duvet and tried to recapture her thoughts.

The image of her father's face re-formed behind her eyelids. She remembered throwing her arms round his neck and being cross that something was in the way, between them, hanging round his neck, bin ... *somethings* – she hadn't known the word adults used. They were special to him, like one of her favourite toys, and she was only allowed to touch them and look through them when he was with her. She had wondered why he had his bird watching glasses with him: she knew you couldn't see birds when it was dark outside. *That's strange,* had been her naively fleeting thought. He had kissed her again, tucked her in and turned to go, pausing briefly in the doorway to look back at her. *Oh how I clung to that look.*

She tugged more vehemently at the duvet, resenting her lack of personal space. A cloying feeling in her stomach echoed the sensation of her six year old self, curled up under the sheet and blankets – a strange sense of foreboding or sadness for which her tender years had been unable to find vocal expression. *It was just odd. I felt something was wrong and I just ignored it, ignored my intuition. Is that where I learned it? Is that when I started avoiding looking into the truth?* When she had woken up that the morning, she knew. Daddy had gone taking all his belongings, including his precious binoculars, and it would be thirty years before she caught up with him again. Nothing was said that she could remember. It was as if he had never existed. He had been erased from her life. Her mother had just carried on the normal routine as if nothing out of the ordinary had happened. When Cheryl tried to recall if she had asked about him, or what she had been told if she did, amnesia confounded her. *Maybe I just shut down? Isn't that how children cope with bereavement sometimes? You see kids on the news, in war zones, just carrying on, playing amongst the rubble of their lives. Maybe that's what I did? It's so strange that I can't remember – as if someone took the folded newspaper of my life and cut it, so that when it opens there's a hole in the middle where part of the story should be.*

Cheryl still felt tired under the weight of the duvet. She didn't want to think about starting the day. Besides, it was Sunday morning. Tom and Zoë, being teenagers, would not be surfacing before lunchtime, if then. Nothing needed to be done before *The Archers' Omnibus* started at ten except, maybe, feeding the cats Merlin and Melchior.

A deep sighing breath almost took her back into drowsy reverie... so inviting... so unfair that sharpness and pain should stop her – gentle pawing, with claws not quite sheathed. 'Merlin!' she hissed at the intruder. 'Not now! Later.' She pushed and registered the *thwunk* of substantial black cat hitting the floor before rebounding to knead ever more insistently on top of her. Ross snorted and turned over, taking the duvet with him, Merlin still attached. Now cold, and with a pair of green eyes penetrating her conscience, she gave in and got out of bed.

The Sunday papers were on the front doormat. As far as Cheryl was concerned, in suburban middle-class London, Sunday morning was invented for leisurely cups of tea with the papers whilst awaiting the rumpty-tumpty-tumpty-tum theme tune of *The Archers* on Radio 4. It was a comforting Sunday routine, something to anchor the week, and had been in her life from childhood. Her mother had always listened – it had played out in the kitchen while Cheryl helped wash up the breakfast things. *No dishwasher and sleeping past lunchtime in those days!*

'Sunday morning equals *The Archers*. Period.' Cheryl had opined recently during a discussion in the Channel 9 bar after a shift. Her preference for spending her Sunday morning thus absorbed met with derision from the twenty-something production trainee.

'Isn't that a bit ... old fashioned – *The Archers*?'

Cheryl had defended her Sunday sanctuary.

'It may sound it, but it's not! If something has been going since 1950, it's got to keep current and gutsy. It's got something like sixteen thousand episodes under its belt; it holds the record for the number of times a programme is listened to over the internet. Even the general election didn't budge it from its regular transmission spot. So that's no *has been*. Anyway, I bet you watch *Eastenders* or *Corrie*?'

'Do me a favour – *Corrie*? – *Eastenders* every time.'

'Oh, I see. So it's just a matter of which community we prefer to emote through? Working class aggro, or the catastrophes in the countryside. It's all schadenfraude, anyway. A bit like comedy; you laugh or watch because you're glad it's not you.'

'Whatever—'

'It's got depth, continuity—'

'Yeah, well that's right up your street, then!' The trainee retreated back to the bar, leaving Cheryl in peace.

Job done!

So Sunday mornings were sacrosanct. Cheryl was preparing her second pot of tea when she heard Ross's slouching slippers scuffing across the kitchen flagstones. Despite her current uncertainties, she turned into his embrace. *No point starting a fight. It's a heart-to-heart we need.* He still smelled of sleep – that pleasant warm skin odour, the idiosyncratic scent of a familiar partner. He pushed her hair back and ruffled it slightly as was his habit. She didn't mind this morning. She'd put it back how it should be later.

'Hey, how'd it go yesterday? Sorry I wasn't around when you got home.'

'Fine. It was fine. Cold when I got home with that wind. Were you working on the shoot?'

He nodded and shook his head almost in one movement: 'Marie-Claire,' he said with heavy emphasis, denoting resignation and frustration.

Cheryl had never met the star of his latest film, but she knew the story well enough. Maire-Claire Devine, née Deborah Swale, had been hot property and the fodder of tabloid press gossip ever since her début on the public stage as the nubile teen star of *Deep Dark Love,* which had hit prime time television three years ago: a sensational and successful drama series exploring a middle-aged man's obsession, and the devastating manipulations of an under-age teen temptress. Now eighteen, television's wild child had come of age, littering a trail of hard partying and speculative affairs in her wake. Her destructive and indulgent lifestyle was fuelled by her unfettered earning power, mitigated and obscured in the worst of its excesses by her father's PR agent. Daddy – Don Swale – was an actor turned MP and his hapless PR agent was in regular employment distancing Don from his daughter's antics, or finding a way to make the details disappear.

For months Cheryl had listened to Ross's concerns about casting her. On the one hand, her notoriety would bring instant publicity. On the other, he would have the daily experience of directing her and controlling her tantrums. In the end, producer power and financial considerations triumphed. He had to concede and she was cast in the lead role. Ross had already endured months in rehearsal and in the studio with her where, true to form, she had been a temperamental nightmare. And starting tomorrow, they were away on location for a week.

Cheryl tightened her hug, her earlier discontent softened by compassion. No wonder he was tense. The memory of Miss Skinny-Jeans resurfaced.

'Good luck,' she said pulling away. Rather you than me. Got any ideas on how to deal with her?'

'Nope. I've got two stage managers to guard her like sheepdogs and tip me off if she starts going wild. If it's really bad, I'll have to take her out to dinner and read the riot act.' He smiled fondly, 'I know our two have their moments, but at least we can talk things through with them – they do eventually appear to listen.'

Cheryl turned away to put the kettle on. 'Tea?' This was no time to examine the subject, but she knew what the twins would say. Ross was creative and fiery, with a short fuse. He flared instantly if annoyed, and then ten minutes later could scarcely remember what the fuss was about. Cheryl was slow to ignite, but once pushed to the point of showing anger, erupted like a volcano. Once she had overheard Tom and Zoë agree that Dad blew his top at the drop of a hat, but if Mum 'went off' they knew they were in real trouble. She poured the tea and set two mugs on the kitchen table.

'Do you want the magazine, or the main newspaper?' she enquired, before broaching what she wanted to say next.

'Either, don't mind.'

He was going on location for a week. Cheryl knew only too well about locations. She'd been on enough herself before the twins came along. She was a Director's Assistant back when she met Sheila, a wardrobe mistress and now her best friend, on location in some godforsaken town on the North East coast. A soggy winter shoot on a sorry little drama that failed to attract many ratings when it finally aired. Sheila and Cheryl had cemented their friendship hiding in the laundry cupboard of The Grand Hotel. They had become horribly drunk on mulled wine, and then spent the entire evening trying to ward off the unwelcome amorous advances of an equally inebriated props man, finally hiding amongst the bed linen, and dissolving into fits of tipsy giggles every time footsteps approached and faded away. They had been friends ever since. Gossip co-conspirators. Drinking buddies, a mutual shoulder to cry on.

Locations meant late nights, early starts, travelling for days, sometimes weeks. And as a single, she'd loved it. Sport; costume dramas; comedies; seasons of summer specials; touring the South coast with a crew of technicians whose motto seemed to be: o*n location doesn't count.* One-night-stands, quick flings, summer romances. It was all pretty inevitable, and inevitably far too common and complicated. Their wives probably knew, too, and turned a blind eye. After all, *what the eye doesn't see* ... She assumed they knew. Perhaps they were naive. Maybe they didn't know. It had never really been Cheryl's business and she was careful never to get caught up in it. The lamest proposition she had ever received was from one hopeful camera assistant who knocked on her hotel room door late one night, or early morning to be more precise, in Barcelona:

'I've forgotten my toothpaste. Can I come in and have a *squeeze* of yours?'

'No! Bugger off!'

And, of course, TV directors were the prize catch for any footloose and fancy-free female with a predatory eye. Yes, she knew about locations.

'So, when I've listened to *The Archers*, do you want me to help with your packing?'

'Huh? ... Oh, um, yeah,' he mouthed absently staring at the headlines. Then he engaged, and looked up at her; unruly blond mop of hair, scorching blue eyes –now framed with laughter lines – broad shoulders underneath a black T-shirt with silver Hollywood logo.

Who couldn't have fallen for him?

'Yeah, that would give me time to take a last look through the scripts again. You are a darling,' he added as an afterthought. 'Thanks.'

His suitcase wasn't the enormous one he sometimes chose. After all, it was only a week. Cheryl packed and folded jeans, shirts, socks and then turned her attention to underwear. Right on the top she smoothed his red silk boxers; (she'd chosen them as a present last Christmas) he loved the feel of silk, she knew. She hoped they would remind him of her while he was away.

It wasn't the threat of a fling. If Cheryl delved deeply into the alarm systems of her psyche, she'd known about the likelihood of that all the time, but didn't want to bring the knowledge to the surface. To acknowledge it would mean taking some course of action. Years ago she had decided ignorance was wedded bliss. If she didn't think about it, then they didn't exist. And *maybe* they didn't exist. She listened to friends and colleagues furtively sharing their forays into their partner's phones to check for secret texts or indiscrete photos. They scanned the call lists for unrecognised numbers, projecting infidelity into the ether, whether it was fact or fantasy, twisting their reality into contortions of suspicion and anger. Cheryl didn't have a jealous nature. She puzzled over her lack of this seemingly insatiable drive to discover something amiss. Trust is what makes a relationship special. The odd booze-fuelled fling in a distant hotel, she reasoned, whilst undesirable, was not a deal breaker. An affair of the heart, on the other hand, was! Ross's mobile was right there, on the bedside cabinet, next to the suitcase. He was downstairs in his den checking the scripts. He would be hours. All she had to do was pick it up. It was in her hand now, the black screen waiting to awaken and reveal its core knowledge. Cheryl put it back unopened, exactly where it had been, at the precise angle.

That's what years of working in continuity does for you. Her lips stretched into an ironic smile. Everything remained the same; the picture of her life remained unchanged.

Besides, she had a secret of her own, one she had even found hard to share with anyone, except Sheila, and then only the skimpiest details. Not that anything had *happened.* It was a fantasy, just a fantasy; like window-shopping – looking, admiring, but without any intention of actually getting involved. In fact, she hadn't even been looking for it, yet somehow it had leapt upon her and taken over her mind. For the past two months, Cheryl had been in love – *no, let's be realistic* – *infatuated like a lovesick teenager. He's everywhere I go: the supermarket, Soloman's Café, even in the park while I'm jogging.* It had created a schism in her life. The more she felt drawn towards him, the less comfortable she was with Ross. Was this guilty secret the nail screeching down the blackboard of her marriage, or the uncertainty of the girl on the doorstep?

Did fantasizing count as adultery? The more Cheryl tried to unravel her tangled thoughts, the further into anxiety she dived. *It's one thing to indulge in a concocted fantasy, something to daydream about; but yearning for someone who was real, tangible, where something might, in theory, actually happen, that's dangerous ground. A dangerous liaison.*

Cheryl gave the contents of the suitcase one final appraisal before closing the lid and zipping it shut. While Ross was away, she had planned lunch with her friend, Joanna, and two days later with Sheila. Plenty of time in-between to clean the cupboards, jog around the park if the weather permitted, and treat herself to a coffee at Soloman's – *where I might see him.* Not that he even noticed her as far as she was aware.

She tore an old travel label from the suitcase handle. Thank goodness the need for anonymity held her in check. No one would know besides herself and her guilty conscience. Despite her gut-wrenching disappointment that she couldn't take any step towards turning her fantasy into reality, this was a comfort. Nothing must show, not even a smile in his direction, not a gesture.

Cheryl didn't remember feeling the thunderbolt hit. Or a piercing pain like Cupid's dart, but it must have happened. The day after she'd first noticed him leaning back in the soft squidgy sofa at Soloman's, reading *The Guardian*, the only intelligent broadsheet available amongst the array of tabloids in the news rack, she seemed to have lost all sense of balance and reality: she was totally obsessed. He'd initially caught her attention because he was relaxing in the very sofa she had earmarked for her own pleasure. If questioned, she might have said he had an aura about him, an air of mystery and something else, which she couldn't define, but somehow could feel, right in the heart of her. Still transfixed, Cheryl had noticed his dark shoulder-length hair, flecked iron grey, and in the fleeting moment when he had looked up, taking in her arrival in the café, his slate-grey eyes seemed to sparkle and almost smile. She began going back more frequently in the hope he would be there. She wanted to sneak a photograph of him, but didn't dare. Firstly, he might see her and think she was a freak. And secondly, what if Ross happened to look at her phone and ask about him? *I'll just have to hold his image in my mind. Oh God! Why can't I let go of this? I can't even tell Sheila how bad it is. What's the matter with me?* What made it yet worse was that she had never before felt this way about anyone, including Ross. Not even on their wedding day.

Leaning forward in thought, her left hand sank into the softness of their bed and she was aware of the pressure of her ring. Yes, she had loved him. Yes, she meant her vows. But the circumstances were a long way from a romantic idyll as they awaited the imminent birth of Zoë and Tom. Cheryl had always thought that high-octane passion was something confined to the film screen, or something that happened to someone else. As a teenager, she never seemed to attract the boys she yearned for; much less did they ask her out. She was never one of the popular crowd. She was the type who met someone through a friend or a club, and then they worked at getting to know each other. Textbook. True, her first encounter with Ross had been unusual. *But that wasn't a lightning strike. More a bird strike!*

Twenty years ago, being something of an adrenalin junkie, Cheryl had gone to a theme park for the day and chosen to ride whatever gave her the greatest G-force thrill. Her companion for the day was Katrina, a work colleague who wanted to take her two young children for a day out. While Katrina escorted her children on the little rides, Cheryl buckled up for the white-knuckle and scream trip. They had agreed a rendezvous for tea at four.

It was her third trip around The Bat Trap, a twisting, looping high speed roller coaster that reached giddy heights before plunging deep into a cave, corkscrewing down through the dark tunnel to what looked like an impossibly small opening at the end - the Bat Trap - and thence back up to the stars. Cheryl had whooped, shrieked and laughed her way round twice already and calculated she could just fit in one more go before tea. Being a single rider, she stood in the separate queue from the groups waiting to be loaded onto the ride. Single riders avoided the long wait in the normal queue. They had their own entrance and were used to fill up gaps left by friends and family groups. The empty coaster rolled forward with the restraints raised, jaws waiting for the riders, four abreast, to settle into the belly of the flying Bat. The theme park staff motioned to her to come forward, and to her joy she saw she was being ushered onto the front row of seats. Riding front or back, in Cheryl's opinion, were the best options. Either a great view of the track, twisting into the oblivion of apparently empty space in front, or the kickback G-force of being on the tail of the ride. Of the two, front was her absolute favourite. On this occasion there was a bonus. A couple took the two far right seats. Cheryl was on the extreme left, leaving one central seat vacant.

Please don't let it be some smelly geek.

She had shared trip two with the odour of overexcited teenage armpits. Her fairy godmother answered her prayer. Cheryl found herself loaded next to an attractive blond man with a grin of expectation to match her own. She had noticed him a little way behind her in the singles' queue. All locked and loaded, the Bat took off and delivered a front row ride to meet all expectations, and more. Halfway round the loop Cheryl felt a thwack on her chest. She couldn't look down to see what it was as they swept into the dark of the Bat Cave, so it wasn't until the ride came to a halt and the restraints released over her head, she realised she'd been smacked right in the heart by a large incontinent bird who apparently liked blackberries.

'Oh shit!'

'Yep, it certainly is!' her blonde hunk agreed.

Cheryl could see his eyes roaring with laughter even though he was trying to maintain a concerned demeanour. Cheryl searched her pockets for a tissue to stop the mess dripping any further. Nothing. He came to her rescue.

'Here. It's a serviette from the café. I have used it I'm afraid, but ...'

'Thanks. It's hardly going to matter what it's been used for when I'm going to mop this up. Oh yuk.'

'It's supposed to be lucky, you know.'

'Well, right now, I can't see how. Oh Lord, I'm going to have to buy a T-shirt or something from the shops. I can't wear this, I stink.'

He produced a second serviette from the depths of his jeans pocket and proffered it towards the mess.

'Ross? Ross! What are you doing?'

The woman behind the railings, which bordered the exit, raised her voice proprietorially. She beckoned him to join her and her two young children.

Oops, sorry! Cheryl didn't want to cause her benefactor any trouble, and besides she was desperate to find something else to wear and wash off the stench.

'Thanks for your help – you'd better go. Sorry, your wife seems annoyed.'

'*Not* my wife. And yes, she seems annoyed.' Ross raised conspiratorial eyebrows, smiled and exited past her.

Well, that's a shame on two counts. He's gone to deal with his shit, and I'm covered in it. Cheryl found herself a pink T-shirt in one of the theme park gift shops, and turned up for tea with Katrina fronting a huge white bunny motif with two appliquéd fluffy ears on her chest. The children loved it and Katrina just shook her head.

'Oh, that's so cute. Can I take your photo?'

'No!'

'Cheryl, that guy over there keeps looking at you. Do you know him?'

Cheryl cast her eyes round the room in the general direction that Katrina had indicated. She could see the man sitting at the far side of the café with his *not-wife* and the two children. Remembering the displeasure of 'She Who Must Be Obeyed', Cheryl made sure she didn't make eye contact.

'Yes. Well, no, not exactly. He was next to me on the ride and offered me something to wipe off some of the bird mess. He was very polite, but I think he thought it was hilarious.'

It wasn't until Cheryl and Katrina were leaving that he made his move. They collided at the door. He seemed to be alone.

'Holy Bat Shit, you look like you're a bunny girl now!' he teased.

Cheryl looked at his mischievous blue eyes and decided she liked his rebellious streak even though he was being rather sexist.

'Oh yes, Batman, or is it Robin? Bat Girl to Bunny Girl.'

'Ross, not Robin,' he pressed a card into her hand. 'Gotta go. Call me. Promise?'

'Well, I'm not sure I should!'

'Trust me. It's okay. Just call.'

And she had trusted him, always. She had taken a risk and called him a week later. They met in a Soho wine bar in central London that Friday evening.

'Hi, really glad you could make it. And hey, you look great!'

'Thank you. That's very kind. The lack of bird poo and bunny ears probably helps.'

'You'd look great in anything.' His smile was charming.

Yes, he certainly knows how to turn on the charm.

Cheryl sipped her wine and wondered how to bring up the subject of his companions on their previous encounter. She didn't want to pry, but she certainly wasn't going to get involved in a clandestine affair. No need. Ross stepped straight in.

'You'll be wondering about the lady I was with when we met at the theme park?'

'Yes.'

'I cannot tell a lie,' Ross put his hand on his heart for emphasis. 'We had been together. But as you could see, it wasn't a happy relationship anymore and, in fact, we agreed to part company on the way home from the theme park.'

'Oh dear, I hope I wasn't the cause.'

'No, not the cause, at all – more a catalyst. Please don't feel bad. It was a blessing. For all of us.'

'The children?'

'Not mine. They're hers from her marriage. Ex-marriage. Nice kids, but they didn't help things. I don't think I'm ready to be a family guy. There are no loose ends. I'm a free man. Honestly.'

Cheryl could still remember the light blue collarless shirt, distressed jeans and immaculate white trainers he wore on their first date. Everything said style with ease. After an hour of trying on this and that, Cheryl had chosen stone-washed jeans, dressed up with a simple tailored white shirt to show off her petite slim figure. She allowed her freshly washed honey-coloured hair to fashion its own shoulder length curls, and accessorized with a chunky turquoise and silver necklace and matching drop earrings. Peeking from her open sandals were her French-manicured toes. With hindsight, they had looked like an advertisement for Mr and Mrs Levi Strauss. The perfect match. And so they seemed to be. At five foot three, Cheryl had fitted comfortably alongside his broad five ten physique.

They had walked along the banks of the Thames in the summer evening. A breeze had made Cheryl shiver. Ross had drawn her closer for warmth and their first kiss was tender.

Cheryl grasped at the remembered magic of that moment. It had been wonderful, indeed. Romantic and caring. Where had that relationship gone? Had it dissolved in domesticated time like sugar in a bitter coffee, and if they made the effort to look deep, to stir up the feelings, could they capture that sweetness again? Or had the drink stood too long and become cold – stale beyond redemption? Certainly, it was nothing like this burning compulsion she had after one look into the enigmatic eyes of a complete stranger in Soloman's Cafe!

She yanked the suitcase off the bed so vehemently that its impact with the floor rattled her jewellery on top of the chest of drawers. Her world shook. She froze hoping no one would come. She wasn't ready, not composed. This was crazy, they should make the effort; dump their hectic media schedules; take time to talk.

Perhaps it's the allure of forbidden fruit? Middle age. A midlife crisis? You're pathetic, Cheryl!

No one in the house seemed to have reacted to the case crashing to the floor. The effort of lifting the suitcase became too great, inertia and resignation causing her shoulders to slump.

A yawning gulf of disconnection seemed to be opening up in her mind's eye, with her on one side and Ross on the other; the hole filled with the humdrum habits of daily existence and the formulaic behaviour that passed for a happy family life. When Ross was at home, Cheryl was frequently out, taking the twins to the many activities that seemed to her to be essential to their personal growth. Ross only acted as chauffeur when Cheryl had a clash of appointments and asked him to step in. Even then, she had leave notes detailing where they should be taken, and cash to pay for entrance fees and refreshments. Zoë was a key player in the school senior netball team, which meant after-school practice and matches every weekend. Cheryl heard the tale from Zoë after one Saturday's league match:

'Mum, I'm so pissed off with Dad.'

'Darling, please don't use language like that about your father. What's happened to upset you?'

'He only spent the whole match in the bar with his paper. We won, and I scored three times! All he could say was *well done, that's my girl.* But I know he wasn't watching.'

'Well, I'm sorry that happened, darling, but you know I don't think Dad meant to miss your match. He probably just got absorbed in the paper and lost track of time.' Cheryl hoped that Zoë didn't see right through this cover story. She was only too well aware that if Ross wasn't interested in a person, a place, or an event, he would simply disengage. If he had been taking Zoë to a film, it would have been different. He would have been the first to leap into an animated dissection of the cinematography, the lighting, and the plot with her afterwards. After all, her plan after taking her exams was to apply to film school, and this was something he could help her with. He lived and breathed film and television; big screen, television screen, computer screen. Ross's life revolved around images.

Tom enjoyed art and attended extra classes after school. Sometimes he also joined Sheila on her allotment – he too seemed to find great satisfaction in growing things. Often he combined these activities, and sat at the allotment drawing leaves, buds and flowers.

'Those are so good, darling,' Cheryl commented when he came home one day bearing three new watercolours along with an armful of sweet corn. Ross was supportive of Tom's art, too.

'Great composition. I really like that one of the tree. You should look into doing fine art. Have you asked your art teacher about studying it at university?'

Tom looked evasively at the floor.

'Well, I could, but, you know I'm also thinking about agricultural college. I'd like to do something working with trees.'

'Trees?' Ross was genuinely puzzled.

'Yeah, conservation and ecology. That kind of thing.'

'Hum, interesting. Well, look at all your options.' Ross tried to mask his disappointment that his son didn't want to follow him into the arts field. It seemed that Zoë was destined to step into those shoes. She excelled in media studies.

Tom knew.

Cheryl gripped the suitcase handle, extended it and wheeled it towards the door. The whole family seemed to be facing crossroads and choices. This was no time to go off the rails. *I just need to keep things stable. It's only a year before the kids finish school. If I can just hold on until they're through their exams and off to university or college, then ... I'll see how I feel then. I feel so ... what do I feel? Stifled? No. Work is great and the twins seem very happy with their friends and at school. My heart just sinks as I arrive home. I can't go on like this. It will have to get sorted out. But not yet. Not yet! I must make the effort to keep things stable.*

She caught her reflection in the mirror on the rear of the door. Peering at herself, her right hand raked through her fringe, pushing it back. No lines on her forehead – yet. Quick glance down – figure's all right. Her attention zoomed into her reflected eyes. Did they seem lacklustre somehow? It seemed to her that there was a vacancy behind them, where the person ought to be.

Ridiculous! You're imagining things. Dinner: A really lovely evening meal with Ross on his final night before going on location with that crazy actress. That's what she'd do. She wouldn't coerce Tom and Zoë to join them if they wanted something earlier. It was just a phase, and it would pass if she could just *keep calm and carry on.*

CHAPTER THREE

Cheryl finished texting Sheila shortly after Ross departed for his location shoot. They were due to meet for their lunch date in two days' time. Contacting Sheila always felt so reassuring. They had an unspoken connection and understanding despite their backgrounds and lifestyles being completely different. She could picture her friend's chaotic kitchen and imagined her rifling through her pen jar for a red crayon to mark their lunch date. They were both planning to do their Christmas shopping this week – it was the only opportunity they were going to get, thanks to an endless round of school concerts and Christmas bazaars interlaced with work.

Sheila was still a wardrobe mistress, as she had been when she and Cheryl enjoyed their tipsy evening in the hotel laundry cupboard on location all those years ago. Elfin-featured, tousled, a natural tawny, Sheila liked caring for things. She always had. Furthermore, she had discovered as a child she had a gift. Not that she realised it was a gift until she went to school, where it became obvious not everyone shared her talent, nor did they like her for it. They called her a freak, not a reputation she enjoyed. So Sheila quickly learned to keep quiet and pretend she had just been playing make-believe. The fact remained she could heal things with her hands, and sometimes just by thinking about them.

Cheryl had often listened to Sheila's tales of her modest childhood home and how it had irritated their neighbours with its ramshackle and run-down appearance. The garden grew wild, with an unpruned willow tree that cascaded over the front drive, and which every autumn shed enough leaves to carpet the pathway from the front door and shake a leafy doormat of welcome out onto the pavement. One particularly abundant leaf year, a formal letter of complaint arrived from the council informing them the tree was a health hazard and someone in the street had complained they had slipped on the fallen leaves. The owners had a week to sweep up and trim back the tree.

Compared with Cheryl's easy and unremarkable early life, Sheila described a lonely childhood. She was a misfit. Her schoolmates weren't the only ones who thought the Davenports were weird, and a nuisance. The family didn't fit in amongst the trim line of little bungalow-style houses. Her mother Clara had an allotment: about three hundred square yards of land, rented from the local authority, where she grew a variety of seasonal vegetables for her family of four – her carpenter husband Josh, and her three children Stephanie, Samuel, and Sheila. Having all their names begin with the letter *S* hadn't been intentional. They just seemed to come to her in the middle of the night, as if the unborn had whispered their preference in the inner ear of her mind. But it proved a boon in later years when it came to the time consuming requirement to sew name labels – '*S. Davenport*'– into their school clothes; they could be handed down from one to the other with only the need for the occasional spot of invisible darning.

Sheila was her first-born and so accompanied her mother to the allotment from the outset. It was her kindergarten, her playground, and later her refuge. It was also her tutor. She would help to push the seeds into the compost in the pots, and together Clara and Sheila would make a game of singing them a little song for their birthday and willing them to grow strong and delicious. They would cup the pots in their hands as they did this, and Sheila found that her hands grew warm as if her heart were shining through them.

Unlike Cheryl, who had an English degree, Sheila had never courted academia. Sheila followed her artistic inclinations, undertaking a three-year fashion design course, specialising in her final year in textiles and costume. It was during this time of study that she came across the reason her hands would heat when she placed them on someone or something that needed help. Sheila discovered reiki.

It was the late 1980s. British history was about to enter the era of what later became classified in popular parlance – thanks to comedian, Harry Enfield's successful television character – as 'Loadsamoney'. This comedy character typified the boorish behaviour of many men at that time, unaccustomed to wealth, who due to the booming prosperity of the decade, suddenly found themselves with large wads of cash. 'Loadsamoney' vaunted his spending power, indulging in vulgar and wanton consumerism without regard for environmental impact, or the sensibilities of anyone around him. It was the anthem of the times. Financial confidence was rampant and bankers' bonuses were stratospheric. Anyone who espoused the esoteric or healing arts was patronisingly and pityingly side-lined in the category of a loser who had failed to get with the programme. It was an era of loud ostentation and lavish excess; in which quiet contemplation, intuitive guidance, and compassion had scant credence.

Sheila's art college was holding a pampering evening to raise money for cancer relief. This was as close to compassion as this era of hedonism was likely to get. The irony that those whose excessive cocaine consumption, coupled with their long stressful working hours to fuel this lifestyle of greed and overindulgence, were the very ones who would probably benefit most from some healing, was still in the vaults of destiny. A lesson they might have learned from the humble oyster, which so often accompanied their jeroboams of champagne. The oyster, prized in pursuit of sensual pleasure, and even more so when its struggles to dispel an irritant chip of grit, cause it to grow its coveted pearl. Only through its pain, can the oyster grow the beautiful jewel.

Sheila hadn't been planning to go. Pampering sounded like false fingernails and expensive chemical-laden lotions. Nonetheless, she had given in to the peer pressure of her flatmates and found herself wandering through the classrooms where she was pleasantly surprised to find Indian head massage, reflexology, and a reiki master called Mark.

His leaflet on reiki explained the universal life force to the uninitiated. It described the energy that runs through every creation on the planet and beyond –the unity of life. If it has an atom, it is susceptible to reiki. If Mark were talking to teenagers, who tended to place the sharing of such cosmic knowledge on a par with Santa

Claus and the tooth fairy, he might simply ask them if they had ever seen *Star Wars.*

'Well, the Force is with you.'

'No way? You can do the Yoda thing? That's way cool!'

To which he'd reply, no, he didn't lift star fighters out of swamps – well, not this week at least – but the principles of being in harmony with all living things and channelling the immensely wise and powerful life force that connects and supports the universe, with the intention to help and heal anything or any situation was, indeed, pretty cool.

Sheila stood with the leaflet in her hands, and merely thinking about this energy made her hands heat. Somehow, she already had this connection and she wasn't going to leave until she found out why. She waited in the textiles classroom, which had been temporarily turned over to therapists, for the two women currently with Mark to decide whether they thought reiki might be a form of voodoo, and therefore incompatible with their image as ladies who went to church for Christmas Eve, Easter, christenings and weddings. They chose not to risk being drawn into something they could neither quantify nor understand.

One never knew where these things might lead ...

Sheila had no such qualms. She didn't need to quantify or verify reiki's existence. Whatever reiki was, she had it, and it had brought her nothing but good so far. Having accessed the energy since childhood, it had never occurred to her that reiki might be something that could be studied, or learned. It struck her now that this veiled view was quite odd. Why had she never explored what it was, or where it came from? Odd, indeed, but that's how it had been, so there it was. She glanced through the leaflet, which traced reiki's origins from Japan, through Hawaii and thence Europe.

But still, Sheila was puzzled. 'I've always been able to feel a sort of energy in my hands, ever since I was a little girl. How can I do that? I'm not Japanese or American and I don't remember anyone in our family talking about having any sort of training. Mum and I just did it. How can that have happened?'

Mark confirmed that everyone has the capacity to work with reiki energy, but some people are born naturally attuned to the energy vibration.

'What is called having healing hands. Might have got you burned at the stake in earlier times! Nevertheless,' he explained, 'it is always preferable to have some knowledge and control over its use, and that's why you study with a master to get reiki *attunements* – that's what hooking up to the energy source is called.'

For Sheila this opened up a world of possibilities. *I wonder what else I can do with this if I study it formally? Wow! I feel as if I have some strange connection to something old. I've read about people remembering past lives. Maybe that's it.*

'How do I get these attunements?'

Mark indicated the back panel of the leaflet. 'I run weekend initiations from time to time. There are three stages. The next reiki one course is in a couple of weeks. Get in touch if you're interested.'

Two weeks later Sheila had her reiki one attunement; followed by reiki two some months later. And a year after that, she finally became a reiki master in her own right.

Once she had the additional control of the symbols and had honed her ability to send distant healing through time and space, Sheila's healing abilities really took off. There was a point when she wondered whether to step away from her life in television and espouse her healing completely. She thought about it long and hard. She meditated whilst walking to her allotment, and while sending energy to her seeds and plants. In the end, she decided the upheaval and loss of income while she established herself in a practice would have too great an impact on her family. *Maybe I'll do it when the kids leave school.*

So, Sheila kept reiki as her hobby. She shared the knowledge that she practised it with friends, none of whom enquired too deeply. *They think it's like a religion. Perhaps they think I'm going to coerce them into something dark or 'woo woo'.*

Cheryl had listened to Sheila's story as if listening to a play on the radio. Somehow she couldn't connect it to *real* life. It wasn't that she disbelieved her friend's experience; it just seemed a bit *odd.* When she stopped to think about it, Cheryl was fascinated by how different their life paths had been. Yet they had such a deep friendship, as if some unforeseen force wanted them to be together. Cheryl's family hadn't even been churchgoers, never mind connected to some universal force. Somehow the thought made her uncomfortable, although she couldn't quite pinpoint why. *Maybe I just like to be able to see proof. It could be wishful thinking.* She recalled Sheila asking her to be a guinea pig for her friend who was learning tarot one teatime. She had declined, and had pushed the muffins between them to politely mask her unease. Offers of reiki had been similarly rebuffed. Sheila hadn't seemed surprised, none of their television colleagues who knew about her gift ever asked. It was all a bit strange. Better avoided.

Their everyday lives were very different. Cheryl's home could have been a magazine feature. Ross wanted a fashionable home for entertaining, a reflection of his standing amongst the television glitterati; Sheila joked that she had to take her shoes off when she visited. Her own kitchen, the battered wooden table littered with cups of tea and assorted newspaper cuttings, was usually their meeting place for a conspiratorial gossip. They didn't even have to go along the road: if they took the passageway at the rear of their houses, they could cut through the network of alleys once used by tradesmen. The back wall of Sheila's garden had a back gate which lead through to the herb patch and chaotic scented cottage garden, created with baskets, tubs, old Wellingtons and any other creative junk Sheila happened upon. Even an old loo had been pressed into service to contain the aggressively invasive roots of peppermint and spearmint. Cheryl had once cracked her shin on it in the dark. And, by way of security, wind chimes assaulted anyone walking up the loudly crunching gravel path. Cheryl had jokingly enquired: 'Any fairies at the bottom of your garden?'

'Of course! And elves and gnomes and salamanders' Sheila replied with a cheeky grin leaving Cheryl unsure whether she was joking or serious. They always had fun, even after all these years, and they shared everything –

even their deepest secrets. Sheila had been the first, outside Cheryl's family, to hear Cheryl was unexpectedly pregnant with twins, and terrified by the prospect of motherhood. She had been her bridesmaid once Ross proposed shortly after they found out.

Yes, indeed, they'd weathered the years together.

Now, as Cheryl gathered her things for her daily routine, her dearest friend stared at the red-ringed lunch date on the calendar. Sheila's intuitive connection to Cheryl was shouting that something was out of balance. She sensed an undercurrent, above and beyond the usual bumps and bruises of everyday married life. For a start, Cheryl seemed to have fallen in love – or perhaps lust – with a complete stranger. It seemed more tangible than a simple crush on a film star or some actor in the studio. A *frisson* of claircognisance raised her downy arm hair into goose bumps. She was glad they were meeting for lunch, maybe she'd be able to assess whether her concern was well founded.

CHAPTER FOUR

Cheryl was late! She hated being late. Punctuality and timing were her bread and butter. Ross's PA had called just as she was leaving to ask if he'd left his favourite aftershave at home. After ransacking his bathroom cabinet, Cheryl ran back downstairs with the news that he must have it with him. His PA sounded as irritated by having to ask as Cheryl felt about the unnecessary delay. Lunchtime was always busy and she sat impatiently tapping her steering wheel, willing the car park queue to move on.

*

Joanna Short waited for Cheryl in the restaurant, filling in time with a quick text to her agent. Short was a ridiculous misnomer in her case. Gangly – at five foot eleven she was bordering on undateable – even in flat shoes, men found her intimidating. She always said she felt extremely grateful to the Almighty that He, She, It, Whatever ... had delivered Richard, her husband, into her life. Plain Jay is what they had taunted her with at school, like a plain Jane. And it was true. She knew it was. Mousy hair, dead straight, totally lacking in seductive curls. Not a single facial feature that went with any of the others. Her big, round, hazel eyes would have been fine with high cheekbones to set them off, but in her long, narrow face they were protuberant, and positively stared. Her nose was a disaster: too big and Roman, like a cliff overhanging her broad mouth.

None of my features is too bad on its own, she'd told her reflection in the mirror that morning. *It's just when they all get together.*

So, plain Joanna she was, and glad of her job in radio where her finest asset, her voice, had always commanded immediate attention.

Deep, soft and sexy. A touch of liquid gold, read the description on the demonstration CD issued by her agent. He was careful not to include a photo. Her voice said Marlene Dietrich, and the name of the game was marketing. If clients wanted to book a sultry blonde, hers was the voice they'd choose.

Joanna might be the celebrity voice that every household in Britain could recognise, even if they couldn't put a name to it, but she had to admit to a prickling of jealousy as she spotted her friend nimbly winding through the bistro tables towards her. To Joanna, Cheryl seemed to have it all. Small-boned, brown eyes, a well-balanced, straight nose, which didn't draw attention to itself. Honeyed and generally tousled hair, with some lighter streaks expensively provided by the hairdresser every six weeks or so. Neat figure, small hands, small feet, small appetite. While everything about Cheryl said delicate, she was clearly not: she had given birth to twins, in a marathon nineteen-hour labour; she ran a house, held down a job; and jogged round the park every day.

They had met following a major decision in Cheryl's life. Cheryl had given up work when her twins were born, imposing their own demanding schedule, which in no way allowed for the erratic hours working in television entailed. She did miss the social aspect of working, but going back to her job, as a production assistant, with its unpredictable and long hours, wasn't an option. Besides, having been out of the industry for five years, she had lost a great deal of her old confidence. And then she saw a course in radio presentation advertised. She'd loved it and couldn't wait to try for a job.

Joanna had been in the studio of Radio Judd on the day Cheryl had come for an interview, and they'd asked her opinion afterwards. Already a seasoned presenter, Joanna had an eye for talent and had offered to mentor Cheryl if they decided to take her on. She could recall Cheryl's reply to the standard interview question:

'Why do you want to be a radio presenter?'

'Er ... because I like talking to people?'

Joanna could see that Cheryl had immediately thought better of this reply, but in fact, it was the perfect response. A week later Cheryl found herself in the hospital basement being shown round the low-roofed corridors lined with ducts and cables, and into the tiny studio of Radio Judd, St Judd Hospital's radio service. Someone had teased her by asking if she believed in ghosts and the spirit world, adding that the room used to be the morgue. Cheryl had looked askance. Was it true? Well, it had been a morgue, but no one had ever seen a ghost ... yet!

'We only have a skeleton staff,' they'd joked. 'Joanna will be here to keep you company to begin with anyway. You'll start off doing *short* pieces.'

Joanna had laughed dutifully at this play on words, even though she had heard it many times.

'You know, the sort of thing you get in women's magazines. The patients can't cope with anything too long or in depth. No one wants to concentrate for long when they're ill.'

Their friendship and Cheryl's first step on the road to becoming a professional voice over had started there.

*

'Hi. I'm so sorry I'm late.' Cheryl breathed as they hugged.

Joanna and Cheryl had made a pact to meet once every three months for lunch. A pact they'd kept, barring illness and other unforeseen domestic disasters, ever since they'd met at the hospital radio station all those years ago. After Sheila, Joanna was Cheryl's most regular and closest companion. But, unlike Sheila, there was a distance, a glass window through which the world could gaze and draw its own conclusion of Joanna, but never be invited in. Joanna was not a woman to divulge her deepest self. Cheryl had sometimes wondered if there was an aspect of Joanna that she wanted hidden, some covert secret. Or, maybe she was just shy? Impossible to tell. Besides, they never had time to talk at length, despite the fact they both made a living from doing just that. So, they had made a resolution to make some space in their overcrowded lives. Sometimes, when they felt particularly jaded, they'd make it a 'health lunch' – their antidote to the 'power lunch. They'd take sanctuary in a health spa for a swim, sauna and possibly a quick back massage before lettuce leaf lunching over herb tea. But today was a grey, drab autumnal drizzle-fest. It called for more robust fare. The comfort of a warm casserole accompanied by full-bodied red wine.

Cheryl divested herself of her grey heavy-weave jacket. It seemed to have enveloped her with its mood, as she flopped down in the chair to the left of her friend. Joanna looked calm and composed, as always. Cheryl felt anything but. Their drinks arrived and they clinked glasses and set about studying the menu.

If only I had the amount of space in my life that Joanna has, thought Cheryl enviously. *She's always on time. She can do the things she wants, when she wants. No children. No scatter-brained husband. Richard is either away or abroad on business once or twice a month. Just imagine having the whole house to yourself. No one changing programmes every thirty seconds with the remote control. Joanna could have a candle-lit, scented bath without someone shouting through the door, demanding to know where the things they'd dropped had magically been put away. No packed lunches, no school run…*

Joanna's husband, Richard, was the meticulously tidy type.

It irritated Cheryl to realise she was jealous of her friend. It wasn't as if she wanted to escape the twins. Never having been the maternal type before their birth, she had grown to love them as she nurtured them through their formative years. She loved the way Zoë reminded her of herself, with her drive to explore in search of adventure, even if that simply meant escaping through the fence into next door's garden. Tom she loved for his gentle artistic nature, which began to emerge as early as pre-school nursery. He brought home paintings that expressed how his day had been in colour and contours: sharp and red for a day of childhood tiffs and tantrums, green and blue in patterns and curves for good days. His trees were extraordinary for his age. She loved them both to distraction. She couldn't even contemplate something happening to them. Stories involving children on the television news made her stomach knot. No, she just wanted a bit of space – time off in acknowledgement of long and distinguished service to the family. And she had a plan. What if she and Joanna went somewhere together? A spa break, or a yoga holiday? Joanna could certainly afford it, and she had the time, too.

'Alright?'

'Yes.' Cheryl smiled back.

Joanna's eyes detected the lack of sincerity. Cheryl couldn't lie if her life depended on it. Joanna's raised eyebrow said it all.

'Well, no.'

'So, give!'

'Oh, it's nothing really. Just family things. You know …'

Joanna didn't. She waited for Cheryl to continue.

'Just … Ross giving me a hard time this morning. He phoned from location because he didn't have some of the shirts he wanted. Then, just as I was leaving to come here, his PA called to see if he'd left his aftershave behind. Honestly, men! And then Zoë announced she needed some red cardboard and green tissue paper to take to school for an art project, just five minutes before we leave. One of the cats hocked up a hair ball in the hall and, of course, Tom's lumbering teenage foot trod in it and spread it half way round the house.'

Cheryl thought about Joanna and Richard's tidy feng shuied lounge, high-end kitchen, and white marble bathroom. The latter had been carefully designed to overlook the garden yet not be overlooked itself, so they could have candle-lit baths and look straight out on to the grotto and terrace without having to close the blinds. They didn't have any pets. Richard abhorred pet hair anywhere.

'I mean, I love them all,' it seemed to help Cheryl to say this out loud. 'But I just need a break. In fact, that's something I was going to talk to you about. I don't suppose you fancy extending our lunch date thing into a weekend away somewhere, do you?'

Joanna's taught expression suggested that the idea made her uncomfortable. Cheryl was puzzled; she'd thought Joanna would jump at the chance. She had no ties, and had often mentioned that she didn't feel like going away on her own when Richard was away on one of his architect's conferences.

'Well, yes, it sounds like it could be a great idea.'

Cheryl sensed Joanna didn't really mean it. There would be a corollary.

'The only thing is … I've got the prospect of something quite big coming up. I don't really know what the dates are yet. I love the idea. But I can't really say yes at the moment, because I just don't know.'

'Well, at least you're not saying no.' Cheryl tried to lighten her disappointment. It was unlike Joanna to be so secretive about her work; she was normally very open with Cheryl about that, because there was no danger

Cheryl would attempt to steal one of Joanna's clients. More than could be said for some of the other jobbing voices out there. The mere mention of a campaign and they would be pitching on your turf with a demo CD, their CV and a follow-up phone call before you could say: *supercalifragilisticexpialidocious!*

'No, I'm definitely up for it. It's just the timing might be a bit awkward at the moment, that's all.'

Cheryl realised there was no point in pushing Joanna further.

'Okay, just let me know when is a good time for you and we'll head for the sun! But what I need right now is a large mulled wine with lots of bits floating in it to prove it's been made properly!'

Joanna agreed that was precisely what they needed.

CHAPTER FIVE

The conversation hadn't gone well. Cheryl had to admit Ross's timing had something to do with it. It came on the aftermath of a screaming row with Zoë when dinner was about to be served. The row followed a call from Zoë's school to inquire why she was absent without a permission note. The latter was easy to explain, Cheryl hadn't written a note. The former involved a boy and an alleged day at an art gallery. Cheryl was fairly certain the boy was fact, and the art gallery fiction. Cheryl grounded Zoë who stormed up to her room, and then served Tom's plate just as the phone rang. Her tone was less than warm and welcoming; she didn't want to share the row with Zoë. Cheryl felt the details of any domestic discord could wait until Ross returned. He was an admired and attractive man away on location surrounded by who knew what temptations. Home, Cheryl felt, should be a port in the storm and not another squall on the horizon. He wanted to share his day and Cheryl was usually a sympathetic listener. In uncharacteristically lacklustre tone she gave him his cue: 'Good shoot? Get everything done?'

In reply, she was regaled with the tale of the delay while props found a vintage car that *would* start; heard the saga of the endless re-takes because it was a period piece set in 1918, when commercial air traffic hadn't even been thought of.

In Pursuit of Perfect Timing

'It was completely quiet when we did the planning visit,' the location production manager had whined in self-defence. 'The wind was blowing the other way. They were all taking off and flying south.'

And, of course, the cat ran off into the bushes the minute they put it on the garden wall for the leading lady to stroke. Which accounted for the strange sight of the entire crew on their hands and knees, backsides in the air, 'puss-pussing' in all the gardens in the street, holding out leftover bacon from the caterer's bin. Anyone walking past might have thought they had stumbled on some strange local ritual.

Usually, she relished all those location stories; echoes of her former life, told with great drama and a few embellishments for effect as Ross unwound. He was accustomed to being centre stage and in command. 'Mr Apollo,' Cheryl sometimes joked.

Ever the raconteur, he loved having an audience prepared to laugh in the right places and applaud the finesse and aplomb required to coax a performance from an artiste or overcome a technical hitch. Tonight Cheryl's attention was below par and she knew he would feel it. When his tone chilled in response, she called on her professional expertise and summoned warmth into her voice to fake what she didn't feel and they parted on amicable terms.

Zoë was clearly not coming down to dinner. Tom finished his last mouthful and pushed back his chair. 'Please put your plate *in* the dishwasher, not just near it, Tom,' she reminded in irritable tone. The dishwasher door slammed harder than was necessary before Tom made his exit to join Zoë and hear the full story of her day.

Cheryl looked at the tepid contents of her plate and pushed them around with a fork, before letting the utensil drop in a petulant gesture. Aware she would have admonished either of the children for such behaviour at the table, she sighed and leaned back into the chair.

A flush crept up her neck, as a feeling of shame assailed her. Had her anger with Zoë been disproportionate? How much of her fury was unexpressed frustration? Zoë had skipped school; *she* had excused herself from a routine staff meeting to spend an extended lunchtime languishing at Soloman's, where the source of her romantic longing was also lunching. She had scarcely been able to nibble a blueberry muffin, so consumed had she been by his presence. She tried to work out what he might do. Clearly, he had free time on a weekday. His long fingers held the newspaper. She peeped over her coffee to watch his eyes. She wondered if he noticed.

Indeed, how much of her angst had surfaced as anger at Zoë? Cold dinner was scrapped into the bin, cold comfort food. She made her way up the stairs to reason with Zoë without the histrionics. As she approached the door, she could hear gentle sobbing under the music. Her hands instinctively joined in prayer position in front of her mouth. What was happening in this house? There never used to be this tension. As her hand reached to knock on Zoë's door, she offered up a prayer of thanksgiving that she was having lunch with Sheila that week. Sheila was so calm – her sounding board, her confident. Yes, thank goodness for Sheila.

CHAPTER SIX

November 23rd had been a very strange day. Cheryl had a gut feeling that something very big was starting to unfold, but she didn't know what, and that made her feel even more insecure. First of all there had been a shocking revelation during lunch with Sheila. And then dinner was accompanied by its own unpalatable surprise. She felt she was getting only half the story. In fact, Cheryl was reminded of the joke: 'What's worse than finding a worm in your apple? Finding half a worm.'

Lunch with Sheila was at Manhattan's, a fashionable department-store restaurant favoured by ladies who lunch while their cleaners finish preparing the house for their return.

I've done it!

Cheryl stowed the Christmas shopping, unwrapped in the department-store bags, under the table.

I've actually got all of it. Even a gadget for Ross. The most complicated hand held gadget the shop assistant could come up with.

The smile on Cheryl's face gave the harassed waiter hope.

'Yes, two very *large* gin and tonics, please.'

She watched for his reaction. If he thought she was a lush, he didn't let it show on his face.

Sheila was going to be late according to the text message on Cheryl's mobile. Or to be more precise:

'Stk in trfic, wl b 10 min l8'

In Pursuit of Perfect Timing

There should be evening classes: texting for over thirties, TOTS, Cheryl mused. *I'm so out of touch, I'm a dinosaur.* Although in truth, text-speak irritated her at a very core level. Logically, there was nothing she could find wrong with it. After all, it took her an eternity to type a message in full, including an aeon to find the correct punctuation mark. So long, in fact, that whole species could have gone extinct and the next step in evolution evolved before the send button was pushed. Maybe it was her training – her English degree, and the discipline of script writing and voicing – but grammatical inaccuracy and sloppy pronunciation always produced a gut level reaction totally out of proportion to the offence.

(It occurred to her that she sounded like a stalwart member of the newspaper complaint letter brigade. Those middle class defenders of morality, rightly or wrongly typified as living in the South Eastern town of Tunbridge Wells, who reputedly put pen to paper at the slightest provocation, in support of *proper* behaviour and the status quo. Yes, Cheryl might have joined the ranks of Disgusted of Tunbridge Wells', had she lived there. It was a slightly worrying thought.)

Cheryl's eyes followed the waiter as he worked his way between the immaculate white tablecloths. Everything was very formal, with silver cutlery and opaque glass screens dividing the room into sections. The leaf motifs etched into the glass matched the damask tablecloths. Not Cheryl's scene at all. She was more a jeans and bistro girl. But it was convenient for today as she and Sheila were both in town to tackle the Christmas shopping. And, apparently, they were not alone.

Is that Joanna's head?

The hair was right and the height. And then the woman looked up at her companion.

Yes, that is Joanna. The face was unmistakable.

Cheryl hadn't noticed her as she struggled with the shopping on the way in. And Joanna was tucked behind one of the glass screens, with someone *who certainly isn't Richard!* Cheryl could only see the rear view. A luxuriant head of dark hair, cropped at the nape of the neck, just above the sea blue casual linen jacket that screamed expensive chic. Cheryl hadn't met Richard often. He travelled a great deal and girlie lunches were anathema to him. But she knew that he was sparsely blond, and his suits always immaculately pressed; he wouldn't sport a crumpled linen look, even at the weekend.

Perhaps it's someone from work?

And then it happened. They reached across the table and joined hands. They leaned forward, gazing into one another's eyes. A long thin hand caressed Joanna's cheek and brushed provocatively between her lips. This was no work colleague! Cheryl, who had been on the brink of making contact, stared and then looked down.

Oh God! How embarrassing.

She wondered whether she should leave and go somewhere else. But what if she couldn't contact Sheila? And she was sitting in the centre of the dining room. Joanna only had to look up and she'd see her. Cheryl leaned down, grabbed a shopping bag and feigned looking at the contents while she changed seats so that her back was towards Joanna. She risked a furtive glance over her shoulder just in case it had been an apparition.

No doubt about it. As if fate were making it perfectly clear, Joanna and her date rose and prepared to leave. Cheryl spun back, head down. For one moment she thought of covert observation. *What would James Bond do?* Could she use her spoon to act as a rear view mirror to see what was happening? But rampant curiosity or no, she didn't dare. Sitting in an elegant dining room apparently admiring yourself in a spoon was bound to attract *attention of the wrong kind* in every possible meaning of the phrase.

No wonder she didn't want to come on holiday with me! She'd need her spare time for this new relationship while Richard was away. Joanna! Who'd have thought it? What a dark horse? Well, her secret's safe with me.

She kept her back turned until the gin and tonics arrived and she was certain that Joanna and her companion had left. Cheryl sipped and tried to look composed as Sheila flurried across the room, in an undignified riot of ethnic scarves and jingling jewellery.

'Sorry! Bloody traffic!'

*

That night, Cheryl served dinner early to avoid a repeat of the previous night. Zoë and Tom had wolfed down their plates of pasta and were already upstairs when Cheryl gave up staring at her plate and decided to cover it up and save it for tomorrow's lunch. She had no appetite, in part due to a substantial lunch, but that had been six hours ago, ample time to digest. She just felt a void, void of appetite and a strange disconnection from life around her. Surrounded by an outpouring of enthusiasm for gatherings, gifts, and the commercial Christmas clamour, normally she would be right amongst it. Hadn't she just celebrated a successful shopping spree? Her face stared back at her, reflected in the golden orb of a Christmas tree bauble; a parabolic distortion of her truth, luminous and attractive on the outside, yet fragile and hollow. She so wanted to grasp this elusive discontent, to grapple with it, see its component parts and sort it out, but it remained an enigma. Turning the orb in her hand, watching the unique marks of her supper-greased fingerprints tarnish the pristine surface, she reflected: *Was it possible that one intangible fantasy could cause all this unease, or was it something else, deeper within her?*

The phone rang.

Ross sounded very jovial. It was all going very well, but they were a little behind. They would overrun and were negotiating two extra days. He was sorry. Yes, he knew they had arranged to go to a drinks party, but she could go alone, couldn't she? He was planning something special to make up for it. He was sure she would love it. He had to go; that noise in the background was Marie-Claire enjoying all the attention she could arouse in the bar.

Cheryl distinctly heard her call Ross's name. 'Love you, love to the kids, gotta go, honey, it could get wild!' She put the phone down. Re-planning her weekend – alone – she wiped the print-marked Christmas decoration and hung it with some stars and a home-made angel that Sheila had given her over lunch: 'Someone to watch over you,' she'd laughed. Cheryl swished at the tassels and the angel's bells tinkled. Were angels real? Sheila believed they were. In that moment, Cheryl wished she did, too.

True to his word, late Monday afternoon, Ross returned full of his exploits, and bearing an elaborately wrapped box which contained a midnight-blue beaded cocktail dress. He looked on with boyish glee as the tissue rustled away, watching Cheryl's reaction. It looked expensive. He assured her it had been. 'Put it on!' She hardly felt she did it justice with little make up and her hair down, but she had to agree it was a beautiful dress, if a little too large in places. *I've lost weight. Never mind, better that than too tight. It'll give me room to breathe if I put on a few Christmas pounds.*

'It's beautiful, darling.' she acknowledged his enquiring gaze.

'So you like it?'

'Yes, of course!'

'Will you wear it to the office Christmas do on Friday?'

'Yes. Do you want to show me off?' she pried with humour.

'My darling, you don't need me to do that, you always shine, whatever you wear. And, of course, I want everyone to see you are worth a top designer label.'

The party was on Friday night; it was an elaborate affair in an empty studio, with a false floor laid to prevent damage from stiletto heels, a laser light show, music, and lavish catering. Santa was in a separate room for the children. Cheryl had been to the hairdressers and invested in a manicure to do her dress justice. After his initial bonhomie, Ross had been rather distant for the rest of the week. Cheryl understood his pressing edit schedule, but once home he'd absentmindedly stroked her head or, when prompted, given her a hug with none of the enthusiasm of his arrival home, and certainly no intimacy. He came in late, and slept in late. Cheryl was about her daily routine before he appeared in the kitchen. If she were honest, she wasn't completely disappointed. Maybe after the party it would be different?

Cheryl and her designer dress certainly attracted compliments. Wasn't she looking good; I must take what you're taking; that's a fabulous dress, where did she get it? Ross's PA, Martine, certainly took notice.

'Wow, Cheryl, you look great! Fabulous dress! It's a perfect fit, too!'

An overtone of envy in her voice, perhaps? There was something – the smile was too forced and didn't extend to her eyes.

'Yes, well, it was a bit on the loose side – don't tell Ross, but I nipped to the tailor to have it taken in.'

'Oh, goodness! No, of course, I won't say a word.' Martine's eyes betrayed her again before the conspiratorial hollow chuckle. Cheryl's stomach lurched. Had Martine made the size error when she bought it? If she'd been out designer shopping, that meant no shooting. Where had Ross been? She looked over Martine's shoulder and caught his eye. He strode over.

'How are my two favourite ladies, then?'

'I was saying how great Cheryl looks tonight,' Martine looked up and shifted her weight onto her back foot.

'My wife always looks fabulous,' he planted a kiss on her cheek, arm proprietorially around her shoulder. 'Martine, I need to introduce Cheryl to our new publicist, would you excuse us a moment?' Martine inclined her head and pulled a knowing smile. Cheryl found herself escorted into the fray wishing she had chosen a larger drink.

CHAPTER SEVEN

At the television studio the Sunday film had another forty minutes to go. Cheryl was down in transmission chatting to Robin. The presentation suite was a tiny room, packed with monitors as a backdrop to the vision-mixing desk. Some monitors showed the clocks that identified which item was cued and ready to go. The two large central screens showed the picture that was on air, the second being a preview facility, which allowed Robin to take a look at any of the clips before transmission. The minimal ceiling lighting was carefully focused on the desk, avoiding shedding any light on the monitor bank. With Christmas a week away, there was the addition of tinsel around the monitors and a flashing, nodding Santa on top of the monitor stack.

The conversation lulled. Cheryl found herself leaning back against the dark rear wall of the suite, going through the same list of possibilities she had been sifting for the past two months. Santa flashed hypnotically.

She'd casually asked around the studio about the girl on the doorstep back in October. She was careful not to reveal the full story; just that she thought a girl had a crush on Ross. People shrugged, were dismissive, or changed the subject. Just once Hilary, the MD's personal assistant who got all the gossip, took a breath, paused as if to say something, and then diverted onto something trivial. Cheryl wondered what she had thought better of saying. But without concrete evidence she clung to the life raft of belief that Ross might have been telling the truth. Perhaps the girl was just an infatuated acquaintance. But where had Ross been on that extended weekend shoot? Her initial pleasure in wearing her designer dress had been tainted by the possibility that it had been an expensive gesture to assuage a guilty conscience. She had gently enquired about the circumstances of the purchase and was fairly certain that Martine had been sent to buy it. Was *that girl* involved? Cheryl kicked away from the wall, restless with irritation. Suspicion gnawed at her. Was she right? Santa nodded. She reached forward around Robin and stopped him,

'Sorry, it was driving me mad.'

Robin shrugged. Did he know? Did they all know, except her? How to find out? The uncertainty was maddening.

And then, there was Joanna.

It isn't anyone from work. Can't be anyone Richard knows.

He'd always struck Cheryl as the jealous type, and he was extremely astute.

He'd notice something if it was someone he knew.

Richard was a complete control freak.

So, where did they meet? And how long has it been going on?

Cheryl felt as if all the certainties of life as she had perceived them were open to challenge.

Joanna and Cheryl had met for their usual lunch, the first since Cheryl had seen her at Manhattan's.

They exchanged their greeting hug, and were ushered to a table at a local tapas bar. As they colluded over the ordering of a selection of sharing plates, Cheryl looked at Joanna as if meeting someone for the first time.

That's what happens when strange meetings make you wonder how well you really know those closest to you.

Cheryl was aware she was projecting her issues with Ross onto her friendship with Joanna. She focused back on Joanna's face. Despite knowing her for so many years, Joanna could still put on a mask so securely that even those closest to her found her inscrutable. Cheryl could detect nothing amiss. But she couldn't quite leave it alone.

'This is nice. It seems ages since we managed to arrange lunch, what with Christmas almost here.'

Joanna smiled and agreed.

Cheryl tried a different tack. She dared not be too obvious.

'I don't get the chance to indulge myself in too many lunches these days. The older the twins get, the more they seem to need me. You'd think it would be the other way around, wouldn't you? It's a good thing we have a regular arrangement or I'd never get away at all. Although I did have a nice lunch with Sheila, while we were doing our Christmas shopping. That's the last time I treated myself.'

Joanna lifted a large forkful of spicy mushroom to her mouth and savoured the moment.

'Mm, yes it is good to enjoy a lunch. This is scrumptious – have you tried that plate?'

Hopeless. Either Joanna is avoiding the conversation or she's oblivious to what I'm fishing for.

Cheryl felt a bit hurt that her friend hadn't confided in her. *No, make that very hurt. But then, if I were cheating on Ross, would I risk telling anyone? Even Joanna?*

She knew for certain that the answer was *NO!* She played out the scenario like a movie role in her mind, feeling the situation and the emotions. Cheryl found the idea of living with deceit almost incomprehensible. She couldn't even tell Sheila the full extent of her infatuation with her mystery man. She wore her heart on her sleeve, so how would it be possible to carry on daily life if she let an attraction evolve and allowed herself to become intimately involved with someone else? She would end up blurting it out in a fit of guilt, which would achieve nothing but salve her conscience and cause catastrophic pain and anger to her partner. No, for Cheryl, it would have to be *end the relationship first*, and then move forward into a new one. Joanna was a dark horse, indeed.

On the other hand, I haven't told any of my friends the full story about that girl on the doorstep, either. Somehow it had made her feel ashamed. As if she had been so lax about her relationship that she had allowed it to happen. *Cuckolded! I know that's only for men who have been cheated on. But, oh how that sounded more like the feeling I had! Made a laughing stock, diminished.* To tell anyone about it would feel like being publicly shamed. Again she wondered what Hilary, the MD's secretary, wouldn't say. *Perhaps the only person who didn't know is me?*

She brought herself and her thoughts back into the present.

'Everything all right?' Joanna asked with a slightly more earnest note in her voice than would have been expected from someone enquiring just about the food.

'Oh ... sorry … miles away. Um, just thinking about some loose ends at home.' Not exactly a lie. Cheryl didn't like lies. She couldn't tell whether Joanna believed her or not. She had a feeling that Joanna didn't.

'That's okay then. I just thought you looked a bit – well, troubled. Here, try the tomatoes.'

Cheryl spooned the tomatoes and their garlic and herb juice onto her plate. She had thought she knew her friend well, but she hadn't an inkling of her secret life. She and Ross were invited to Joanna and Richard's Christmas cocktail party in two days. *The masks we wear. Oh well, it's her choice, but it's going to be as awkward as hell – it's straight out of a soap opera.*

*

Christmas came and masqueraded as a happy family affair. Everyone opened presents, the meal worked perfectly and then they all went their separate ways. The twins either watched TV or stared into their phones. Cheryl flopped in front of the big film, and Ross wandered in an out from time to time. Christmas wasn't his favourite time. Cheryl suspected he found the holiday week an unwelcome distraction when he could be getting on with the film edit.

It's all right, Cheryl placated herself. I've had to work a couple of shifts this week. It's just how the business is. We've always had a fragmented family life.

But there was something else, she could feel it lurking as January progressed into the trough it always did in the weeks after the effervescence of Christmas and New Year.

She turned out the kitchen cupboards as emotional salve.

Ever since he'd returned from the location shoot, Ross had been even more withdrawn Cheryl thought. Yes, he was often like that when he was immersed in a big project but when she analysed it, he seemed moody and more reclusive.

She found mould hidden behind one shelf.

He would close the door to his office-come-den and disconnect from family life. When she was at home with the children at night, he would be out and often came in very late. She didn't want to deal with garrulous ramblings and tried to be asleep when he came home. If she wasn't, she feigned sleep. Sometimes he had the taint of alcohol on his breath, other times he seemed agitated and restless and would sit up watching TV into the small hours. On the odd occasion that she did make the effort to enquire, he would reply that he had been drinking with friends and they had gone back to someone's house afterwards.

The cupboard cleaning felt cathartic. Perhaps it was her imagination.

Television attracts gregarious characters and late nights were part of the culture. Cheryl had done plenty of carousing herself in her younger years, and though she found Ross's behaviour irritating, she said little beyond an occasional barb over breakfast. It wasn't a lifestyle choice for her any more. She didn't miss it, but if Ross wanted to continue to espouse it, that was his business. *Just so long as it didn't have a negative effect on the children,* she once told him in response to his grumpily hung-over mood. That was her boundary line.

Valentine's Day waved on the horizon and Cheryl wondered how she was going to negotiate it. She had been browsing the cards and the incongruity of buying one grated. If Ross wouldn't talk, then she'd have to find a way to do something about their growing estrangement. It couldn't go on – it sapped her energy.

CHAPTER EIGHT

The deadline was approaching and the office lights still burned late into Saturday night. Leaning back from his desk, Harvey Max, the deputy editor of *Celebrity World* smiled. He knew they had a coup, and he was going to work it.

'Oh yes! Perfect for Valentine's Day. A love rat story!' he shouted across the room.

They had the exclusive inside story, and they had the shots. And he could sell the headline to the tabloids. Marie-Claire Devine, MP's daughter, posing as provocatively as you can with a pregnant belly, and spilling the beans – full juicy details included – on the man who'd used her, and then dumped her.

The cheating bastard! Harvey stroked his mouse over the shots. *The lucky bastard, too. Even pregnant she's a cracker. A real life re-enactment of Deep Dark Love. Older man, young starlet. Delicious!*

And it got better. The wife was in television too. Harvey scented fresh blood. He reached for his phone.

'Aiden, get in here. I've got a door-stepping job for you. And book a good photographer to go with you. I want it real and raw!'

CHAPTER NINE

Cheryl stared at the dank February fog out of the bedroom window. She hadn't slept well, and six-thirty was a foreign land on a Sunday morning. Nevertheless, she was awake and the snoring next to her conveyed two things: firstly, she was unlikely to be able to get back to sleep through the huffing, puffing and rumbling; and secondly, she could have the peace of the house to herself for a while. So, as dawn was a while away, she'd decided to give in, saunter downstairs, and feed the voracious Merlin and Melchior, whose desperate meows clearly indicated to any human with a heart they hadn't been fed since, at least, yesterday. It was too early for the paperboy to have dropped *The Observer* on the mat, but Cheryl thought she heard someone in the driveway, so maybe it was going to be her lucky day and he had changed the time of his round. And then, on her way to the kitchen, something very strange happened.

Instead of the thump of a weighty broadsheet hitting the mat, the front doorbell rang.

What the heck? She paused, staring at the letterbox. The bell rang again. Her vision tunnelled; the sensation reminded her of the famous track back and crash zoom in *Jaws* as the shark strikes. She walked towards the door, oddly compelled, her hand hesitated on the latch. It felt timeless, in fact, it was only seconds before Cheryl opened the front door and immediately wished she hadn't. Three blinding bright flashes took away her ability to see for fifteen seconds or more. And reminiscent of thunder and lightning, when you see the flash first and then the thunderclap follows, a volley of cacophonous voices came at her from three sides.

She froze in shock. She couldn't see, but felt the assault in her very core. Fear shot through her like an electric charge. As the blinding whiteout adjusted to suns with smaller nuclei, so that she was able to focus on the scene before her, Cheryl realised she was being door-stepped by a photographer and a couple of reporters.

'Any comment, Mrs James? Cheryl, over here Cheryl—'

FLASH

'How long has it been going on—?'

FLASH

'Did you know—?'

FLASH

Nothing reverent passed through her mind:
HOLY FUCK! WHAT THE? …. JESUS!

Just before she shut the door a magazine was thrust into her hand.

CHAPTER TEN

Sheila had just come in from the woodshed in her garden, which her husband Josh had built in the shape of a summerhouse. Having a carpenter for a husband meant they always had plenty of fuel for the wood-burning stove. Sheila had used last night's candle ends as firelighters and loaded the open mouth of the burner with kindling and logs. It had been burning for ten minutes, which was long enough to get a warm red glow emanating through the kitchen. Her children were still fast asleep and Josh had left before dawn to go fishing with friends, and was unlikely to be back before lunch. Sheila pottered contently around her favourite room running through the possible choices for her day. It wasn't a windy day, so when the door began to rattle it caught her attention. Then she realised someone was trying to raise the latch on the door into the garden. It was still only seven. Alarm shivered through her. She was the only adult in the house and her children were upstairs. Through her fear, her mother-bear instinct kicked in. She looked round, noticed the fire poker, and strode over to pick it up just as the latch finally raised and someone almost fell through the opening into the kitchen. Fortunately instant recognition prevented her hitting Cheryl over the head.

Sheila was genuinely shaken by the sudden entrance, and to find her friend emotionally imploding on her doormat. *Keep calm and carry on* had been her axiom in the past. It wasn't often that Cheryl permitted herself to lose control, and now the floodgates had failed and the vulnerable interior had been breached; Cheryl, paralysed, was unable to swim. Even rudimentary doggie-paddle would have done. But no – this was a full-on, howling, drowning.

'Oh God, Sheila, so … sor … sorry.'

A triple intake of sobs; the sort of incoherent gibbering that distorts the mouth, and turns the face into a drooling mask of misery.

'Sh … Sh … Sheila! Can I come in? I need to talk to someone. They're at the house. Everything's out of control. The children! I don't know what to say. I don't know what to do.'

Sheila dropped the poker and took her friend's weight under the arm. Cheryl released the grip that was holding her up on the doorframe and allowed herself to be assisted to a chair at the kitchen table with her back to the fire. Even with its warmth on her back she couldn't stop shaking.

Once she knew Cheryl was secure on the chair, Sheila returned to close the back door and slide the black bolt across to lock it. This was going to be a private matter and she didn't want any interruptions from *them.* Whoever *they* were, Cheryl had yet to specify. Sheila went to the doorway into the hall, listened to make sure the rest of the house was still asleep, and then closed the door, securing the privacy of the kitchen. She looked fully into Cheryl's eyes and found confusion.

'I don't think they followed me. No, I don't think they saw me round the back. It's the front. The front door. And then they came up the side, by the bins. I hid in the pantry. Slippers. I'm still wearing slippers. Why can't I stop?'

'Stop what, darling?' Sheila asked as she pulled out her brown bottle of Bach Rescue Remedy. Cheryl was making no sense and she knew a couple of drops of the famous flower essence would do wonders for shock.

'Shaking. Why can't I stop shaking?'

'Here, open your mouth; I'm going to put a couple of drops of this on your tongue. I don't want you to swallow – just keep it on your tongue and breathe with your mouth open – breathe it in.'

While Cheryl was breathing, Sheila put her hands on Cheryl's head and held the intention that reiki should flow through her hands. That was all that was needed to start the process. Cheryl's sobs lessened as she breathed in the elixir, and slowly the tremors began to calm.

'My hair's hot! What are you doing?'

'I'm just giving you some reiki to take away the shock. Just let it happen.'

Cheryl sat and allowed Sheila to work on her. She closed her eyes. Sheila sensed Cheryl's fragmented nerves coming back together; she slid her hands reassuringly down onto Cheryl's shoulders and pressed down slightly.

'That's a little better. Now, I'm going to make us some really strong tea. Don't say a word – just sit there. And once I've done that, you can tell me all about it.'

Cheryl nodded her compliance dumbly. Sheila mixed up a strong brew of Indian breakfast tea, and poured two cups, making sure Cheryl's contained a full teaspoon of agave nectar to sweeten it. She used the time to prepare her mind. It would seem her intuition that something was wrong had been accurate. Her heart flooded with compassion. What could have happened to shatter Cheryl so completely? She'd seen Cheryl cope with numerous crises; this was going to be bad. Sheila gently proffered the mug, and Cheryl cupped it with her hands and blew across the top to cool it sufficiently to sip. Sheila watched carefully, concerned to hear what had happened to so devastate her friend.

'So, how are you feeling now?'

'A bit better, thank you. I'm so sorry to barge in this early.'

Sheila didn't interrupt and let her go on.

'You see the front doorbell rang. I thought it was the paperboy or something, and then I opened it and there were all these newspaper reporters shouting and photo flashes.'

Sheila looked shocked but still didn't interrupt Cheryl's flow of thought now that she was coherent again.

'There's a story about Ross having an affair with this young girl.'

'Is this the one you were worried about last year? The one who turned up at your door? I thought you'd sorted that out as someone from work or something.'

'No. No, this isn't her. I don't know what happened to her. I never saw her again. I don't think she was just someone from work, though. I tried to gloss over it, but it was Ross's reaction when she turned up at home – he blushed.'

'Ross blushed? You didn't tell me that. I'm sorry, you must have been really hurt.'

'Well, I hoped it was only a fling.' Cheryl's words accelerated like a runaway train as her distress re-emerged. 'And I had no proof of anything, I asked around and I think some people knew more than they let on. I thought Hilary was going to tell me something and then she just turned away. I just let it go.' The train crashed into the buffers. Cheryl hung her head a little. 'But now, after today, I realise it probably *was* something to worry about.'

'So, these reporters, what did they want?'

'He's all over *Celebrity World* for having an affair with the girl who starred in his last film.'

'Oh my God! Not that MP's daughter, Marie Claire … what's-her-name?'

'Yes, that's the one.'

*

It had been just over an hour since the door-stepping, but for Cheryl it felt like time had frozen; the scene swam before her, ethereal and unreal, as if she was watching herself from afar.

The commotion on the doorstep had woken Ross. By the time he scrambled downstairs, a tousled, grumpy presence, Cheryl had blocked out the press gang with the solid oak front door, shrouded in the night-time velvet curtain. Muffled disturbance could faintly be heard in the drive.

She leaned against the curtain, as much for support as to hold back the invaders. The magazine, *Celebrity World*, gloated with lurid headlines:

In Pursuit of Perfect Timing

BRUCE AND BRONTE IN NIGHTCLUB FRACAS!

DEBUTANT REVEALS RAUNCHY ROYAL ASSIGNMENT

MARIE-CLAIRE DEVINE'S TRUE-LIFE DEEP DARK LOVE SECRET

It was the picture of Ross that caught her eye. Turning to page five, as instructed in smaller print below the headline, Cheryl read on:

Marie-Claire Devine accuses award-winning director of leaving her holding the baby ...

Love rat Ross James ...

Cheryl looked up, straight into Ross's enquiring gaze.

It couldn't be. Surely this couldn't be happening? Not here. Not to her family. This only happened in soap operas, films, novels.

Ross in his den. Ross coming in late. Ross tired and distant. No – No – NO!

Like Alice in Wonderland, the whole delicately balanced pack of cards was tumbling on top of her.

'What?' He said. 'What the hell is going on? Is there someone out in the drive?'

Instinctively, Cheryl knew Ross's irritation masked his reaction to what he was seeing. He was in default defence mode.

Cheryl wanted to scream *You Bastard! I trusted you. I gave you the benefit of the doubt. I never nagged or pried. How could you be this stupid? This ... this cruel?* But no words would come out. He started towards her. A step too far.

She engaged her vocal chords: 'All those late nights. You lied. You weren't at parties. You've been with this girl!' Cheryl slapped the magazine for emphasis and waved the picture at him. 'You've been lying all the time. You liar. You cold-hearted, calculating bastard! You've been lying to someone who's your partner. I'm supposed to be your best friend. Your wife! Bastard!'

She threw the magazine at him. It flailed through the air, missed and landed on the floor at his feet as she pushed past and strode to the kitchen, only to catch sight of one of the reporters leering through the side window. Evidently, the gate from the drive to the garden had been left unlocked. Cheryl fled into the walk-in pantry and cowered.

Oh God, make them go away! Make it all go away!

*

Sheila listened to the morning's events aghast. She knew Ross and how cavalier he could be sometimes. But she had never expected he could behave like this: 'Did he say anything?' Sheila asked, hoping that getting the broader picture might help her frame a way of comforting her friend.

'I think he said: "I'm so sorry". And then he went and locked himself in his den. I suppose I should have gone to find him, but I was trapped in the pantry.'

'How long were you there?'

'Oh, I don't know, it's hard to tell, about fifteen minutes I suppose. I crept out and looked around. I couldn't see them in the garden any more. Then I just wanted to get out of the house. Just go away, somewhere where the situation didn't exist – some kind of bubble or vacuum. Does that sound silly?'

'No, it doesn't, sweetheart.'

Silence.

'How did you get out without the press seeing you? Had they gone?'

'Back gate. I wasn't going to risk the front. They might still have been there, I didn't know.'

'Oh, of course.' Sheila searched for how to bring up the next question.

'Um – Zoë and Tom, are they ...'

'Sleepover. Oh God! I should call. What if Alex's parents have seen the papers?' Cheryl groped in her pocket. 'My phone's in the house,' she wailed. 'How I am going to get—'

'Stop, stop! I can do it.' Sheila gently ushered Cheryl back down into the pine kitchen chair, in front of the basket of unwashed leeks.

'I have Alex's number. Just promise me you'll sit there while I go and call. It will be easier for me to explain than you having to relive the experience.'

Yes, she's right, some part of Cheryl's brain spoke. *You're still a gibbering mess. And you wouldn't get past the first sentence.*

'OK, it's sorted.' Sheila explained on her return. Alex's parents are going keep the papers out of sight. And when you're ready, I'll drive you over there to collect the twins. And then they can stay here if things are too difficult at home. Let's just take it as it comes.'

Cheryl had no other response but to revert to a further paroxysm of tears.

CHAPTER ELEVEN

Ross paced the floor in his room – his den, his sanctuary, his refuge from the world. Wasn't this where he came to get away from it all? 'What a bloody mess!' he yelled out loud at the picture of a girl on the wall, his favourite Roy Lichtenstein print *M-Maybe*. 'Just when I thought it was all over, now this!'

Marie-Claire had been trouble right from the start. He hadn't wanted to cast her. Even with two stage managers watching her, she'd gone wild. Something had to be done. He'd taken her out to dinner, reasoning a paternal approach and some firm boundaries might turn the tide. Failing that, he would threaten to sack her and get another actress.

He remembered that night. How could he ever forget? It hadn't gone well.

He suspected Marie-Claire was already high before he ordered a bottle of expensive champagne to go with the meal. Her petulant outburst had made them an unwelcome centre of attention at his private club. Following the rage, she collapsed in melodramatic sobs, so overwhelming that he felt obliged to accompany her home in a cab to make sure she didn't go even further into histrionics and self-harm - one of her destructive traits that Daddy's PR agent had managed to keep from the front pages. Once through the door of her dockland penthouse, Marie-Claire had changed tack. Sobbing gave way to wheedling and seductive pouting: surely Ross wouldn't deny her a little fun? A little stumble, so that Ross had to catch her. Arms round his neck, she'd said she felt faint. Pressed so hard against him, the perfect package of slender and seductive woman – and slender as she was, she was well endowed – *Yes, she'd been the ultimate temptation.* It had been like holding a living fantasy. Her tactics were unsubtle and deliberate. Ross knew he should just leave. Somewhere in the recesses of his mind his conscience told him he looked like a cliché in a second-rate drama. He was a renowned director nearly twice her age. She was a celebrity wild child who changed men as often as her underwear. But she was so tempting, and he'd had most the bottle of champagne – it had been a long time since he'd enjoyed that kind of spice and excitement.

Through the alcoholic veil, it had never occurred to him that he was stepping straight into the role of Nigel Peters, the male lead in *Deep Dark Love,* the drama which had catapulted Marie-Claire into the spotlight in the first place. With hindsight he wondered how he had been so gullible, or so desperate for approval or validation. *Classic components of a mid-life crisis.*

That's where it had started. After all, it was just going to be a bit of fun – just one night. A fling. It wasn't going to last. *Oh, fucking hell, why didn't I just leave it at that?*

But it had turned addictive and dangerous; Ross had found a renewed zest for life. He became a regular guest at her 'soirées', often getting home late, fuelled with champagne and the occasional line of cocaine. Despite her high-octane life, Marie-Claire experienced a kind of escapism in Ross's company. He became a port in the storms she created around her.

Two months later, by the end of the film, they were no longer having a fling – they were having an affair.

Maintaining privacy and avoiding the press became a game. And they played it well, keeping the appearance of director and starlet. Amongst the cast and crew there were murmurs. Daddy's PR agent threw red herrings to the press to throw them off the scent.

Ross did wonder from the depths of his den, at home, whether Cheryl had any idea. *She doesn't' say anything. How could she know? There's nothing unusual going on, apart from some evening, after-shoot parties.* However, once the filming was finished, Ross had been forced to be more inventive with his cover stories. He'd been to dinner with a prospective producer and then gone on to a club.

'I'm getting too old for this,' he remembered explaining to Cheryl to cover his jaded appearance at breakfast. 'I can't keep up with these youngsters anymore.' Wry smile. She'd just looked through him and walked away. He had wondered whether she knew. There was a cool distance between them. *Perhaps just as well* had been his thought at the time. *And it wasn't a lie. It was the truth.* Keeping up with Marie-Claire was a challenge, and his body was beginning to flag. In addition to the odd line of cocaine, Ross had added Viagra to his regime.

It might have been the drugs, but he had found himself uncharacteristically possessive and jealous.

Of course, she's all over the tabloids connected to designer-stubbled boy band celebrities, he'd reasoned. *All part of the P.R. smokescreen.*

His gut tightened as he paced and recalled the unsettled, gnawing feeling that wouldn't be reasoned away. On top of late nights, he'd had months of sleepless ones. Insecurity had become his four o' clock in the morning companion. Insecurity teamed with guilt, and quite often they invited *fear of the consequences* to the party. Sleep definitely wasn't invited. *God, I was exhausted.*

Ross was used to calling the shots in his relationships as well as behind the camera. He'd resented the stories in the press showing her with teenage boy bands.

Marie-Claire knew. She made sure her phone was never around to be probed.

And then, inevitably, it happened. She got careless. *Yes, no wonder she used to hide her phone in the drawer. Lucky I heard it vibrate.* In the shower Marie-Claire hadn't heard it.

Ross read the texts.

He'd thought afterwards that the ensuing row was as spectacular as a scene from any drama. Accusations were thrown. Abuse was hurled. Ornaments dramatically – if mercifully inaccurately – flung. The door slammed as Ross had stormed out having told her a few home truths.

'You bastard! You ain't going to—' her parting words were cut short as the door connected to its frame.

He'd gunned the engine of his Audi: *The ungrateful little slut! Thank God it's over, anyway. She was getting too much trouble.*

That's how he'd viewed it: *A lucky escape.*

And that should have been that.

But now it wasn't. Ross stopped pacing and gripped the window ledge. How was he going to sort this out?

I've seen Cheryl angry and upset, but I've never seen her look like that. Shit, what am I going to do?

CHAPTER TWELVE

And so the week began. Sheila and Cheryl collected the twins from their sleepover. They complained loudly down the driveway at being summoned to come home and exchanged looks as they wondered why Mum wasn't driving herself and why she'd brought Sheila. Sheila tactfully went to turn the car round while Cheryl explained to them that there was a story in the papers about Dad.

'So what?' sulked Zoë, still resenting the change of plans. 'He's often had a profile in the Sunday mags when he's got a film out.'

'Darling, this one is a bit different.' Cheryl paused; she'd rehearsed what she was going to say on the drive over with Sheila. *Not too much detail, just the bare facts.* 'The papers seem to have a story that he's involved with one of his actresses.'

'What? Dad? With some old slapper?'

'Zoë, shut up!' It was Tom who leapt in before Cheryl could counter. *Bless him, he always sees the best in people.*

'Thank you, Tom. That's enough.' Cheryl managed to speak and give him *the look*, which had always been her way of indicating they had overstepped the mark. It calmed the air before inter-twin warfare broke out. She put an arm round both of them, being at once referee and comforter.

'No, it's the girl from his latest film.'

'The tramp that's the MP's daughter? Please tell me it's not her? God, she'd make anything up for a bit of publicity.' Zoë raised her teenage eyebrows to heaven.

'Do you believe it, Mum?' Tom asked.

There's a million-dollar question. And one Cheryl would rather avoid right now. She wouldn't utter a platitude that it was a fabrication when in her heart she feared it was true.

'Tom, I don't know what to make of it at the moment. There were reporters at the house this morning, and I haven't had the chance to talk to your father yet. I'm sure there's an explanation.' *One of which is it's true.*

The twins picked up on her unspoken thoughts and went silent, a state that lasted all the way home. Neither Sheila nor Cheryl felt able to make conversation until they reached the driveway. There was no sign of reporters.

'Thank you,' Cheryl hugged Sheila.

'Let me know what you need. Promise?'

'I promise.'

'Do you want me to come in with you?'

'No, I've got to face this, and it's probably best if it's just Ross and me. But thank you so much for being here for me.'

'Always.'

Cheryl nearly broke down again in Sheila's warm embrace. She just caught herself in time and ushered the twins into the house. There was no sound apart from Merlin jumping down from the kitchen counter.

Oh Lord, I forgot to feed them.

'I'm just going to feed the cats. Run upstairs with your sleeping bags and put anything that needs washing in the laundry basket, please.'

For once the twins complied without a word of protest. They sensed this was a situation outside their range of emotional experience. Reverting to childlike defence, they shut it out and went to hide in their rooms.

Cheryl, good as her word, fed the cats. Still there was no sign of Ross. She wondered if he was lurking in his den or whether he had gone out. The former was more likely. She was just wondering whether to knock and look inside when the door opened.

Here was the moment Cheryl had avoided for months – had dreaded – the moment to face it all. But somehow, strength was building inside her, as if a pilot light had been lit, her own inner core of strength. Now was her chance to speak her mind and sort things out. The truth began to percolate to the surface of exactly how deeply unhappy she had been for a long time, even before her infatuation. Irritation with Ross had festered into resentment. The gulf in their lifestyles had ensured that this estrangement had never been addressed. And if she was so unhappy, Cheryl reasoned, then probably so was Ross. Which would explain it. But did she want to do anything about it? Or make a fresh start? And how much of that was due to her continuing infatuation with a stranger?

I had a fantasy man, and he acted out his fantasies. Guilt. That's what that lurking feeling is. It feels like a grey slimy ball oozing between my thoughts. I'm hurt and angry, and I've a right to be. But I'm not as white as snow, either.

Everyone might blame Ross, but Cheryl wondered how much she had contributed to their predicament.

'So, they've gone, then?'

'Yes.' Ross looked at the floor. A crestfallen boy in place of the usual confident man. 'We need to talk,' he said.

'The kids are upstairs. I've told them there's a story in the papers. We'd better go back in your room, I don't want them eavesdropping.'

Ross closed the door behind them and motioned to Cheryl to take his leather swivel chair by the computer. He stood at the window gripping the ledge.

'Is it true?'

Ross raised his head, a man about to take responsibility for his actions. 'Yes.'

An uncomfortable silence followed as Cheryl allowed all her suspicions, her hopes, and her doubts to rise.

'Is it your baby?'

'I don't know. I'm pretty sure there were other men.'

'And the other girl who turned up on the doorstep?'

'Yes.'

So I was right. Through all the distress and disappointment, a small comfort. *Are there others? How blind have I been?*

'Cheryl, I'm sorry. I am *so* sorry.'

'So am I.' Cheryl meant it. She wasn't so much angry now, as resigned. She had tried for so long to hold out, to hold things together, to keep calm and carry on. And now, the effort seemed pointless and the burden of carrying it had worn her out. A Stygian gloom enveloped her.

'Are there any more I should know about?'

'No, and that's the truth. What do you want to do?'

'I don't know, Ross. Right now, I don't know anything. I need time to think.'

'Okay. I'm so sorry,' he repeated.

Cheryl summoned all her energy to rise out of the chair, walked out, and shut the door behind her. The clock in the lounge said ten. In the space of a few hours her life had changed forever. Too exhausted to grapple with the situation any more, Cheryl went upstairs to lie down, and she wouldn't be listening to *The Archers*. She'd had enough drama for one day.

CHAPTER THIRTEEN

In Solomon's café, Mark carried the iced water and two double-shot, very macho espresso coffees over to the table where his friend and workshop colleague was waiting, casually leafing through the red topped tabloid headlines.

Mark raised a dark ironical eyebrow, arching it towards his short-cropped black hair, which showed scarcely a trace of grey despite him being in his fifties. It was a habitual facial expression, which amused friends and pupils alike.

'You look like Mr Spock,' they often teased. 'You don't get your power from Vulcan do you?'

Indeed, Mark did somewhat resemble that fictional master of logic, being tall, dark and slender with long Vulcanesque fingers, which he easily configured into the 'live long and prosper' salute in response to the taunts. Today his hands guided the tray of drinks to a safe landing on the table. Red tops were not his friend, Stefan's usual read; he was only reading one today because it was a free copy in the newspaper rack beside him. He flicked the paper closed as Mark released the tray.

'The mess some people make of their lives,' Stefan observed, shaking his head at the tabloid headlines:

MARIE-CLAIRE DEVINE AND HER
DEEP DARK LOVE …

'All *they* want', he slapped the page, 'is to profit from someone else's pain. Somewhere, there's a family torn apart and for what? It's time the world grew up and we dropped this greed for instant vacuous celebrity and all the crap that goes with it.' His slate-grey eyes crackled with anger, then instantly softened.

Mark agreed wholeheartedly. He didn't need convincing and was surprised that his usually laconic friend was so agitated by the lunacy of the world at large.

'Sorry – hobbyhorse. I know it won't change unless the public refuse to buy it. If only they knew the power they had. Enough of that,' he gestured, 'let's get down to business.'

Mark passed the coffee, nodding in accord.

'So, where are we going to hold this workshop? Your place? Mine? Or do we hire a room?'

CHAPTER FOURTEEN

On Monday, Sheila took all the children to school. Cheryl had phoned and spoken to the headmistress and the head of senior school. They were very supportive and advised maintaining a watchful but normal routine. Cheryl tried to do the same herself. At work, people either muttered, 'I'm sorry', or shot her sympathetic, slightly knowing looks. The first Saturday night at work after the story hit the press had been the worst. Cheryl was determined to go in and face everyone.

It has to be done sometime, better get it over with.

Remembering how it had helped on the morning fate had knocked on her door and delivered the truth with the Sunday papers, she had bought herself some Rescue Remedy from the local chemist. Cheryl was glad of its help as she walked into the control room and sat in her booth. Everyone's sympathy had somehow taken her back to the original shock, and she was in danger of emotionally falling apart. By meeting other people and acknowledging the news through their reaction, she was re-living that Sunday morning. Alone in the booth, away from the need to put on a brave face for her children, Cheryl struggled to hold everything together.

The light in the booth flickered, imitating a warning strobe. On the small screen in front of her a murder was being committed. Cheryl witnessed the whole thing and hardly noticed. She could see what was happening clearly enough as she stared blindly at the dingy night scene. She was aware of the click clack of the woman's high heels on the concrete, walking faster than fashion shoes allow towards her car in the deserted underground car park. The shoes, ill-suited to taking long strides, were designed for mincing and sashaying across carpets and catwalks. Cheryl was vaguely aware the woman has good reason to walk quickly –

She has witnessed a crime. Cheryl's eyes watched the woman increase her pace to get to the distinctive, flip-painted Mini, which shines with every colour of the rainbow as the light changes. A car to stand out from the crowd. Now, it might be her nemesis, making her an easy target. Cheryl stared vacantly as the woman looks around to see if she is alone. She sees nothing but the buzz and flicker of a malfunctioning ceiling light. Her key fob opens the car door, the clunk echoing from pillar to pillar.

Too numb to care, disconnected from the scene in front of her, Cheryl closed her eyes for a moment, waiting for what would come next.

On screen, in the empty echoing car park, a bony wrist appears from behind a concrete pillar clutching a long kitchen knife, which glints in the intermittent fluorescent glare. A tall, bulky figure shadows the woman in front of Cheryl's sightless eyes. The musical crescendo flooded the booth. Chery's lids scrunched as she winced at the terrified scream, which stabs out of the speaker on the shelf. The screen flickered as Saturday night's murder mystery claimed its next victim. The sickening sound resonated in her own stomach. A woman in anguish.

Resigned to re-enter the world outside her inner sanctum of numbness, Cheryl opened her red-rimmed eyes, and focused on the small colour screen eighteen inches in front of her, aware that tears had scored trails through her carefully applied make-up. A forlorn attempt to appear normal.

Oh, shit! What must I look like?

She dabbed at the damage with one of the crumpled tissues on the small ledge in front of her. Soggy evidence of her emotional incontinence through the evening.

Get a grip!

The pain caused by sinking her short nails as forcefully as possible into the palm of her hand in the hope of causing a diversion from her mental anguish, failed in its purpose.

Come on, for heaven's sake! You've only got two and a half minutes!

A disembodied voice spoke into the headphones she was wearing: 'Cheryl? Are you okay there?'

Cheryl was glad it was Robin on duty with her tonight. He was kind and didn't ask questions. In her announcer's booth, clad and muffled with soulless grey carpet, Cheryl had hoped she would be able to cut herself off from reality, to shut down her emotions and focus on the job in hand. She glanced up at the clock in front of her …

in two minutes ten seconds …

The window of soundproof glass with carefully directed lighting afforded Cheryl a view of Robin. Fortunately, she reflected, his view of her was more restricted, as only a script light, designed so that she could see her script without the light shining on the rack television monitors in front of her, illuminated her sanctuary. She was aware of Robin staring at her profile outlined through the glass.

'Hi, Robin – fine – standing by.'

Well, that was an ad-lib if ever there was one! Of course, I'm not fine; I'm an imploding emotional mess! But I had to face coming back to work sooner or later. Hiding at home won't help anything. Again the pain from her embedded nails failed to effect the desired distraction. *I'm damn well falling apart and Robin knows why. Half the bloody country knows why.*

She forced a smile, hoping it was true that the act of smiling would trigger a chemical reaction in the brain – a serotonin release – that really made you feel better, despite the circumstances.

'One minute to you.' Robin's voice in her headphones made her jump. Panic took over.

Is my voice steady? Deep breaths. Alternate nostril breathing, deep breathing: Hell! Any kind of breathing! Come on, you can do this! You can do this! You MUST!

Cheryl trawled through every trick, every titbit of training she had ever learned in her ten years as Channel 9's announcer. The music for the closing credits began to play. The red light glowed in the tiny soundproof voice booth, indicating that the chunky phantom-powered Neumann microphone, slung from the ceiling in its cradle, was now live to air – the microphone that gives every television voice over and radio presenter their close deep and sexy sound, as if they are sitting right in front of you. Cheryl knew the secret to working well with a Neumann is to cuddle up so close you can lick it. In return for this intimacy, it delivers the very core essence of the voice; every click, spittle and nuance; every smile, every frown, every tremble. She took the last steadying breath and spoke.

'And you can see the concluding part of this week's murder mystery tomorrow at the same time. Stay with us here on Channel 9 as we kick off an hour of comedy at home next with *The Soul Sisters.* Just pull up a sofa and get ready to smile.'

The red light faded out. Robin's voice spoke through her headphones:

'Thank you. Fancy a cup of tea when we're into the next one?'

'Oh, yes please, Robin.'

The commercials rolled on with their ersatz happy families. The advertising jingles jarred and jangled in her ears, a discordant orchestra. She licked her lips, and swallowed down a sour taste of humiliation and disillusion brought up by the contrasting irony of *her* home situation. The concept of corporate illusion and aspirational happy living rolled on. Jibes, every one seeming to confront her with the fiasco unfolding in her world outside the booth. Cheryl reflected briefly on the reality beyond her screens, knowing that the television audience would be going about its business of chatting, making tea or heading for the bathroom, whatever was needed to be ready for the start of the next programme. Those who remained would be gazing at the screen, the advertising messages either rolling over them or sinking into their subconscious.

None of them would give a thought to the voice that went before – to me Cheryl thought. *For once anonymity is my ally.* She reached for her make-up and re-examined her distressed appearance in her small compact mirror. *Thank God I'm not in vision!*

In Pursuit of Perfect Timing

As the night wore on, Robin was kind and undemanding. He said nothing, made cups of soothing tea, and kept a watchful eye to help Cheryl through the shift. Her concentration clearly wasn't as sharp as normal.

Whatever happens now, Cheryl thought as she sipped one of Robin's brews, *it's never going to be the same again. It's like getting over a death. A grieving process.*

*

Something had to be done, that much was very clear. Last week's scandalous revelations made sure there was no hiding place now. As ever, Sheila was her sounding board, a grounding dose of kindness and common sense, and the final catalyst to make a decision.

'Darling, I'll be here for you whenever you want, day or night, but what you've been through is not your average, everyday affair. You need some professional guidance.'

After wrestling with the potential possibilities and abject lack of sleep, Cheryl knew Sheila was right. Finally, fortune smiled like a ray of sun in the aftermath of a storm of gloom. Her shifts allowed her free time during the day, so she managed to get an appointment with her local marriage guidance service within two weeks.

The counsellor assigned to her, listened with empathy, quietly making notes. The tissues sat comfortably on the small table between them. In the small, off-white counselling room, the furniture was shabby yet comfortable. A five-bar electric fire wrapped its warm hug around the room. The clinical white waste bin at the side of Cheryl's enveloping wing back chair was already a quarter full. This was her first appointment with Relate. Even after going back to work, facing that first shift on air, thereafter going through the motions of normality, her bulwark philosophy of keeping calm and carrying on was a tactical failure.

'Eighteen years. Ross and I have been together for eighteen years. Twenty if you count the dating stage'. Cheryl's voice trailed off, disappointment and self-reproach soaking away her vocal vitality. Another soft white tissue, with balm for sensitive noses red raw from crying, mopped up the tears.

'So,' the counsellor said when a hiatus seemed to have blocked the flow of further thought process, 'it might be helpful to recall how you used to feel about each other.'

Cheryl closed her eyes and almost hypnotically surrendered to the memories. After their first date, news had travelled fast. They were invited to all the media parties. Everyone's golden couple. The envy of singletons and the target of the happily hitched, who never tired of hinting that they would like to know as soon as Ross popped the question and Cheryl set the date. Despite the pestering of married friends, they felt no need to rush into a formal arrangement.

They had been living together for just over eighteen months when they were invited to stay with Ross's friend Max and his wife Heather, for a week in their Cornish cottage. For once the summer weather was kind, and the week with Max and Heather had been going really well until Cheryl started to be sick. She couldn't work out what had caused it. She didn't eat shellfish. She'd had the same meals as Heather the previous day. Looking back, she had felt a little unwell a few months earlier. But nothing like this. On the fourth day, Cheryl was feeling so awful that Ross drove her to the nearest hospital. They ran checks and took blood samples. Finally, a doctor pulled the curtain round the outpatient's bay, consulted his clipboard, and gave them the news. Cheryl was pregnant, probably with twins. A scan would confirm it.

'Oh shit!'

The doctor watched her to gauge her reaction. He looked across to Ross who looked equally dumbfounded. Cheryl looked at Ross too, and then back at the doctor.

'How? I'm on the pill.'

The doctor looked through his notes, filtering the information she had given him.

'Well, you have mentioned that you were nauseous a few months ago, and it is possible that you vomited up the pill before it had time to enter your bloodstream, which would have left you unprotected,' he paused, looking at Cheryl's expression of continuing bewilderment and concern.

How bloody stupid! How could I let this happen to me?

Unsure, the doctor continued, 'I'll give you a moment and then I'll come back for the discharge papers. Could you sign them at the bottom, please? And you'll need to make an appointment with your own doctor when you get home.'

'Ross?' Cheryl was suddenly afraid. They had never really discussed having a baby. Never mind having two babies. *Why had they never discussed this? Other couples worked these things out before they got married. But we're not married. Oh my God, what if he wants to leave?*

Cheryl was not particularly maternal. She had never hankered after children or cooed over babies. Everyone told her it was different if they are yours. Ross had left the woman with children he'd been with when they met. *I'm not ready to be a family guy.*

What if he wanted her to have an abortion, or leave? They didn't have any agreement about this. Neither of them had expressed a wish to start a family. They'd been fine enjoying the relationship as it was. Cheryl's thoughts spun at an alarming speed making her feel even sicker and she felt tears welling up. Ross's arm on her shoulder made her jump.

'Cheryl, you're shaking. Darling, come here,' he pulled her upright on the bed into a hug. 'It's all right – I'm not going to run. Don't cry. Don't get upset. It'll be all right.'

Tears of relief, gratitude and confusion continued to pour out of Cheryl as she berated herself. *Why didn't we ever talk about this? What are we going to do? What if I can't work? How are we going to survive? What kind of mother am I going to be thinking like this? I'm twenty-eight years old and I'm still not ready to be a mother. How do other women do this? They always sound so happy to be pregnant. And what about the birth? Twins! Oh God!* Cheryl went round and round the situation, seeking any straw of comfort, throughout the whole car journey home.

*

The morning sickness continued for the next six months, and Cheryl found herself acquainted with every drain grating between the car park and the short walk to the studio, as she stumbled out into the daylight and regurgitated her breakfast. Afterwards the day would settle down, so she was able to carry on working until the final six weeks.

Ross's proposal wasn't the romantic moment that most women hope for –although there had been moonlight, as they sat looking out of the villa dining- room window talking through the future.

'What do you want to do? Do you want to get married?'

'Um, well, I think we ought to. I know a lot of people don't, but it will just make things easier,' Cheryl ran her hand over her progressively rounding belly.

'Okay,' Ross took Cheryl's hand with his left hand, his right hand produced a tiny blue velvet box he'd secreted somewhere under the table. He placed it in the centre of the table between them, took her other hand and then looked up to hold her gaze.

'Cheryl Dryson, beautiful lady, will you marry me?'

'Oh Ross,' Cheryl looked back into his eyes and saw only love and sincerity. 'Yes!'

Their accord was sealed with a kiss. Despite her misgivings about marriage being more of an entrapment for women than for men – a belief that was the legacy of her father's departure and the years watching her mother struggle to support them both – Cheryl felt at peace.

Cheryl and Ross's wedding was a low-key affair; neither of them wanted a big white fuss. The local registry office was set in a grand old Georgian house with a beautiful and secluded garden for family photographs. *Well, some of the family! Others were significant by their absence.*

'Walking down the aisle six months gone!' her aunt tutted down the phone as she declined the invitation. 'Anyway, it's too late to arrange flights. Besides, who would care for the garden? It's crucial deadheading season.'

Cheryl's mother came with her cousin. Both Ross's parents made the journey from their separate homes and behaved with courteous civility throughout. Cheryl's best friend Sheila was her bridesmaid.

'A bridesmaid is a virginal young girl. *She* should be a matron of honour,' Ross's brother Joseph corrected tartly. He had made time in his diary to arrange his trip from Ireland, where he ran a computer business. 'A ...' he paused to choose the least offensive phrase he could muster, '... a mature woman is more appropriately called a matron of honour.'

Joseph was single, or bachelor, as he'd probably prefer to be defined.

Cheryl could understand why he remained unattached. Joseph was as anal as Ross was extrovert. As Ross tossed back a handful of peanuts from the bowl on the bar, Joseph looked on aghast. He would *never* risk eating something from a bar – what if the person before him had been to the toilet and not washed their hands? Cheryl could read the distaste in his body language; the drawing back of his torso, the held breath, and the wide-eyed stare following Ross's hand from bowl to mouth.

Thank God for Sheila and her sense of humour and sanity! Lord, how absurd; here we are, marrying each other and this strange and fragmented family. An odd fit. I wonder what kind of family we will be, Ross and me? Her hand instinctively reached to connect to the duo of potential she was carrying inside. A *frisson* of misgiving and self-doubt passed through her in the wake of her prospective mother-in-law and her own mother, as they sallied across the room in a show of solidarity; women who had weathered divorce. *What kind of mother am I going to be?*

Ross's best man was his great friend Max, whose Cornish cottage had been the start of the road to matrimony. Small, discreet and elegant is how they described their wedding, captured in an album of informal unstudied photographs; frozen moments of conversation, off-guard expressions and the one obligatory you-may-now-kiss-the-bride pose.

*

The twins came into the world early one March morning and changed her life forever. *It's true. It is different when they're yours.* Cheryl was so relieved that she did love them; even when they screamed in unison or at separate intervals. They were exhausting, and a huge learning curve. Tom, the elder by ten minutes, was quieter and Zoë more forceful.

At least, Cheryl thought as she battled her way through chaotic days, *I'm not going to be tormented by doubts in my thirties, wondering if I want another child, or not. Fate certainly sorted that one out for me!*

In Pursuit of Perfect Timing

Cheryl had listened to so many of her work colleagues debating, fretting, and failing to arrive at a solution to the question of when is the right time to take a career break, and whether they wanted children at all, and how many? The advent of flexitime and job sharing was a decade away. Having a creative career in television for a woman meant making a choice.

Despite his initial shocked reaction on hearing of their existence, Ross seemed to love them, too. Not that he was around for long periods of their growing up. As Cheryl gave up work for the first years of their lives, Ross drove himself to achieve. His big breakthrough came when he was signed to direct his first feature film for television. What started as a modest collaborative production between a private backer and a well-respected independent production company, became a hot pick. The storyline of lost childhood innocence and corrupt care homes coincided with a front-page real life news story that was very close to the film. *Kiddy Care* became *the* film to see. Ross's reputation was made. And with the kudos, inevitably, came the attention.

'So here we are eighteen years later,' Cheryl opened her eyes and mentally returned to the stifling warmth of the Relate counselling room. *Is it really that hot, or is it me?* Her head was thick, thoughts had to fight their way free.

'And how would you describe your ability to communicate with each other,' her counsellor probed?

Cheryl acknowledged the folly of letting things slide, of emotional denial and complacency. 'It seems an odd thing to realise now. It should be have been so obvious. Not good. We talked all the time, but we never *really* talked about anything of significance. It was always work or catching up with domestic detail and what the twins had been doing while he was away. It was a sort of verbal beeswax to cover the scuffs and scratches without ever having to look underneath to see the real damage.'

The tears erupted again, as if they had a life of their own. 'Oh, I wish I could stop crying. Sorry, I've been like this for weeks. I'm not usually such a cry baby.'

'Please don't apologise. It's quite normal, and it's good for you. So, with this emotional gulf, how were things physically?'

'Pretty non-existent. He's an attractive man. And I still feel I'm quite attractive. It's just the spark has gone. And now, after…well … you know' – Cheryl couldn't bring herself to say it again – 'I can't bear him near me.'

'That's understandable. I just want you to explore the feelings you had before, to see if there is a foundation, something to build on.'

Cheryl explored the vista before her. 'Not much of a foundation,' she concluded ruefully. 'What am I going to do?'

'A step at a time, it's too early to make a decision yet.' Her counsellor closed the notepad to signal this session was concluding. 'We'll pick up from here when I see you next week.'

*

Once home again after her first counselling session, Cheryl's train of thought trailed round the house in her wake like a crying child, wailing for attention. What was the truth? What was her truth? Family life had become routine. The twins were in their teens, she and Ross in their mid-forties. They had navigated their way through life relatively unscathed bar the odd row. Now he'd been unfaithful and she'd been fantasizing about it. Cheryl walked to the mantelpiece over the open fire and ran her fingers along the line of silver-framed photos in her collection: baby twins, toddlers, family outings. The dust of fond memories lingered. Now they were almost grown-ups. In the kitchen Cheryl went through the motions of making coffee; the mug's slogan mocked.

How can I keep calm after this? Slowly, her truth bubbled up *and I don't think I want to carry on.* Once more her truth rose from its hiding place, emboldened now, refusing to be ignored. *No matter how hard this is to face, I want out ... I want a divorce*

*

The following weeks were like living in someone else's life. Cheryl tried to keep calm and carry on. Her ancestors had faced worse and managed. So could she.

It's best for the children, she kept telling herself.

Ross and Cheryl treated one another with polite civility, neither knowing how, nor wishing, to engage the other on the subject. Ross had mentioned that he had hired a lawyer to find out the implications of Marie-Claire's declaration that he was the father of her child, and to see if he could force a paternity test. Cheryl went about her daily routine, reflecting on each task as if for the first time.

It's as if I'm watching myself living from some distant vantage point. Evaluating my day, my life.

And today was the big day for evaluating. Cheryl's hand touched her stomach. Although she hadn't eaten, she felt sick. Confrontation and discord were anathema to her. *I wonder if this is how soldiers feel when they wait for the signal to go into battle?*

After three sessions with a counsellor on her own, it was time for Ross to talk too. For the first time, in the cramped office with its worn upholstery, a fresh box of soft white tissues strategically placed, she sat down opposite him.

'I'm really sorry. I'm so sorry to have hurt you and the children,' he confessed.

Yes, thought Cheryl, *you probably are sorry. And so you should be. But what do you want? Does it match what I want?*

The counsellor looked from Ross to Cheryl.

'Cheryl? Would you like to explain your feelings? As you know, Ross, Cheryl has been for three sessions on her own to talk through her thoughts and try to get some clarity.'

Keep calm and carry on.

Cheryl took a steadying breath and looked Ross in the eye.

She sat upright, allowing her shoulders to fall back and the tension to leave as she breathed out. This was the moment – now. She had trained for this moment over the last three sessions.

'Ross, this isn't going to be easy, for either of us, but I am very clear about how I feel.' Cheryl could see his tension rise. Did he know what she was about to say? 'We haven't been a couple, not a properly bonded couple, for years. You must know that.' His jaw slackened in surprise. She could see that this wasn't panning out how he expected. 'I turned a blind eye to the possibility of a fling on location; after all, I know how easily it happens. I just tried to see that possibility as a kind of blip, which didn't have much impact on a stable relationship. And I also know I'm fairly unusual in holding that view. I just didn't want to know, that's all. On location is one thing, but when it's right under my nose; the girl on the doorstep – everyone seemed to know about *her*, from the embarrassed reactions I got when I asked around. And you lied to me when I asked you; that lie hurt more than the truth. It meant I couldn't trust you. And then Marie-Claire: all the deceit that was woven around that; telling me the shoot was extended; all those late nights. I don't have any trust left, Ross. And I don't feel like I want to stay to see if I can rebuild it. In fact, I know I couldn't have any kind of happiness. I'd be wondering every time you go on location, or have a late night. It's the lies, Ross. I could possibly have coped with the affair if you'd had the guts to tell me.' Cheryl could sense a chasm of understanding yawning in front of him. He'd thought he could talk her round and recover the status quo. 'And then,' she went on, 'there is the impact on the twins. People have been kind, really sympathetic, but they don't want their children coming round to the house. They're embarrassed. Zoë and Tom haven't had a single invitation to sleepovers or outings since this happened. It's just not fair on them.'

… Just so long as it doesn't have a negative effect on the children … the phrase echoed between them.

'So I think a divorce would be best for everyone,' she finished.

Ross's face crumbled. He looked like a small boy left for the first day at boarding school.

Now she'd finished speaking, Cheryl felt almost shocked that he might have considered reconciliation.

Cheryl was sorry too. But she knew now that there was no going back, no patching things up for the sake of the children. The damage was done. This wound was indeed fatal.

And so it was.

When they returned from the counselling session, they called a family meeting in the kitchen and told the twins.

'You see, we've been living such separate lives, and we've talked it through and decided that it will be better if we get a divorce. The atmosphere in this house hasn't been good for the past few weeks.'

'More like a morgue.' Zoë mumbled towards the floor.

'But you must realise that we both love you as much as ever, and you will still be seeing us both when we get things sorted out.'

'Are we going to move?' Tom asked.

'I think so, Tom, yes. Dad and I need somewhere to live and it seems the best way is to sell this house and each buy somewhere else. A fresh start.'

Oh God! They look so sad. This is their home where they grew up.

Zoë burst into tears and ran up to her room. Tom nodded glumly and slouched off behind her. Cheryl felt even worse than she had when facing the truth about her marriage. She would have done anything, had a choice been available, to spare Zoë and Tom this heartache. But there was no other way.

To ease the atmosphere in the house, Ross decided to move out to stay with his friend Max until he found somewhere he wanted to live. The 'For Sale' board braved the winds. And after three months of frantic tidying, set-dressing, coffee brewing and bread making to create the ironic vision of the villa as the perfect family home to prospective buyers, 41 Cedar Avenue was sold. Not wanting to rush into buying anything while she accustomed herself to a divorcée's life, Cheryl found herself planning how to make the best of life in a rented Edwardian terraced half a mile away. The twins and the cats moved with her. As she drove away from the villa with the meowling of Merlin and Melchior in their cat baskets on Zoë and Tom's laps, it felt as if a heavyweight door had closed behind her and a vacuum was waiting to be filled.in front.

A glance in the rear-view mirror confirmed tears rolling down Zoë's cheeks, which she tried to hide by consoling Melchior through the bars of his carrier. Tom's head was down, too, and Cheryl was sure he was trying to hide his emotions.

Oh my sweet darlings. I mustn't cry. Not yet. I've got to look strong for them.

Cheryl bit her lip, blinked back the tears and forced herself to concentrate on the short drive to Trefall Avenue.

CHAPTER FIFTEEN

Joanna and Cheryl's lunch dates had been one of the first casualties of the debacle. In fact, Joanna hadn't been in touch at all, which Cheryl found disturbing and hurtful. *Maybe it's Richard's influence,* she conjectured. *I know he will have been horrified by all the lurid press brouhaha. But surely she could have sent a short text?*

Cheryl searched her emotions to see what she wanted to do. *Did she want to see Joanna? Did she really believe she was just a fair-weather friend?* Joanna might play her cards close to her chest, but Cheryl had always found her to be loyal. On the other hand, there was *that* lunch! *How much do we ever know someone? Do I feel Joanna has truly disconnected from me?*

She recalled the conversation at Sheila's kitchen table that morning. There had been some late spring tulips in a vase, and the first new potatoes waiting to be washed. 'What does your intuition tell you?' Sheila had asked.

'I don't know. I suppose I think she's still my friend. How do you mean, exactly?'

'Well, try this. Put your tea down. Let your shoulders drop, take a deep breath in and sigh it out. Become totally relaxed. And then, tune into how you feel.

Don't think of any question yet, just see how you are. And then, when you're calm and centred, think about Joanna. How does it feel?'

So what does my body tell me? How do I feel?

Cheryl had waited. A warm feeling flooded her chest – her heart chakra Sheila had called it. Cheryl had been spending any free time she had in Sheila's comforting kitchen and was open to accepting any healing and help on offer, even if it seemed a little farfetched.

I'm going to try calling.

The answering machine clicked in after ten rings.

Richards's expressionless voice: 'This is Richard Short. There is no one available to take your call at the moment. Please leave a message after the tone. Thank you.'

She hung up. *That's odd!* Cheryl was accustomed to hearing Joanna's polished performance. Richard, ever the perfectionist, insisted that Joanna record all their announcements.

I'll try her mobile.

The ring tone instantly implied that Joanna was abroad; that long persistent tone that signifies you are dialling Europe or beyond, quite distinct from the shorter *brrp-brrp* of British calls.

Joanna's impeccable tones began to introduce her message service. Cheryl was about to hang up and try later, when Joanna's voice cut in:

'—Cheryl! Oh Cheryl, I'm so glad you've rung. I've been wanting to catch up with you for ages.'

Well that was welcoming enough. Cheryl decided her intuition had been right.

'Where are you? I called home and Richard's voice was on the answering machine. Are you on holiday?'

A pang of annoyance screwed up in Cheryl's chest. Joanna had declined to take a break with her. She tried to breathe it out and let it go. Returning to the present, she focused back on Joanna's voice.

'Well, I'm in France, darling. But I'm not exactly on holiday. Listen, I'm *so sorry* I haven't been in touch. I wanted to, honestly. But ... well, you see ... I've left Richard. And I thought you'd got enough of that kind of news to deal with, without me adding to it.'

Left Richard? Wow! Joanna the dark horse, and with the dark stranger! Who'd have thought it?

'What? Oh my God! Joanna! Are you all right?' Cheryl stalled for time while she wondered whether to mention having seen the pair of them at lunch. And Richard was not the forgiving kind. No wonder Joanna was in France.

'When did all this happen?'

'About two days after Ross hit the headlines. Once we'd made the decision and I faced up to telling Richard, we just fled.'

'Are you alright?' Cheryl repeated. Richard had a cold and ruthless temper, she recalled.

'Yes, darling, I'm fine. And so is Christine.'

'Christine?'

'My new partner.'

Shit! Double shit! Cheryl leaned back on the sofa in her comfortable but tiny lounge. So tiny that the sofa, which had graced her former living room, had to be brought into her new home by taking the window out. Perfect to curl up on in front of the little black cast-iron fireplace, adorned with a selection of white church candles. Her cocoon, her sanctuary; a far cry from the spacious villa.

'Shit! Oh, sorry, I didn't mean to say that. I mean—'

'Don't worry' Joanna laughed. 'I know it's not what you expected to hear.'

'Oh, Joanna, you know I have no problem with anyone being gay. You've known me for years, it's just that, well, I saw you at lunch with someone with short dark hair last year, and I just assumed it was a man.'

More laughter down the phone. 'Ah, so you did see us!'

'Yes, but I didn't think you'd seen me; I hardly ever go to Manhattan's. I was Christmas shopping with Sheila.'

'Well, at least the idea of someone new in my life isn't as much of a shock to you, then, as it has been to some people. Christine and I met at a corporate voice job I was doing. And we were just drawn to each other. It's was like we'd known each other for years, and could almost tell what the other was thinking. Cheryl, it was magical. I've never felt like this before. A real love: I love Christine; I don't have to think about it, I just know it. It's so natural; it just flows out of me every time I see her.'

Cheryl had never heard her friend talk with such heartfelt enthusiasm or warmth.

'Joanna, I am so pleased for you. You sound so relaxed and happy.'

'Oh, I am! I am! And I have some other news, too. Are you sitting down?'

Oh Lord! What else could there be?

'I'm a Mum.'

'What?'

'Christine has a daughter called Leanne. She's such a sweetie. I've moved in with them over here in their gîte and it's all worked out perfectly. It's as if I've been here forever. I just belong.'

Joanna: the career woman with the pristine showcase house and financial high-flyer husband, to Joanna: the gay stepmother, exiled in a French farmhouse. When things change they certainly don't do it by halves!

'Joanna, I am thrilled for you. And totally amazed. I'm still trying to get my head round it. It's like you've almost reinvented yourself.'

'Darling, you're not the only one. *I'm* still trying to get my head round it.' Joanna replied with a giggle.

Joanna giggling? I've heard her laugh before, but giggling?

'So are you there for good? Do you ever come back to London?'

'Well, I am certainly here for a while. Leanne is in the English school over here, and we need to live close enough to take her there. Also Christine has her business based here. She's in apples.'

'Apples?'

'Yes, we're in Normandy – you know – where they make *Calvados*? She exports it to a wine merchant in the UK.'

'So you're not working any more, then?'

'Oh yes, I'm working! Christine has helped me set up a remote studio so I can record and send links to London clients. And I can do live work online, too. It's just perfect.'

Cheryl felt a pang of regret spike her happiness for her friend's new life.

No more lunches. I'm going to miss them. I was looking forward to getting that back in my routine. Some kind of continuity after all that's happened.

As if she were psychic, Joanna picked up on Cheryl's thoughts.

'You know, the one thing I do miss is our lunches. I come back for the occasional voice job if the client really insists on seeing me in person. But what I would love is for you to come and visit out here. Do you think that might be possible some time?'

'I'd love to, eventually. It might be difficult just now. I need to get Zoë and Tom settled after what's happened.'

'Poor mites. How have they taken it?'

'Good days and bad days. They were upset, naturally, and went through a phase of being silent and withdrawn – although, I think they talked to each other, which I'm glad about. And now the hurt and anger is coming out. I have to confess I've been sneakily looking at their emails to get some idea how they are feeling. I feel awful doing it, but—'

'You're only doing it because you love them. Stop beating yourself up.'

This is a new Joanna! Before her leap into family life she would have been sympathetic, but I don't think she would have really understood.

'Yes, you're right. But it still doesn't feel good. Zoë lets me know when she's feeling angry or upset. The doors have been slammed far more here than they were at the villa. It's Tom I worry about. He just keeps it bottled up. I think he uses his art to let it out. He always used to do that when he was little.'

So you're not in the villa anymore?'

'No. I'm in a little Edwardian terraced house in Trefall Avenue. Ross and I talked about me staying in the villa with the twins, but after all that happened, those awful reporters surrounding the house like hyenas, and the publicity, it felt tainted. I couldn't carry on living there. But we're not far away, it's under a mile so the kids can still keep in contact with their friends, and I can still pop round to see Sheila.'

'Well, it sounds like we've both made a new start. Don't leave it too long before you visit. And if I'm planning to come to London I'll let you know.'

'Sure. Oh, I'm so glad we're back in touch. I've missed our chats.'

'Me, too.'

They exchanged a virtual hug over the phone, blew a kiss and hung up.

I'm so glad Joanna has found someone to make her happy. She sounds so different. Free. What about me? I wonder if there will ever be anyone else for me?

Cheryl realised she had had little space to think about her mystery man during all the emotional upheaval and the need to organise the house move. Now, as she stopped to think about Joanna and contemplated her own blank canvas, his face swam back into view and she felt herself remembering his enigmatic slate-grey eyes. A deep sadness and yearning filled her stomach and chest.

Heartache. It really does ache. Cheryl instinctively put her hands over her heart and was surprised to find that it felt comforting.

Maybe I should talk to Sheila about that reiki thing she does? That's what she does; she puts her hands on me to heal. And it feels really good; so peaceful.

Cheryl walked over to the whiteboard in the kitchen and drew a line vertically to separate the shopping list from the *to do* list. Under the tasks of *mow the lawn* and *unclog drains,* she wrote *reiki.*

CHAPTER SIXTEEN

Uranus is squared with Pluto and Mercury is about to go retrograde. An astrological forecast that foretold the coming outlook for the month, not unlike a weather forecast Cheryl thought – only the charts were more complicated. No fluffy clouds or cheery suns. Instead a mass of lines, angles, signs and numbers all of which appeared incomprehensible to a layman, or woman. Cheryl had no understanding of such things beyond newspaper horoscopes, to which she paid little serious attention. However, if when translated, that forecast meant a propensity for major upheavals in the most unexpected aspects of life, she could certainly concur with that. Mark was amazingly accurate. It turned out he was an astrologer as well as a reiki master.

It had been an interesting, and challenging sort of day – in a good way. For the first time in ages, she felt relaxed. *Not just bodily relaxed, that's easy, just get in a warm bath. It's as if the inside of me has relaxed, I don't feel driven, or like I 'have' to do anything. I can just sit quietly and those awful feelings don't keep coming up. I can't remember the last time I just sat, and ... well, did nothing; not even think. Drift ... drift back.* Cheryl felt the soft material of her sofa beneath her knees as she tried to move from a cross-legged to some kind of lotus position. *It looked so easy when Mark did it. One side of me works and the other just won't go. It hurts!* The white A4 paper, with its concentric circles containing glyphs and signs flickered into her sight in the candlelight. *My very own birth chart.*

That morning her spirit had been willing but her mind had still been sceptical when she finally decided to accompany Sheila to one of Mark's open house workshops. Cheryl knew reiki worked, because she had felt the effects as Sheila worked on her. She could feel the heat from Sheila's hands – far more heat than could be explained by ordinary human blood circulation. They felt like a hot wheat bag, soothing and relaxing; and more than that, they seemed to heal the pain in her heart. Not a numbness, but a release, as if it had melted. Cheryl had no idea how this happened but was very grateful that it did. Furthermore, Sheila assured her she could acquire the ability to channel reiki herself if she chose, which is why she had added it to her *to do* list.

Nevertheless, she felt extremely apprehensive as she walked up to Mark's door with Sheila. She stumbled getting out of the car and dropped her keys. She realised she'd forgotten her phone. *What if one of the twins needs me?* She was about to suggest she had to go back for it when she stopped herself. This was an excuse to bolt for home. Once the doorbell was rung, it was the point of no return. *Why I am so nervous?* Her hand rose to brush back her hair, the other brushed down the front of her jumper. Sheila stepped forward first, so Mark greeted her before she introduced Cheryl. The few moments grace allowed Cheryl to form an initial impression.

Oh my goodness! He's very ... imposing. Like a guru. No, like Mr Spock! Oh my God, he looks like Spock! He has arched eyebrows and I could swear his ears are pointed at the top.

She didn't have time to analyse any further. A long thin left hand was presented to her for a greeting. *Oh – wrong hand! What do I do?* Caught off guard, Cheryl offered her own left hand. It felt very strange. Mark smiled.

'Cheryl, I'm delighted to meet you,' he continued to hold her hand and a tingling warmth emanated from his palm to hers. 'Thank you for coming today.'

Just as the left handshake started to feel less awkward, Mark released his grip and opened his arm in an expansive welcoming gesture. 'Come on in.'

Cheryl followed Sheila into a wide square hallway decorated with wooden masks, some kind of small metal symbols on leather thongs hanging at intervals and a beautiful oil on canvas with threads of gold and purple, which caught the light from the room at the far end. She breathed in the scent of herbs and maybe some incense – a potpourri of olfactory sensations.

'White sage and lavender oil.' Mark answered her pondering.

Cheryl looked at him, taken aback. *Blimey! Is he psychic, too?*

'I smudge the house with white sage,' Mark explained. 'It helps remove any negativity. It's a Native American tradition. And I've got some lavender oil on the go in an infuser. Lavender is a great antiseptic and air cleanser in case anyone has a cold. And it smells good, wouldn't you agree?'

Cheryl agreed. Although she was quite used to seeing incense and things on sale in New Age shops, she'd never really explored their uses. *Of course, I've heard of these things. But I've never met anyone, apart from*

Sheila, who actually practises with them – if practice is the right word.

Cheryl and Sheila joined a small group of men and women in Mark's conservatory, the source of the light that had shone through into the hallway. It was purpose built in the shape of a giant upended rugby ball culminating in a point around eight feet high. The glass panels were interspersed with white-painted walls offering niche spaces. There were no chairs, just an assortment of mats, sheepskin rugs, blankets, cushions and beanbags. Being oval at floor level, it was natural to find a seat in the circle. An infuser wafted the scent of lavender from a niche inset in one of the walls. In other niches, which rose from just above floor level in an upward spiral encompassing the room, candles flickered and crystals glinted or radiated a light. However, far from being *otherworldly* the gathering looked quite ordinary. Cheryl wasn't sure what she had expected. *Hippies or strange ethnic clothing.*

There were two women, who Cheryl guessed were in their late thirties, wearing trousers and blouses, one younger girl blooming out of her leggings and tightly stretched tunic top, a similarly aged man in jeans and shirt, and one older man who looked to be sixty or so. As Sheila grabbed a cushion and rug, Cheryl quickly followed suit and sat close to her friend, still feeling out of place in this new environment. Mark followed them in, closed the door and fluidly folded his tall frame into a sitting position.

'Welcome,' he smiled from his place in the circle with his back to the door. A smiling Spock was slightly disconcerting. 'Thank you all for coming. For those of you who are new to this kind of gathering, please be assured this a completely safe space.'

Thank God I'm not the only newbie.

'We're not going to do anything difficult that will make you feel uncomfortable. We are just going to share a guided meditation to take you into a place of relaxation and peace. It's something you can do for yourself, any time you wish. With practice you can even do a quick meditation at traffic lights while you're waiting for them to change, or in the supermarket queue. It always amazes me how many opportunities we are offered to detach from the hurly burly of life each day, if only we are aware that we can.'

That sounds useful.

Mark instructed them to either sit or lie on the floor, whatever was most comfortable, and close their eyes. He invited them to breathe deeply and relax more with each exhalation. Then he took them on a descriptive journey through a meadow, with soft green grass beneath bare feet, to a grassy knoll where they could lie and just let go –listening to the birds, the in and out of their breath, the feeling of the sun on their faces, the scent of flowers. He allowed them to rest there in silence for a few minutes and then guided them back into the room.

Mm, that was nice. I thought I might feel controlled or something. But it was fine. I could do that myself.

Cheryl let out a long slow sigh. Her shoulders dropped back and she allowed her head to incline to the left a little. For the first time in ages, she felt as if nothing was expected of her. Mark talked them through the body's system of energy vortices, or chakras, and gave a brief outline of the influences of each chakra and which colour was associated with it. Cheryl's favourite colour was red.

'Red is the colour associated with the root chakra, the Muladhara, at the base of your spine,' Mark explained. 'It is your sense of security in the world and also your material support. If you hear people talking about being 'grounded', one of the things they are referring to is the need to empower this chakra to get the practicalities of life in focus and working better. It's all very well flying high in a meditation, but if you are not grounded in reality you can really lose track of your life.'

Well, that explains why I've been wearing red. I've lost my marriage, my house and who knows if I'll ever have another romance, at my age.

The thoughts triggered instant emotion into Cheryl's chest and eyes. Her shoulders re-engaged and rose as if she had been re-armoured. The area behind her sternum, which Sheila and Mark had told her was the centre of her heart chakra, from where she could open her heart like petals of an unfurling rose, suddenly hurt as if she had snapped shut a lid and tears welled in her eyes.

No! Don't cry. Don't you dare cry in front of all these strangers!

Cheryl took in a sharp, deep breath to steady herself. *Focus on your tail bone. That root chakra thing. Think red!* It worked. Cheryl felt herself gaining control of her emotions and was careful to keep a grip on them for the rest of the morning. After another meditation, Mark introduced the idea of working with the cycles of the moon and he suggested planetary aspects could influence humanity.

'After all, if our little moon can move whole ocean tides even from a distance, think what a giant like Saturn or Jupiter can do.'

Seems logical, Spock.

The morning came to a close and slowly people said their goodbyes and made their way to the front door. Sheila lingered behind until she and Cheryl were the only ones left with Mark.

'Mark, could I ask you to cast an astrology chart, please?' Sheila enquired.

'Of course, what do you want to know?'

'It's not for me. I wanted to give Cheryl an early birthday present, or you could call it a belated Christmas one,' she laughed. 'She's been navigating some big life challenges lately, and I thought some perspective might help.'

'Sure. Come on into the kitchen. My laptop is in their somewhere. I need to put your dates in. Do you know when and where you were born?'

Finding herself the focus of attention again in this unaccustomed world, Cheryl felt the relaxation of the morning meditation evaporating like the mists of Avalon in bright sunlight.

'Er, yes ...' she hesitated ...'I think Mum told me I was born at around ten at night and it was in Gloucester.'

As they sat at Mark's kitchen table, he tapped in her details and the printer on the shelf whirred into life to produce ten pages of charts, descriptions and summaries which Mark studied for a few minutes before he began to speak. When he did, his words flowed as if he, himself, were plugged into an unseen information source. Her natal chart gave him insight of her life, including her deepest childhood wounds that had matured to become her weak points, her Achilles heel. Cheryl felt her hands chill to clammy. It was so unnerving, she forced herself to concentrate on sitting still. She wasn't sure what her body language might say.

How can he tell that from looking at all those symbols, the planetary alignment at the time I was born? How can that show him my fear of being abandoned: or that fear of speaking my truth comes from a fear of not being liked anymore? How on earth can those lines and charts show him what's going on inside my head? I've only just figured this out myself. This vulnerability, this child-adult who melds and coalesces into friendships and relationships, losing myself, in order to be the person I think they could love? Had Sheila told him? No! She wouldn't betray a confidence.

Mark could see straight through the outer shell, into the primordial soup of her personality. *It's bloody unnerving!* She wondered, furthermore, how Sheila had lived with all this alternative awareness for so long, and yet, close as they were, she, Cheryl, had been so totally closed to it, shut down?

Mark gave Cheryl the printed copy of her chart to take home. 'I know it's a lot to take in the first time you have a reading. Just let it sink in, and take your time looking through the summaries. You can always ask me if you need more help, 'he advised.

Sheila sensed this was their cue to make a move. She was aware she had already taken up more of his time than she had intended, and was grateful he had been able to grant her request. She would settle up later. Unknown to Cheryl, whose mind was absorbed with her chart,

Sheila had agreed to pay Mark for the reading before their visit.

'Well, how was that, Cheryl?'

Cheryl blew out the air in her lungs through puffed out cheeks. 'Extraordinary! It's like walking through a veil or an alternative doorway. I had no idea there was all this *stuff*. Reiki, chakras, colours, astrology …'

'That's just the tip of the iceberg, sweetheart. You can't do it all, but you'll soon find out what you are drawn to. If you want to know more, that is.'

'I think I feel most comfortable with reiki. I can feel that, so somehow it seems something I can accept. Although I am completely blown away by this chart. It's as if I was made of glass and Mark could see right inside. Spooky. Too complicated for me to think about learning. All those lines and colours and planets and glyphs. It would take years!'

'Yes, it does. You could just say you are open to seeing what comes. Look out for signs.'

'Signs? What kind of signs?'

'Well, when you start to accept that there are energies around we can't see, a bit like reiki, and you are not sure it's real, ask for a sign, and you'll get them.'

'Like a road sign?'

'All sorts of signs. Quite often it's a white feather, or a little coin that turns up on the floor. Or sometimes you'll be thinking of a question and you'll hear a song on the radio and the words seem to answer the question. It's as if someone turned the volume up just at that moment.'

'Well, okay. I will try to keep an open mind,' Cheryl promised Sheila and herself as they arrived in her road and Cheryl turned towards her front door.

And now, sitting, eyes unfocused just drifting, she let the thoughts come and go, ebbing and flowing, possibilities and impossibilities. *Sheila believes in angels and fairies and a world that we can't see. I suppose that's what she meant by signs. She means from them.*

*

The first time it happened, Cheryl was amused and a little sceptical.

How bizarre! Cheryl caught sight of the five pence coin on the car seat beside her. *Sheila said I'd see signs like little coins appearing at odd moments, and answers to questions popping up on the radio or in newspapers if I accepted that there is more to life than we see on the surface.* It was all this energy connection. Cheryl had been googling it. A matrix is how someone scientifically minded had described it. The more esoteric evaluations described it as oneness or being in touch with universal law. Scientific explanations delved into quantum physics and string theory. Cheryl's scepticism was taking a battering. She had to admit from her own new experiences that perhaps there might be something in it. She was certainly prepared to keep asking and see what happened.

But pleasant as it might be to feel that someone or something was watching over her; that she wasn't walking alone but connected to some great cosmic network, she didn't see how that was going to help with her consuming passion for Mystery Man. She recalled his mesmerising grey eyes, the outline of his lean torso across Soloman's coffee tables; lean square hands manipulating his newspaper. *What if I actually meet him? Talk to him? How is that going to happen?* Once the initial upheaval of the move was over, Cheryl had tried to recapture some kind of routine. All the advice on alleviating stress carried the same message: exercise counteracts stress by eliminating stress hormones from the body. And she had certainly been stressed. So it seemed a sensible precaution to resume her morning run around the park, and then relax in Soloman's with a juice or coffee.

Not that I'm doing this to actually look for him. But you never know – he might be there. Maybe if I put that wish out to the universe it could give me a sign, like making him turn up?

Sometimes it worked, and other days it didn't. Once Cheryl caught sight of him in the distance as she jogged along the path in the park.

Well, it might be him. I'm too far away to be sure, and even if I really run I won't be able to catch him up before he gets to the gate.

It was a good sprint; Cheryl praised herself for trying. However, when she got to the park gate and out onto the road, he was nowhere in sight. She cooled down with a walk to Soloman's, but one look through the window to the seating area dashed her hopes of an encounter. Another day, just as she was getting into her car after spending an extra half hour lingering over a latte in Soloman's, (thus ensuring she would have to rush to get ready for work) he appeared round the corner with his newspaper and, to her frustration, went into the café.

Bugger! On come on, Cheryl, what were you going to do if you'd been in there? Accidentally trip over him and hope he'd like you. Oh, grow up!

Cheryl continued to debate the possibilities and berate herself for entertaining them all the way to her front door.

Never mind a sign, I need a bloody miracle!

CHAPTER SEVENTEEN

Slowly as the weeks segued into months Cheryl's home life created a new pattern and established its routines. She ran, she worked, she kept house and on alternate weekends found herself at home with only the cats for company until the twins were ferried back by Ross. He was living in a fashionable apartment just south of the River Thames and they had managed to establish a polite bridge of civility over which to confer about their children. After an acerbic exchange of legal correspondence, and histrionic phone calls, a paternity test concluded Ross was not the father of Marie-Claire's child. *So no added complication of a half-sibling for the twins.* However, Cheryl was acutely aware she was approaching another major life milestone. The twins' school year had ended; it was an anxious summer waiting for the exam results.

'I just hope all this upheaval hasn't affected their grades,' she confided to Sheila who had dropped round with some vegetables on one of Cheryl's solo weekends.

'What does the school think?'

'Well, when I went to the open evening all their teachers seemed to think they were on track and should get the marks they need.'

'Did Ross go?'

'No. We did discuss it, and decided that it might be better if he didn't. It's still a bit too soon. I could just imagine all those parents nudging each other and trying not to look in our direction. Zoë and Tom would have been mortified. It wouldn't have been fair.'

'Good call. So have they both filled in their applications for the courses they want?'

'Yes. Zoë has applied to The Film Academy on the South coast, and Tom has found an extraordinary course at Goldsmark College combining botany and art that seconds him to Kew Gardens in his final year.'

'Wow that does sound an extraordinary mix. But Tom was never going to fit the conventional mould, you knew that.'

'Yes, he has always had this vision of combining his art with his love of the natural world. He's often drawing things like the texture of tree bark.'

'A boy after my own heart!' Sheila grinned. 'Except that I can't draw.'

The following week white envelopes with the distinctive red postmarks of the examination board hit the mat. Zoë pounced on hers and ran upstairs. Tom stared at his as if he could read through the paper. Eventually, he took it into the downstairs cloakroom and locked the door. Cheryl waited at the kitchen table. She didn't need Zoë to tell her the news. She could hear the whoop and galumphing of pink Dr. Marten boots bounding down the stairs.

'Yes?' Cheryl enquired of the bright-eyed Zoë.

'Yes! Two *A*s and a *B*. Only needed one *A*. Yes!' she threw herself around Cheryl in a hug. 'Where's Tom?'

Cheryl shrugged.

'Tom! Tom, I've got in!' Zoë yelled heading into the hallway, assuming her brother was upstairs. 'How are you doing? Where are you, bro?'

The downstairs cloakroom lock slid back and Tom emerged into the hall looking glum.

'What's up? Zoë tempered her enthusiasm and put a hand on his shoulder.

Tom sauntered past her, expressionless, into the kitchen looking at his white envelope and piece of paper.

'Tom, darling?' Cheryl prepared herself to comfort him.

Tom's face morphed from bland to an expansive smile.

'Only totally aced it!' he informed the relieved audience of his sister and mother. 'Straight *A*s.'

Cheryl found herself wiping away tears as she watch them doing a victory dance around the kitchen table.

'Darlings, I am so, so proud of you,' she said joining them in a group hug. 'Now, go and phone your father and let him know.'

Cheryl sank back into her seat at the kitchen table. Making tea could wait. She was suddenly aware of the weight of worry she had been carrying. And something else: a sense of an impending vacuum. Of course, she was aware of the empty nest syndrome people spoke about, but in all her striving to carry on, be supportive and worry over her children's futures, she had never stopped to consider how much it would affect her. And now the spectre of being alone loomed out of the shadows. No husband, no children, just Cheryl and the cats. She thought of all the years she had wished for some space, some peace and quiet, and now confronted with that reality, she felt bereft. Merlin jumped up on her lap and started kneading and needling her legs. *Thank God I've still got you.*

In Pursuit of Perfect Timing

Still, she didn't have time to dwell on her new solitude as the time for Zoë and Tom to start the new independent chapter in their lives approached with unnerving speed, as if the time continuum had shrunk. No leisure for lingering in the park and around the café. There was so much to organise. Cheryl made arrangements for student grants, accommodation, books, sheets, towels, and duvets – the list seemed endless. Zoë's course started a week before Tom's, so she was the first to fly the nest. Cheryl drove Zoë the two hundred miles to the South West coast to look for accommodation, and back. And then again two weeks later with all her bags and cases and a food parcel full of the student essentials, baked beans, breakfast cereals, tea and coffee. The last she saw of the gregarious Zoë was her heading down the road to check out the local corner shop.

I wonder how long before she locks herself out?

Cheryl indulged herself in the humorous thought to fend off the escalating need to get in the car and sob over the steering wheel. She managed to drive off, waving gaily, turned the corner, pulled the car over to the kerb and succumbed to her feelings. She was groping around on the floor of the passenger seat for the box of tissues she had secreted away in case of emotional emergency, when she heard a tap on the window. A traffic warden mouthed something that Cheryl couldn't hear.

'You can't stop here or I'll have to give you a ticket,' he repeated when Cheryl opened the window.

Oh for crying out loud! Heartless jobsworth!

Cheryl stuffed the tissue up her sleeve and watched him move up the road to the car in front of her. She watched as the woman in the car blew her nose into a tissue and opened the window, presumably to receive the same edict. Cheryl felt solidarity and outrage.

Prat! He must have seen this so many times, you'd think he could leave us be for a few minutes.

As she drove past the car, she hooted and waved to the driver. She had no idea whether the woman saw her, nor whether her well-intentioned gesture had been received in the spirit it was meant.

Doesn't matter, I know what I meant and it made me feel better. Nothing like a bit of fighting spirit to put heart into one. Gosh, I sound like a First World War propaganda poster.

So that just left Tom. His course was on the outskirts of London, too far to commute, but easily near enough for him to come home for the weekend if he chose to do so. Taking him to his digs didn't feel so much of an amputation. Nevertheless, with them both gone, the house felt uncharacteristically empty and quiet. Numbed by the void, sitting listlessly in the silence, Cheryl found her thoughts wandering to Mr. Mystery with a frequency that was becoming alarming. There were times when she couldn't seem to think of anything else.

Mischief prospers in an idle mind. Who said that? You just did! Keep yourself busy.

Easy to say or think, not so easy to do. One thing she was sure of: getting a divorce had been the right course of action. She ruminated on how it would have felt if it were just herself and Ross.

Worse. Definitely worse. A failing relationship, naked with all its flaws on show.

Now the horror and distress of those months were receding, Cheryl felt a freedom that amazed her. Again, and again she pondered how she had sustained an unfulfilled and unhappy life for so long. From the outside her life must have seemed idyllic: a spacious home in a fashionable area; two beautiful, healthy children; a famous husband; material wealth and her own successful career. She had reminded herself over and over that this was an ideal that many a struggling working mother would dream of. So if she had felt unease creeping up, she'd fallen back on the family motto: 'Keep Calm and Carry On'. *How could she even have considered jeopardizing this life she'd chosen?* Only in the far reaches of the night had she battled with her demons of dissent, whom she dismissed as ridiculous.

Post-divorce, it became clear the mask she had shown to the outside world had not been as deceptive to others as it had to her. Slowly, as time passed, friends felt able to express their true views – they had found Ross arrogant and manipulative. No, they were not surprised by the outcome. In fact, they even went so far as to wonder how she had stuck it out for so long. Cheryl was genuinely shocked. She had assumed they found Ross entertaining and dynamic company. He was well read and had a sharp intellect, which he could use to effect in any situation. Conversely, she assumed they had found her nice but dull. She could always find a kind word for someone, but when it came to witty banter she couldn't seem to conjure ripostes with sufficient speed to impress. Only an hour or so later would she arrive at the perfect bon mot. Good with words, but not with timing is how she saw herself.

How strange that I couldn't see their perspective.

So, here she was, facing the death of the life she had known, single, alone, and confronting the blank canvas of her new future. Now the imperative of taking Zoë and Tom to clubs and activities and school was gone Cheryl had a wealth of free time. Reiki was still there on her *to do* list.

So should I ask Sheila to train me? Or would I be better going to someone I'm not so close to, like Mark?

'What should I do?' she asked Sheila.

'I can certainly attune you to the first level of reiki. I'd be delighted. But one thing you might like is a regular reiki share support group, and I don't really have the facility for that at home. Mark does, though. So maybe he would be better for you for a first attunement. I can always do your reiki two if you decide to go further.'

'Okay, thank you.' Cheryl touched Sheila's arm and squeezed, grateful that a potentially difficult question had been resolved. 'That makes sense. I'll phone him. I'm so glad I went to that workshop with you. Now I've met him and I know where he is, I think I would feel all right about going back. He seems very kind and in tune with how you feel. In fact, at one point I thought he was psychic.'

Sheila smiled and kept her thoughts on Mark's abilities to herself.

'I'm really glad you're going to work with reiki. I think you'll love it, and it does change your life once you start down the road. And speaking of life changes –

completely different subject – I'm itching to know – have you seen *him?'*

Sheila was Cheryl's only confidante on the subject of her infatuation with the man who haunted her thoughts.

'Oh Sheila, I just despair sometimes. Yes, I've seen him in the distance, and I know that he sometimes goes into Soloman's. Who am I kidding? I don't know anything about him. It's ridiculous. Especially at my age.'

'I didn't know falling in love was age specific.'

'It might not be, but I feel like a stalker. '

Sheila shook her head in amusement at this thought. 'Now you have the time, I think you should go along to anything and everything that takes your fancy. Go to films. Go to concerts. Mark does loads of workshops, and sometimes he teams up with other people for two-day events at the weekend. Chances are you will meet a whole new set of people and forget all about this man.'

'I wish. Yes, you are right, of course. That's what I should be doing. Get out and about and get on with it.'

And Cheryl did get on with it. She even went to the cinema on her own if she couldn't find a friend or colleague who was free to go with her. *Actually, I don't mind going alone. I thought I'd look like a sad loser, but it's okay. It's dark, I don't have to share my bag of chocolates, or care if I need a tissue. It's great.*

Along with that choice, Cheryl started to make other changes. She seemed to have bought half a bookshop of self-help manuals. 'I take responsibility for my life and my choices' read the affirmation in red lipstick on her bathroom mirror. That was her way of making sure she started each day on the right note.

So what do you want? She asked her reflection. *Well, I want to cut down the number of shifts at work, for a start. I deserve time to be at home and just be me – more quality time. I've worked ever since I left university. I've always been trying to hit deadlines. No more frantically rushing, trying to balance household duties with work. If I'm going to be at home, I want to enjoy taking care of it. Instead of shooing the cats away because they are under my feet, I'm going to sit and stroke them and enjoy having them around. Why have pets if you don't spend time with them? And, the big one: I'm going to give my full attention to what I'm doing right now, not fretting about the past, and not looking into the future at the next task. Oh God, I'm talking to myself! Is this what lonely people do?*

*

Cheryl found herself one of three who had booked to undergo their first reiki attunement with Mark. She had been surprised, after walking confidently up to his door fully looking forward to her day, that once inside she emotionally fell apart. Tears welled up and no amount of deep breathing was going to quash them.

What is the matter with me? She admonished herself after fleeing into the downstairs cloakroom to dab at her eyes with some loo roll.

However, when she made her way into the conservatory and met the eyes of the other two women sharing the experience, she was relieved to find she was not alone.

'You, too?' sniffed the girl farthest away whom she recognised from her first visit to Mark's house. If anything, the girl's leggings were even more challenged to fit round her solid thighs, and a floral tunic top hugged her ample frame.

Positively Rubenesque Cheryl thought fondly as she acknowledged with a nod and a wave of a tissue that she was also feeling very rocky.

The other participant was a stranger to them both. The modern Miss Rubens did the introductions.

'I'm Maisee, and this is Caroline.'

'Cheryl.'

'Really gets to you, doesn't it?' Caroline offered.

'Oh, I've been all over the place for days.' Maisee agreed.

Cheryl's turn to share. 'I'm so glad you feel the same. I hadn't expected this to happen. Is it normal?'

'Extremely normal.' Mark's comforting voice wafted through the doorway as he joined them. 'You are about to step over a threshold into a new pattern of living. When you receive your attunement later today you may find that the way you deal with everyday life is changed. You are about to shed the outer shell we erect around ourselves to shield us from the pain of life's hurts. And when you initially peel away those layers, it tends to make you feel very vulnerable. Instinctively, our psyches sense this and emotions rise up to the surface. My advice is to allow them and don't hold back. Tears can be very healing and today is a safe place for healing and supporting each other through the process.'

'So are we going to start getting beaten up by everything?' Maisee looked alarmed.

'No, not at all. In fact, you will find that you are better able to weather life's storms. You will start to see them from a different perspective. You see, Maisee, when you scrape everything away, there is only love or fear. When people are angry or criticise or behave badly towards you or anyone else, they are coming from a place of fear. They fear losing something, or they fear you are criticising them. Or they decided that you are making them feel bad about themselves, which is crazy thinking. No one can make anyone else feel. I know we say that sometimes, but it's not true. We all choose how we feel. And we can choose not to take words and deeds personally. We all have free will.'

Mark allowed them to digest this in silence. He could sense all the scenarios playing round in their heads.

'I know it seems a bit of a quantum leap to realise that we can choose all our feelings. It can be done with practice. Don't expect it to happen overnight. Just one day at a time. One hour or minute at a time, if necessary.'

Cheryl frowned: *I know what I choose. I choose to stop thinking about HIM!*

The day progressed with instruction on the history of reiki, discussion of how to use it, and what to expect in the first weeks after the attunement.

'Everything on the planet has a vibrational rate.' Mark explained. 'Rocks and solid objects vibrate more slowly than other things. Think of a glass shattering when someone hits the exact high note. We have a vibrational frequency, too. And what the reiki attunement does is slightly raise your frequency to the same level as the reiki. That's how you will be able work with it after today.'

One by one, they went into a separately prepared room to receive their level one reiki. Cheryl sat as she had been instructed to do, with her eyes closed as Mark moved around her and she could feel him making signs on the palms of her hands. She tried to monitor her progress.

Do I feel any different? Not really; just incredibly peaceful as if I didn't have a care.

Once they were all attuned, Mark instructed them to practise on each other.

'Just place your hands on your partner's head or shoulders and intend that reiki should flow through your hands.'

Cheryl couldn't feel much happening with Caroline or Maisee. Just a warm tingling, a couple of notches up from pins and needles. However, when she placed her hands on Mark's head, she felt an intense energy in her palms. Not pins and needles, and not quite static electricity.

That is bizarre. It's like ... I don't know what it's like. It's just energy; as if I'm microwaving him.

They ended the day sitting in a circle for a quiet meditation to thank each other for sharing the day and for support.

'Don't forget to call me tomorrow to tell me how you're doing,' Mark reminded them. 'You may feel tired, or elated. Or you may feel nothing, at all. Everyone's journey is individual. If you need support I'm always here.'

Cheryl almost skipped home, wanting to put her hands on anything living to test her new powers. All her potted plants were watered and reikied before she slid into bed for the most profound sleep she had enjoyed in ages.

CHAPTER EIGHTEEN

Fortunately, all three of his latest reiki initiates called Mark the next morning before he set out for the supermarket, and he was glad to hear they had all slept well and were enthused about practising their new skills. He slipped his mobile phone into his pocket, just in case they had any afterthoughts and set out.

The supermarket queue must have been designed to teach us patience, or humility, Mark mused. *A chance to practise being non-judgemental.* An interesting challenge, he reflected when you surveyed the haul of crisps, convenience food and fizzy drinks on the conveyor belt in front of you, whilst listening to those who chose them. Harsh words, redolent with criticism and resentment. *Junk food, junk conversations!* Not that the conversation was much better behind him, and that was from people he thought might manage things better. He was shopping with a friend and his friend's wife. Together they had bickered through the vegetables and hissed undertones over the cereals. Divorced himself, Mark wondered why people chose to stay together when clearly the relationship had run its course.

It's not as if they have children. And we're all going back to their place for lunch. Oh deep joy!

But Stefan had been his friend for many years and he felt he owed him the support. Besides, if he could get Marguerite on her own, she was charming. At forty-six she was still in her prime, with flowing black hair and olive-green eyes. Her dress style was unusual and somewhat bohemian. But, it had to be admitted, she was a wonderful vegan cook. Her work as a medical herbalist meant she had created a magnificent garden, abundant with aromatic herbs and flowers, which she used to culinary perfection in addition to putting them in her medicinal potions. So perhaps, if Stefan tended the garden and he commuted between there and Marguerite's domain in the kitchen, it would all be fine. Mark paid for his bottle of organic wine and waited for the unhappy couple to join him at the door.

CHAPTER NINETEEN

Friday morning started well, with sunshine coming in through the window, a nuzzle from two hungry cats, and an affirmation.

I want more magic in my life Cheryl said to herself through the red lipstick writing on her bathroom mirror. *Perhaps, I should start by saying 'mirror, mirror on the wall ...'* She turned to make her way downstairs before Merlin shredded her slippers entirely.

'Okay, okay, guys, I'm on it. Wait a minute!'

Look at me! I'm talking to a mirror and I live with two cats. Anyone would think I was turning into a witch! Well, at least I'd be interesting. Not just another middle-aged divorcée with empty nest syndrome. I need to find myself a date, and the sooner the better.

Yes, there had been plenty of attempts, the visits to psychic evenings, energy and sound healing workshops, tarot classes, even a sweat lodge. *Well, it's different and loads more fun than line dancing or flower arranging.*

Cheryl had never noticed there were so many opportunities in her area. Somehow, leaflets and advertisements seemed to catch her eye wherever she went. At one of Mark's reiki support evenings she even met someone who ran an angel circle. The woman didn't look particularly cherubic or fluffy. In fact quite plain, but very enthusiastic about angels! When she thought about it, Cheryl had never disbelieved in them, but neither had she noticed that they existed. She knew Sheila thought they were real.

It's just I've never really thought that you could actually talk to them or they could talk to me. In fact, I've never thought they'd be bothered with ordinary people.

Vague memories of Sunday school surfaced with ornate stained-glass windows; the archangels seemed to imply they were very remote and saintly, unless you were especially chosen for some godly task, like Joan of Arc.

Not very likely they'd pick me. Cheryl dismissed the idea.

She found that she connected with the concept of energy work best. It was tangible and demonstrable; she still needed to feel that she was working with something she could quantify. Now she had her first reiki attunement, she could feel her hands tingling and becoming warm. No doubt about it, something was there. Something she couldn't see, but was there, nevertheless. Her hands began to tingle as she watered the plant on the windowsill. Did it need some reiki? It looked fine. She gave it a little burst anyway.

And then there was meditation, Cheryl liked the idea of meditation. It didn't require any belief system or adherence to doctrine. It just required the exponent to quieten their mind – something Cheryl found phenomenally difficult to achieve.

Simply close your eyes, concentrate on your breath going in and out, and let your mind rest.

The cognitive left side of her brain, argued with the intuitive expansive right:

Ha! And how do I stop thinking that sitting in this position is uncomfortable. Must stop thinking. Just let go. Left brain shut up. Let your feelings drift by, just allow thoughts to come and go.

My hip hurts!

Mustn't forget to pick up cat food.

Breathe in. Pause, breathe out.

Just stop thinking. Breathe – in…and…out.

Oh be quiet!

Suddenly she understood the idea of a mantra – a set of words that gave her restless left brain something to do. 'Monkey mind' they called it. Give the monkey a pile of beans to play with while you focus on stilling the rest of your thoughts and allowing the creative and peaceful right side of the brain to have prominence, she'd read.

The only time Cheryl came close was first thing in the morning. On waking she found if she sat up in bed immediately, and started the day with meditation before her mind had a chance to jump up and rush around in its pyjamas getting dressed and organising, she could find that calm place, somewhere in the centre of her being that didn't seem attached to her body or her surroundings, or life in general. It just was. She presumed that's what they were talking about when they described the matrix in quantum physics. An existence without form, time or space. An experience of just being.

It was all so intangible, and yet comforting. Nine o'clock had come and gone this morning, and she was still in bed, pondering, wondering. *Procrastinating! Get up! You're going to be late!*

Still chewing on wholemeal toast and honey, she looked at her calendar –

Monday: Talk on Mindfulness

Tuesday: Kundalini taster session

Thursday: Sonapuncture - *what is sonapuncture?*

Saturday: Mark's morning reiki share.

She circled the time for the latter – eight o'clock! *Does Spock ever sleep in?*

Ten past ten. She sipped at the tea, which was still too hot to gulp.

Sometimes she braved the meetings unaccompanied. On occasion, Sheila had time free from her allotment and her family. But mostly Cheryl walked through the doors alone, often finding she struck up conversations with complete strangers who were also solo. Most were *normal* like her. Some were curious.

And some are just plain weird! Like the man who stared without blinking and without breaking eye contact. He repulsed her now as he had done then. Waiting for the tea to cool, she scrubbed at the crusted remains in her food caddy. *Ugh!*

The weird ones seemed to be there for some egotistical reason. Maybe they thought it might make them clever, or mysteriously attractive, or better than their fellow beings? Perhaps they were hoping to meet someone to date? *In their dreams!* The rinsed food caddy leeched suds on the draining board. Most of the practitioners teaching the classes stressed humility, forgiveness and non-judgemental living. Cheryl wiped her hands dry and reached for the hand cream.

Thank goodness most were simply kind, openhearted and really good company, and *maybe a bit lost, like me?* The soothing scent of lavender hand cream was a comfort. Cheryl's favourite lecture had been the Law of Attraction. *Attraction, oh yes!* She threw herself wholeheartedly into imagining what it would be like – no! – What it *is* like – to be with *him*. That's how the Law of Attraction worked; the teachings of *Abraham* and *The Secret* assured her. She now had the videos, and the books to keep her focussed. You have to live and *feel* as if you already have whatever it is that you desire. *Desire!* It was driving her mad. This was insane; she didn't even know him!

Yes, the classes and meetings were fun, but there was no getting away from the truth, that she hoped *maybe* she'd bump into *him*. Although, why he would be there she had no idea, just an instinct that he was part of that alternative world. Looking into the mirror last night, wiping the cosmetic mask away, she realised that somehow she looked different. She had paused mid-wipe and peered at herself. She had almost wanted to prod the image to see if it did anything different. Did she look different, or, was it the way she viewed herself that had changed? Any shift had been subtle, stealthy, a slight tweak on the steering wheel of her life. Essentially, she was still Cheryl – the one who went to work, shopped, cleaned and worried about her children from time to time when they hadn't messaged or called. But, she wasn't the same. Inside, looking out, her interpretation of what she was seeing had morphed. *Same landscape, different perspective. Altered reality?*

My filters have changed – yes, that's it! And, damn it, I'm late!

She grabbed her bag, the car keys, vaulted a cat, which zigzagged skilfully in front of her along the narrow hall. The heap of partially read books on the hallstand mocked.

'Where do I start? It would take lifetimes to read you all!' She yelled at it.

Louise Hay she loved. *Change your attitude, change your life.* A no-brainer really. It made so much sense, why had she not seen that before? Many of the authors seemed to have been through life crises and dramatic upheavals that had required them to make major shifts in the way they lived. *I'm with them on that one!* There was a strong common denominator running throughout. They all advised changing the way you care about yourself in order to experience a happier life, and the advice that Cheryl most espoused, how to attract a soulmate. But what about *the* soulmate? There was only one contender on Cheryl's horizon.

She snatched *Lovescopes* from the pile and rammed it into her bag to dip into in the pauses between the programmes during her shift. She could devour its lengthy and detailed description of the characteristics of the astrological star signs and how relationships work between them. She could fantasize about which star sign he might be. Moody creative Cancerian, fiery flamboyant Leo, or quixotic Gemini perhaps?

'Oh, I give up …' she said to the clouds as she ran for the car, flinging her arms open in a dramatic gesture, releasing the whole longing to the winds. The car keys arced out of her grasp and clattered onto the tarmac. 'Damn! Oh, I wish, I wish …'

You should be careful what you wish for. You might get it her intuition cautioned. *Shut up!* her left brain admonished, *you're late!*

CHAPTER TWENTY

Cheryl relived the past ten hours with a mixture of bewilderment and joy. She and Sheila had been at one of Mark's reiki gatherings. It was only nine-thirty in the evening and they could have gone to the Coach & Horses or the Flowerpot for a drink. But neither of them could be bothered to walk past Solomon's, and Cheryl went to the counter to order two hot chocolates. Sheila chose the seats.

'They'll bring them over in a—' Cheryl's breath seemed to have stalled; her voice departed.

'Cheryl? What on earth is the matter?'

'It's him.' She uttered in something between a croak and whisper

'Which him? Oh my God! *Him*. The one you've been besotted with for months?'

'Yes!'

'Where? Over there at the table?'

Cheryl eyed the dishevelled and slightly paunchy man pawing through a book.

'No! Give me a break, Sheila – how desperate do I look?'

Their giggles made the man in the booth beyond look up. Sheila caught the enigmatic grey gaze and saw it connect to Cheryl's hypnotised stare.

'Oh, *HIM*!'

Perhaps conscious he was the subject of their conversation, the man reverted his gaze to his table and the papers he was checking.

'Oh my God, he's so .... well ... you! He's gorgeous, and there's something else ... I don't know, otherworldly about him. I see what you mean about being a mystery man.'

As Cheryl looked down, he looked up. Sheila took him in; his appearance and his energy.

'He's noticed you, too. Do you ever speak when you see him in the park?'

'No! How could I? I don't know him.' Cheryl's voice belied her confusion, yearning and note of desperation.

'Well, you could smile at him!'

Cheryl chanced a look up. He mirrored it.

Cheryl swam into his gaze and smiled. He mirrored her.

Cheryl felt herself dissolving into a pool of girlishness. Her eyes shot back down.

'I've forgotten how to do this. And anyway, I'm a grown woman. I can't behave like this. Sheila? Do you think he knows I fancy him?'

A pause; punctuated by Sheila's sigh.

'Darling, if you had *take me, now*! scrolling in neon lights across your forehead you couldn't be more obvious.'

Sheila laughed into Cheryl's shocked expression. 'And you know what? I'm going. I'm going to leave you here all alone, with him.'

'What—!'

Sheila made a great show of wrapping her multi-coloured scarf collection around her shoulders, followed by an overtly elaborate goodbye kiss, and before Cheryl could protest, she called to the bar to cancel her order and was gone.

Oh crap. Now what? Nothing. That's what. I'll just sit here feeling totally self-conscious, burn my mouth trying to gulp hot chocolate, and leave.

She couldn't help stealing a peek over the rim of her mug once it had arrived. Their eyes met again. A decision was made. In one swift movement he closed the document, then stood up and headed towards the door.

No! Not the door! He's coming over here!

'Hello.'

Dumbfounded silence. Cheryl's countenance betrayed complete emotional shock.

'I hope you don't mind me saying, but we seem to bump into each other rather often. I've noticed you go running and I sometimes see you in here when I walk past. In fact, if it wasn't the corniest line ever, I'd say: *do you come here often?*'

Despite her efforts to look neutral, Cheryl's smile lit her face from the depths of her heart.

Oh my God! He's been noticing me, too!

'Well, no ... um.. actually I don't come in *here* very often, well, sometimes, occasionally,' Cheryl floundered. 'It's just that I, we've, just been to a reiki meeting.' She was suddenly afraid that this might be an off-putting statement. *Did he even know what reiki was?*

'Ah, would that be at Mark's?'

'Yes! Do you know him?'

Obviously he does! Stupid question. Pull yourself together.

Yes, he knew Mark and he had studied reiki himself.

'So, are you a reiki master?' he enquired.

'Heaven's no! I've only just started. I did my reiki one about a month ago.'

'Ah. How are you finding it now you're attuned?'

This is astonishing. Not only am I talking to him, we're discussing reiki. Never in my wildest dreams did I see that coming!

'It's been really good, actually. I was a bit wiped out and sleepy for the first twenty-one days, you know, as some people are. Apparently, I'm one of them. Must have needed the rest. But now, I love it. It's given my life a whole new dimension.'

And it's brought you to me.

'That's great! I'd love to hear more about it. May I join you?' he gestured towards the space opposite her in the booth.

'Oh, yes, please do!' *God I hope I don't sound too inviting, too forward. I have no idea how to do this anymore.*

Cheryl watched him rather more intently than she intended as he came down to her height and slid onto the faux leather banquette opposite her. Close up, his eyes were mesmerising; slate-grey flecked with crystal highlights and seeming to hold a wisdom and intuition that was completely unnerving. Cheryl's mouth was dry and her throat seemed to be closing, rendering further speech raspy. Choosing to avoid speaking for a moment, she became aware of her rapid tremulous breathing. She noticed her hands fiddling with a napkin and stopped them. Fortunately, the cause of her speech impediment broke the silence.

'So, are you using your reiki?'

'Um, yes. Yes, when I first went home, I seemed to be reikiing everything; water, plants, food, me... It's almost as if I've discovered an alternative universe.'

'Good description.'

'Are you a reiki master like Mark?'

'Yes, I have done my masters. A long time ago, long before I met Mark.'

Their conversation continued to meander through metaphysical lanes and lands for half an hour, and Cheryl was pleased that she could converse with a little knowledge about her brief flirtation with tarot and crystals and sweat lodges. He was very engaging on the subject of nature and shamanism. He had a particular interest in woodlands and trees. He could list all their medicinal properties. Cheryl felt a novice in his world, but was gratified and emboldened that he seemed impressed with her career in television. Finally, Solomon's staff began to rattle chairs as they tidied them under the tables, covered the pastries and started dimming the lights.

'Time to go, I think,' Cheryl's mystery man acknowledged. So at fourteen minutes past ten, they found themselves on the pavement in the autumn drizzle.

Now what do we do? I don't want this to end. Cheryl desperately clung to the moment. 'It's been really fascinating talking to you,' she truthfully remarked.

'And you. I feel as if I've seen behind the scenes of my television. I had no idea. Listen, it's a very murky night, and I think I've kept you out longer than you intended. I don't like to think of your walking alone in the dark. Would you like me to walk you to your door?'

Can I believe this? It's as if someone is pulling strings.
'Yes, please, that would be really kind, if you don't mind. It's only a few streets away.'

'My pleasure.' He walked her home. Their steps echoed on the damp empty pavement, punctuating their polite conversation. When they arrived at the crossing point, he extended his arm, protectively. Even though it didn't touch her, the impression of an aureole cloak wrapped her shoulder. Cheryl hopped over a puddle at the opposite pavement edge, swinging her arm. Their hands brushed. Shivers ran through her that had nothing to do with the night air.

As they arrived at the low wall topped by black metal railings with fleur-de-lis finials, which pointedly guarded the little garden and tiled pathway up to Cheryl's front door, her heart hammered. She had wondered whether she dared ask *the question* with every footfall of the way from the café to her threshold. Was it the inevitable question? Was he expecting it?

'Would you like to come in for coffee? Or hot chocolate?'

'Got anything stronger? Coffee with a shot of brandy?'

'Of course.'

Cheryl's hand fumbled the lock, trying to recollect what state of household disorder might greet them. She made a point of flicking the switch to the upstairs light, so that it would cast softly down into the hall. *Just in case.* Her tiny front room had a dimmer switch. She ushered him in.

Cheryl wondered if they were both speculating that *coffee* might be a euphemism. He flexed his weight from one foot to the other, and she noticed his hand stroke his black-jeaned thigh. Was he nervous, too? Why? What was he feeling? She could only play a waiting game; she had never been one to make the first move. Already she had been far bolder than caution advised: *I've just let a complete stranger into my house in the middle of the night. I know nothing about him, except I so want him to be here.*

'I'll just get the coffee. Please do sit down and make yourself comfortable. I won't be a moment.' In the kitchen she switched on the kettle and poured two brandies. *I should have put some music on. I wonder what he likes?* She took the brandies through to the lounge.

The cats were befriending him as he crouched to scritch their ears.

'Oh, I see you've met Merlin and Melchior.'

Faint amusement fleeted across his face. 'Oh, a pair of wizards!'

Cheryl put the brandy balloons on the low coffee table, and crossed the room to flick on the CD player. 'What would you like?' She motioned to the vertical rack of cases. 'I have—'

'Whatever there is will be fine.'

Cheryl looked up; he was watching her with such intensity. She didn't look away. Sliding her hand down the remote control without looking, she pushed the play arrow. The disc whirred to select the sultry intro of Phyllis Nelson's 'Move Closer'. The lyrics could have been written for the moment. He smiled and held out his arm, inviting her to dance. He was even stronger than she imagined, and yet gentle as he pulled her to nestle against him. She could hear the kettle reach boiling point in the kitchen. She let it click off. Her head leaned into his shoulder. She guessed neither of them wanted coffee now. They swayed together as the song suggested. Cheryl let her hands feel the long muscles of his back. *Oh my God, I can't believe this. Am I dreaming?* She flexed her fingers. *It was real!* Three and a half minutes went by in a moment, and the song finished. What was next – it was always set to random? She felt his hand stroking her hair. Warm breath nuzzled her crown. 'Addicted to Love' rocked into play. He laughed at the discord with their mood. His grip tightened as he led the jive. Every distance, every joining, their eyes never lost contact. The cats scattered away from their frantic feet.

Cheryl found herself breathless by the end of the song.

Laughing, he pulled her to a hug. 'Brandy break!'

Her head turned to look at the table. His hold scarcely loosened. She looked into his eyes as they parted to elbow length, still mesmerised by the moment. Music played, neither noticed, captured in mutual silence. Delicious indecision. He was here. It was perfect. She didn't want to pull away. He was smiling. He had creases around his eyes creating frames of kindness. His head tilted to the right, as if he was searching for a decision. She risked reaching up to rest fingers on his lips. She felt them kissed with tender intimacy.

Brandy was forgotten.

His ran his fingers through her hair and gently caressed behind her ears. Her breath shivered through her throat as she savoured the moment. *The Law of Attraction works! Thank you, thank you, thank you,* Cheryl remembered to say to whichever part of the universe had arranged this, just before she raised her chin to his kiss. Their lips touched tentatively, the kiss deepened. His embrace grew stronger. Cheryl responded kissing back with fervour, stroking her hand through his hair and round the nape of his neck. His hair felt surprisingly soft, and then her fingers found the contrast of masculine stubble along the line of his jaw, back to smooth and moist as she ran them across his lips as they drew breath. She registered the scent of evergreen trees and damp nights – the scent of woodland.

He whispered into her ear. 'Wow.'

A soft sensual motion stroked her leg. Melchior wove between them. She tried to ignore it. A set of claws impaled his leg. He winced – and then laughed.

'They're very protective of you.'

'Sorry, they're used to having my undivided attention.'

A pair of orange eyes stared from the sofa, where Merlin had taken up pole position.

'Let's make a run for it!'

Laughing and teasing, he chased her up the stairs, stopping halfway for a passionate embrace and a bout of soft love-biting, before they made it into her bedroom.

Melchior and Merlin, thwarted and confounded by the closed door, listened to the soft, sweet cry of abandonment from their mistress. Whisperings of tenderness; ecstatic fulfilment.

Afterwards, as they lay in each other's arms, she fought to stay awake, to watch him sleeping; *I don't want to miss a thing.*

Watching his closed eyes, his gentle breathing – the rise and fall of his chest, speckled with grey hair, angular yet square and comfortingly strong shoulders, Cheryl couldn't quite believe what had happened even though she was lying next to him. Her feelings of joy overwhelmed her; she didn't know she had that kind of all-consuming passion in her. It felt like free fall, terrifying, exhilarating.

And so here she was, the morning after. Her whole being was buzzing with joy. Should she wake him? No! The longer he slept, the longer she had to savour his company.

One slate-grey eye opened and then another and laughter lines framed them both.

Thank you, Cupid, fate, angels ... whatever... he's gorgeous!

'Good morning'. A soft voice with the trace of an accent she still couldn't quite place. Irish, or West Country perhaps, legendary home to Merlin and Arthur?

'Hello.' Cheryl replied rather shyly. *What would he think of her in the morning light?* The archetypal concern of every woman.

Actions spoke, he pulled her towards him and enfolded her in an affectionate kiss.

'Good morning, gorgeous lady.'

His words were poetry, but didn't match the truth in his eyes. Or was there something in his tone? Cheryl sensed there was something. He seemed hesitant – remorseful, perhaps?

Oh God. I'm such a fool she started to berate herself. *I shouldn't have just jumped into bed.* Her stomach twisted with disappointment as she wondered how to extricate herself with any form of dignity.

He stepped into the pause; this time his voice matched his demeanour:

'This is so unexpected. Yesterday I was just out for a coffee and now, I have to confess, I feel quite in awe waking up to a famous voice-over artist. It's a bit surreal.'

Cheryl laughed with relief.

'I can assure you celebrity and being in the public eye is all gloss and varnish, and nothing to be in awe about.' Her recent brush with celebrity gossip was still raw. 'Whereas, you – you seem so knowledgeable about reiki and crystals and trees and all those things we were talking about. It's just a sort of hobby, or interest for me. It's fascinating to meet someone who works with it. And I'm such a novice, I am a bit embarrassed to admit that I still don't quite understand *what* it is you do?'

Her mystery man raised himself up onto his right elbow so that their eyes were level, giving Cheryl another chance to take in his lean toned physique. She followed the line of his arm muscles to his hands, which were a curious mixture of a workman's and an artist's or creative designer's: slightly rough and the nails not manicured, the thumbs, where they joined the palm, squared and angular, yet with long and artistic fingers. Cheryl remembered seeing this conformation in many of the hand imprints of film stars which were immortalised in the concrete of the famous Hollywood Boulevard. She had to admit she had a *thing* about hands. And shoulders. Men may worry about other parts of their anatomy, Cheryl, however, loved the feel of snuggling into the perfect shoulder, and she always noticed a man's hands and how they expressed his personality. Did she want to be caressed by them? *Yes*, was the answer to the question in this case.

His voice spoke to her heart, too, with a mystical timbre: 'Well, there is a reason for that. I don't tell everyone *exactly* what I do. Especially not until I know them better. Some people find it difficult to comprehend.'

'Oh?'

'The truth is: I'm a wizard'

'What! You're a *wizard*! Really? I mean, they *really* exist?'

'Oh yes, they exist! My professional name is Arcturus Wolfe.' He smiled at her wide-eyed expression.

'But of course, you can call me Stefan'.

CHAPTER TWENTY-ONE

Despite repeating the phrase: *patience, patience* to herself all morning, Sheila kept reaching for her phone and putting it down. Maybe she could call round? 'No, that would be too intrusive.' More searching. 'But, what if Cheryl isn't all right? I could have left her with a complete maniac. Although, he looked okay. But ...' her thoughts went, round and round.

Just as Sheila hovered her hand over the phone for the umpteenth time, it rang.

Please be Cheryl.

It was.

'Sheila?'

'Yes'.

Who else would it be? Sheila thought with uncharacteristic irritation. She realised that being the catalyst for whatever she was about to hear had happened after she'd left the café was making her tetchy.

'So?'

Silence. Followed by a squeal. Sheila tried to sort distress from joy. And joy won.

'Oh my God! Thank goodness. Did you speak to him? Did it go well?'

'Oh Sheila, you genius. Better than well.'

'So, you met and chatted? Are you seeing him again?'

'Sheila, he's only just left'.

'What! Holy crap. Cheryl, you certainly go for it. Don't get me wrong, that's not a criticism. I'm just gobsmacked. You're normally the cautious one. You sound so happy. I'm so pleased for you.'

'Sheila, I haven't ever felt like that. Ever. I feel like singing, dancing, crying with joy. I can hardly believe it. I even had to go and sniff the pillow to catch his scent and make sure it wasn't a dream.'

'Too much information!' Sheila laughed.

'So who is he? What's his name? What's he do? Come on, I want the whole story.'

So Cheryl traced the steps from Sheila's departure from Soloman's café, to her little house.

'It was so strange. As if some weird force was at work.'

'Wow! That intense!'

'Yep. And you'll never guess what he does?'

'Writer?'

'No.'

'Poet?'

'No'

'Am I warm?'

'Nope.'

Cheryl giggled.

'Anything arty?'

'No, still cold'.

'Um, eco warrior?'

'Well, getting a bit warmer, I suppose.'

'Something green?'

'No. More in your area of expertise.'

'A reiki master?'

'Getting warmer…'

'Astrologer?'

'Cooler …' Cheryl's tones reflected the game, rising and falling with the direction of temperature.

'Oh, Lord. Um, a sound healer?'

'Noooooo!'

'Cheryl!' Sheila mock shrieked. 'What?'

'Try magic.'

'What?' He's a magician? Like a kids' entertainer?'

'No!' Cheryl left a theatrical pause.

'He's called Arcturus Wolfe, and he's a wizard!'

'Seriously?'

'Yes! I'm surprised you haven't come across him. He knows Mark, apparently. They're planning some sort of energy workshop together.'

'But his real name isn't Arcturus, is it? Is that his magic name?'

'Yes. He's called Stefan'.

'Gosh. I'll have to quiz Mark to find out more about him. So how did you leave it? Is he going to call you?'

'Yes, I really hope so. He said he would.'

'Do you have his number?'

'No, but he's put mine in his phone, so I will when he calls.'

That's odd, Sheila's intuition cautioned. But she thought better of voicing it.

'Oh, Cheryl. I'm so pleased for you. You realise we will have to meet for a celebratory drink?'

'Oh, absolutely!'

CHAPTER TWENTY-TWO

'I'm using the dishwasher, today. When I've got so many people, I reckon it's actually more environmentally friendly than multiple bowls of water' Mark explained, almost apologetically.

'Sounds good to me,' Stefan raised his hands. He hadn't been worried about it anyway.

'Thanks for the tea. I'm glad we've found an alternative venue for the workshop. It looked as if it could all go pear-shaped for a while. I'd better get going if you've got a house full of people on the way for your reiki support evening.'

'No problem. There's a quarter of an hour, yet. If you don't mind me saying so, you seem on good form today?'

Stefan inclined his head to one side. A smile warmed his features.

'Yes, I guess I am.'

'How's Marguerite?'

The smile faded.

'Oh, you know. Okay. Pretty much as usual,' Stefan shrugged, leaving Mark wondering whether his friend's good mood was due to an improvement in their relationship, or something else.

'Good. Good. I'm glad things are all right.'

Stefan gathered up his file of papers, closed his laptop and rose to leave. There was something in Mark's tone he couldn't quite fathom. It puzzled him.

Maybe it's just my conscience niggling me, he reasoned. He felt uneasy that he'd been unfaithful. But, in truth, things were so strained and difficult at home, he couldn't really believe that it was so wrong to take some comfort elsewhere. *Pretty much as usual,* summed it up. It was usually pretty grim and he didn't want to extrapolate any further. Besides, at the moment, he didn't care. He was still enthralled by the memory of his night with the beautiful lady he had admired so long from a distance. It had seemed a blessed fate that Cheryl kept crossing his path. He had watched her graceful running in the park and been inexplicably drawn to her. More than a physical attraction, she had a resoluteness in her stride and the few times he'd seen her closer, a beauty in her eyes.

Some man, somewhere is probably very lucky he'd told himself. And left it at that. The night they finally spoke at Soloman's he was alone for the weekend. Marguerite had gone away for a conference and their parting had been acerbic and disagreeable. Even so, if he hadn't seen Cheryl smile at him across the room and then remain alone with her hot chocolate, he might never have seized the moment and chanced a conversation.

Magical, totally magical he breathed in the memory, knowing that in reality it might never be repeated. He had promised to call, and he was a man of his word. But whether they would ever meet again was a matter for conjecture.

He and Mark had been friends for years; Stefan could usually read Mark's moods.

Mark knows me so well, I wonder if he's sensed something?

*

Mark closed the dishwasher and turned to accompany Stefan to the door. He definitely felt there was something Stefan wasn't saying.

'Well, take care, mate. Send Marguerite my love.'

'Sure. Will do.'

A *frisson* of something intangible.

They shook hands and Mark gave Stefan a friendly slap on the shoulder for good measure as he stepped through the door.

In the minutes that followed, both men mused on what they felt the other hadn't wanted to say.

Mark shook off his suspicions and headed to the conservatory to prepare for the evening's meditation. He was half way through tidying cushions from the floor ready to run the vacuum cleaner over it, when the doorbell rang.

'Hi Mark.'

'Thanks for coming early, Sheila. It's been a busy afternoon, and someone's only just left. I haven't done the conservatory yet.'

'No problem, that's why I'm early.'

'Cheryl not with you today?'

'No, she's got a work shift tonight.'

Sheila had always liked going to Mark's house. It had a feel-good factor, like an instant welcoming hug. The porch was surrounded by honeysuckle, which gave a fragranced welcome to his stone-clad cottage. It had once been a woodcutter's cottage; the wood had long gone, felled to make way for housing. But the cottage retained its individuality and stood alone at the end of the cul-de-sac, where it still annexed a small wooded area to the rear.

In the conical wooden conservatory at the back of the house, the glass roof allowed sunlight, or moonlight, to flood down upon the occupants. In the centre of the floor, a glass circle surrounded by a brass ring, sheltered a hollow, which housed a phial of water from the holy Chalice Well in Glastonbury. Cushions and flokati rugs lay scattered in rainbow abandon.

Mark's philosophy as a master/teacher demanded that he offer regular sessions of ongoing support for initiates at whatever stage of their journey. Tonight, was an open support group for reiki students to practice giving and receiving, and Sheila, now attuned by Mark as a reiki master herself, whole-heartedly agreed, and always turned up to lend a hand. And she found there was always something new to learn from the group.

'The teacher learns from his pupils, as they learn from him,' Mark had told her when she became a master.

Oh, how true! Sheila thought. *It's not until you try to be a teacher yourself, that you realise what it was you wish you'd asked your own teacher. You think you know until someone asks a question and you can't think how to answer. You know you have the knowledge, but knowing how to apply it to answer the question is a real test of how well you have assimilated your training.*

So, as the monthly meeting slowly convened, Sheila handed round tea, and wondered how she was going to bring up the subject of Stefan if she could find a moment alone with Mark at the end of the day.

CHAPTER TWENTY-THREE

The cursor blinking on the computer monitor acted as a flashing focus, like a cyber-candle flame, sending Cheryl into a meditative daydream. Her mobile phone sat on the desktop waiting to ring. So far it hadn't.

On her screen it read:

My incredulous heart in your slipstream
Fluttering behind you, on gossamer thread
A fragile kite, trembling lest you cut it free
To buffet in the sharp winds of life.

Poetry had poured forth from Cheryl ever since that night.

Me writing poetry!' she marvelled. Cheryl hadn't written a poem since her school days.

And I love it! I just love writing. I've done writing for work; scripts and stuff, but that was work. This is writing for joy, expression, and inspiration. It feels so different.

Cheryl leaned back against her chair, closed her eyes and let her mind fantasize about how life might be. Cheryl James, the poet and writer who lives in a country mansion with two cats and a wizard.

Wow, it feels like a fairy tale!

Could it really happen to her? If books like *The Secret* and *The Law of Attraction* were to be believed, it could.

Really? Truly? Can I allow myself to trust in all this?

Cheryl had to admit that part of her heart was still shrouded in caution.

Best not to get carried away – yet.

But already, it had inspired her to do something rash. Well, rash by the evidence to date of her conventional life as former wife-mother-wage-slave. She knew she could write short scripts for TV, and had done for years. And, it appeared, she could write more creatively of late.

What if I could write something really significant? Really say something that mattered? So, what matters? And come to that, why does it suddenly seem to matter that I write something of note, at all? Cheryl noticed her hands were clasped in front of her chest. To the outside world she would look like she was praying. *How bizarre, is that?* A colour formed in her thoughts: orange. Was it her thoughts, or …? The whole thing felt surreal. She closed her eyes, and experienced the colour again. There seemed to be an entirely separate internal dimension, another Cheryl. Finally, her body forced her to breathe. She hadn't even realised she was holding her breath. *It felt as if I was suspended somewhere. Really weird.* Her brain's practical left hemisphere came on line again and refocused on her question. What to write? Was this simply a form of catharsis? Did she want to write about her journey through divorce? In truth she couldn't think of anything she might say to help others that hadn't already been written – and probably better expressed. No, it was more than that, Cheryl decided after mulling over her thoughts and consulting her feelings. They seemed to have merged somewhere in her chest to become 'theelings'; they started as thoughts and then transformed into feelings. *Have I just invented a new word?* Well, if she wanted to be creative, then it would need to be fiction. Cheryl James the novelist sounded alluring. However, a novelist with no idea whatsoever for a story wasn't going to end in glory, and somewhere in the depths of her understanding, a novel didn't feel quite right either.

No, what I want to say, to express – to share, is this different way of looking at life that seems to have grown organically around me ever since my conventional life blew itself apart. But how? A blog?

Cheryl's idea came to her in the middle of the night, *as these things tend to do.* Thankfully, at one of her meetings, someone had suggested she keep a notepad and paper beside her bed to jot down sparks of inspiration. The kind of flash of inspiration which illuminates the night so vividly that you're positive you will remember every detail the next morning, only to wake groping for even an inkling of the idea, and come up with a complete void. The light bulb had, indeed, gone on at precisely four forty-four in the morning. Those were the numerals displayed on the clock radio as she fumbled on the bedside table in search of writing implements and her notebook. She had rediscovered the notebook in a suitcase when moving. It had come from a market stall in Florence years before; the heavy hand-cut plain paper was bound in a printed leather jacket and could be tied with two leather thongs. It felt luxurious, the tool of a true creative soul, and Cheryl had been keeping it for a special occasion, which is how it came to be stashed, and forgotten, in a suitcase. So, at four forty-four, eyes unfocused, squinting in the sudden light, she clicked the golden metal ballpoint pen into action and started to write on the blank pages of her notebook.

The next morning, when she woke, groggily drifting into consciousness, it seemed she'd had a dream. A very lucid dream. She rolled over and felt the knot of the leather thong around the notebook press into her flesh. *No, it wasn't a dream!* Her left hand drew the notebook from under her hip and pulled it up where it could be opened. She had a good outline to work on; furthermore, she knew what had sparked the idea.

The week before Cheryl had re-encountered the woman who said she worked with angels. Cheryl had expressed a mild interest. Or to be more accurate, she hadn't expressed a disinterest, which had opened a floodgate of information flowing her way whether she liked it or not, and had found herself receiving an angel-card reading. Somewhat unnervingly, like her astrological chart, it seemed to by-pass her outward persona and look directly at the character within. Was this woman psychic, or really working with angels? Perhaps both?

Cheryl still wasn't sure if she even believed that angels existed. Somehow the whole idea seemed muddled with fairy tales and Father Christmas or faeries at the bottom of the garden. Things you were told as a child, which turned out to be disappointingly fantastic. However, now that she acknowledged that energy forms exist which most people – *except clairvoyants maybe* – cannot see, it didn't seem to be beyond the realms of possibility that angels *might* exist.

'After all,' the woman had explained, 'they are messengers. The word angel comes from the Greek *angelos,* which means messenger. You can't see the signal that brings someone's voice into your mobile phone, can you? Well, it's the same with angels. You just have to find the right frequency to pick up their messages and talk to them.'

'Well, maybe?'

'Try talking to your parking angel next time you need a space outside the house, or in a busy car park,' the angel enthusiast suggested, leaving Cheryl unsure whether she was the subject of a joke or whether the woman was seriously proposing that she sit in her car talking to the ether.

However, as she left the meeting, Cheryl was aware that the likelihood of a space being outside her house on a Friday night in her narrow road of Edwardian terraced houses, where every household had one or sometimes two cars – a road designed for horses and carts, not vehicles parked on either side of the road leaving a single central lane for travelling –was remote.

Still wary of mixing fact with fantasy, Cheryl sat in her car after the meeting and spoke to the sky. She figured if angels were going to be hanging around anywhere, that's where they might be.

'Okay, I'll try. If you're my parking angel, I want a space right outside my house tonight.' She remembered her manners just in time. 'Please.'

I know reiki is real, she reasoned. *I can feel it in my hands, and it makes perfect sense that there is a life force running through the planet. The planet is alive and so are all the plants and creatures on it. It's been known and documented for centuries. It's even been scientifically proven recently. It can be seen with special photography. But angels? Well, I'm willing to give you a try. S*he aimed the thought at a looming cloud.

As Cheryl's car turned into her street, the cars hugged the curb, bumper to bumper as far as she could see. As tightly packed as shoppers in the queue for a New Year's sale; each aggressively guarding their pitch, not giving an inch. Her heart sank a little. It would have been nice to believe in angels. Comforting. It was beginning to rain.

Oh well, only one thing for it. Drive along the road into the next one and see if I can find a space there.

It wasn't until she had almost reached the middle of the road, a few feet short of her house, that the amber light of a car indicator started flashing, headlights flared and the car pulled out in front of her, leaving a parking space.

Right outside my house!

If there really were angels, Cheryl concluded, they had a sense of humour, teasing her and leaving it until the very last moment to act. She remembered to say *thank you,* as the angel lady had impressed upon her.

But it could just have been a fluke.

The third and fourth time it happened, Cheryl started to take things seriously. Maybe Sheila was right and they did exist? Sheila wasn't an airy-fairy sort of person – quite the opposite – she was intensely practical. But she believed in them and she wasn't even religious. It just seemed so intangible.

Okay, you've got my attention, now. So what do I do next? Talk to you?

Silence.

This is going to be a one-way conversation, then. Cheryl supposed. *I'd better research how other people tune into them.* As soon as she typed the subject into her computer's search engine she found reams of articles.

Too much information! And it's all so confusing: thrones, virtues, powers, coloured rays, cherubim, seraphim, dominions, dimensions ... God! (Sorry, hope that didn't sound like blasphemy. I was actually talking to you, so maybe it's okay). How could any ordinary person work their way through all that? It would take years to learn. You'd have to spend half your day researching which angel to talk to. Always assuming you did want to talk to one.

And then, it hit her. At four forty-four in the morning.

If I quite like the idea of talking to angels, but I don't want to spend a lifetime studying to find out how to do it, and which one to pick, maybe lots of people do? The research said that fifty two per cent of people believe in them. What if ... what if, I wrote some kind of book that made it easy to know which angel to talk to at the precise moment you needed to talk to them? Like a kind of time line, portable angel-card reading?

The next morning, when Cheryl looked at her nocturnal scrawls, she found she'd even written down a title: 'Perfect Timing'.

Sitting in front of her computer, she started to catalogue all the information she would need. Angels of the hours. Angels of the days. Angels of the months.

It'll give me something to keep my mind off waiting for the phone to ring.

And then, another example of synchronicity struck.

Cheryl saw an advertisement for a course, an Italian holiday writing retreat in Tuscany.

Yes, yes, yes, yes, yes! She jiggled in her seat. How wonderfully childish it felt.

Cheryl loved Italy, and Tuscany in particular. Many years ago on a family villa-holiday, they had visited Florence for the day and she had treated herself to that notebook from the San Lorenzo street market, famed for its leather, silk and cashmere. The children had whined about being taken round the art galleries and artisan shops. Ross had quite enjoyed practising with his new camera, capturing the light and the vibrancy of the ancient Ponte Vecchio spanning the river Arno. Cheryl, however, drank in the whole city, home to the famously mendacious boy, Pinocchio; incomprehensibly delicious cakes and ice cream at Caffè Rivoire in the Piazza della Signoria; Michelangelo's David; and the Uffizi gallery. And as the day ended, she had climbed all four hundred and sixty-three steps inside Brunelleschi's mighty dome at the Basilica di Santa Maria del Fiore, still unsurpassed as the largest brick dome in the world. Even the name sounded romantic: The cathedral of St. Mary of the Flower. Cheryl stepped out onto the tiny exterior gallery, two hundred and ninety-five feet above the Piazza del Duomo below, just as the sultry Tuscan sun set over the horizon and every church bell in Florence rang. Cheryl's heart rang with them. She was enraptured. There and then, she had vowed to the sunset that one day, she would return.

The course details were perfectly timed. The leather notebook seemed a good omen.

Tom and Zoë won't be back from university until the following week. I've got a little money left over from the house sale. And the rest? Oh, blow it! I'm just going to put it on my credit card! I'm going!

Cheryl's right index finger clicked on the final confirmation button.

Now there's just one thing needed to make today really perfect. Come on phone, ring!

Right on cue it played her chosen ring tone from Vivaldi's *Four Seasons.* The screen read: *Number unknown.*

CHAPTER TWENTY-FOUR

The only way to talk to Mark, it seemed, was to linger longer than necessary over the washing up. Only one of the group remained, and he was deep in conversation with her. Sheila wondered how much more feigning culinary clearing and flailing about with a tea towel she could sustain. Finally, the door clicked shut and Mark returned to his kitchen.

'So, you have something to ask me?' he queried. 'I haven't seen that much ham acting with a tea towel since I was ten and tied one on my head so I could pretend to be Lawrence of Arabia.'

Sheila was glad of the good humour to ease her approach to the subject.

'Well, yes. I do have a something I have been meaning to ask you. I have a friend who was talking to someone you are planning a workshop with.'

'Oh?'

'Yes, um, I think it's a pagan or maybe shamanic sort of thing. He's a wizard, apparently,' Sheila tried to sound neutral.

'Stefan. Yes, we're planning it for next month. Do you want to take a flyer for your friend? I think I've got one here.' Mark rummaged through a heap of untidy paperwork on the table until he located a plastic folder.

Sheila accepted a couple of posters and glanced through the details.

'Yes, that's him,' she agreed, as much for her own satisfaction as Mark's. The photograph was very flattering and the light brought out the enigmatic quality of his eyes.

'It's strange; I've never seen him around. Is he local?'

'Yeah, pretty local. He lives about three miles away. He's a tree wizard. He likes working with tree energy. And his wife is a medical herbalist.'

Wife! Sheila stared at the poster trying to compose her thoughts and wondering what to say next. She had a horrible suspicion she might look flushed. She hoped Mark hadn't noticed.

Finally, she managed: 'It looks great. I'll certainly pass it on, thank you.'

Mark had noticed. Sheila was one of the calmest and most emotionally centred women he knew. He recalled his recent meeting with Stefan, and the feeling that there was something unspoken. Coupling that with the discord he had witnessed at first hand in Stefan and Marguerite's marriage, he hazarded a question of his own.

'Well, I certainly hope she'll come along. It's only half sold at the moment. Has she done any of this kind of work before? Not anyone from the reiki circle, is it?'

Sheila's mental defences went to red alert. She took evasive action rather than tell a lie.

'I think they just met over a coffee one day, and the workshop was mentioned.'

Mark sensed she was prevaricating, which further raised his suspicions. And why would Sheila need to remain behind to talk to him about a workshop alone?

'Okay. Maybe I'll meet her if she signs up.'

Sheila nodded, and made her excuses. It was late. He had things to do. All the way home she fretted and searched for a way to tell Cheryl that the love of her life was a married man.

Mark took his cup to the table and stared at the poster of Arcturus Wolfe.

'Stefan, what have you got yourself into?'

And his thoughts drifted to Marguerite.

CHAPTER TWENTY-FIVE

Watching Marguerite engrossed in her herbs, experimenting with a new recipe she had acquired whilst away on her weekend course, Stefan felt a melancholy he hadn't experienced since his mother's passing.

Stefan had always felt protective towards his mother and she alone had supported him when he discovered that he had a way of looking at the world, which separated him from his peers, and often engendered ridicule. As a teenager, he found himself acting as head of the household following his father's abrupt departure with a work colleague. Stefan and his father had been at odds: Percival Wolfe, ever the logical statistician, made it quite clear that his son's nonsensical ideas about ley lines and tree hugging were to be quashed whenever they arose. So it was that most of Stefan's childhood had been lived in a covert inner world.

The past weekend had marked the anniversary of his mother's death. At the time of her funeral fifteen years ago, he had been distraught, and yet unable to display his feelings. Looking back, he assumed this was due to a mistaken belief he had to be strong, to demonstrate some British stiff upper lip. He had felt he was now effectively head of the household and had to take charge of the funeral.

He did his best to comfort his younger sister, whom he found sobbing alone in the empty family home once the mourners had departed. There was an age gap of ten years, and although Stefan felt protective towards her, they had never been particularly close. He had left home as soon as possible. As far back as he could remember, they had little in common. He was almost reclusive in his world of books and nature while, even as a little girl, she relished glitter and glamour and kept a diary about how she would travel the world and marry a prince.

Well, part of the dream came true; she trained as a travel agent and lived abroad. Nevertheless, when she returned for the funeral, he had wanted to share the pain, to tell her that he felt the hurt keenly too, that losing the one person who had believed in him seared like a hot sword into his heart. But he couldn't. The *coup de grace* was the grudging impersonal note in the card sent by his father to be read out to relatives – a social obligation and brief expression of condolence from the ever correct Percival – that had the effect of clamping a lid on his son's emotional reactions. Stefan choked back hot acid bile, which rose into his throat as he read it out. He was afraid he might actually be sick.

Now, sitting in his office at home, watching Marguerite through the doorway, he acknowledged the timing might well have had a bearing on his unprincipled behaviour of late. *Perhaps, I've got to the stage where I don't care any more. I just wanted to be happy, to share some passion and tenderness. I don't mind being solitary, I'm used to that, and I enjoy it. But love, sharing love and ideas and enthusiasm for life with someone is so fulfilling. Soul food. The only person who made me feel like that was Mum, and then Marguerite for the first year or so. And now, I feel like I live in a dank grey space where nothing grows. I'm breathing in cobwebs and struggling in the web.*

The uncomfortable thought sent him back into his reverie. Following his father's departure, his mother became occupied with bringing up his young sister and so he spent much of his time left to his own devices. Far from being lonely, he remembered feeling he had been intellectually released, and used his freedom to expand his knowledge of nature and spirit energy. *All those walks in the wood, the light streaming through the trees. I used to spend hours just sitting with my back to the giant beech, just daydreaming and absorbing the sounds of nature.*

Once he gained access to the internet he quickly discovered like-minded people. Just knowing he was not alone in his *alternative world* was a great comfort. One exchange of views led him to find *The Grimoires*, an essential handbook, which explains everything a young wizard needs to know. He discovered that the use of grimoires dated back to ancient Mesopotamia where magical incantations were inscribed on various cuneiform clay tablets. The name derived from the Old French *grammaire,* which applied to any book written in Latin; by the 18th century it exclusively denoted a textbook of *magick.* Within the pages of such volumes, a student wizard could find instructions on how to create amulets and talismans together with magic spells and invocations. Such was the awe with which these tomes were regarded, the books themselves were believed to hold magical properties. He knew he had to be part of their world somehow.

In Pursuit of Perfect Timing

All those jobs – delivering newspapers, digging gardens, chopping logs – anything I could do to save the money to get to Italy.

Stefan recalled contacting the community of wizards in the remote hills of Italy, which he felt in every fibre of his being, was the place to complete his training.

Even with the money he saved, his journey there had been a real trial. Travelling and eating on a meagre budget, nineteen year old Stefan bussed and sofa-surfed his way to Dover, through France, and finally hitched a ride across the Franco-Italian border as far as Bologna with a lorry driver. One of the wizard community had business there and had agreed to meet him in front of the Palazzo Comunale in the Piazza Maggiore, Bologna's central square. Stefan stood there, a gangling youth with his scruffy rucksack containing a few clothes and weighed down with his grimoires, notebooks and treasured samples of tree bark. He had been instructed to wear something yellow.

God, I remember I didn't have anything yellow and I had to persuade the lorry driver to give me an empty yellow plastic sack.

The massive clock on the Palazzo tower struck two, the appointed time. No one came. Stefan sat on the yellow sack until three, feeling by turns dejected and panic stricken, and was considering how he might hitch a lift home again, when a robust man in country clothing strode across the square gesticulating wildly.

'*Oddio mi dispiace molto, c'ho la testa di merda, mi sono dimenticato!*' Seeing Stefan's incomprehension he switched to English. 'Oh God I'm so sorry, I am shit for brains. You are Stefan, yes? Come, come.'

In Pursuit of Perfect Timing

They squeezed into a tiny Fiat with Stefan's bag of precious books perched precariously on the roof rack and set off out of the city into the hills of Tuscany. The community had taken over a small farm about a mile outside a village. Stefan was glad to discover that some of the twenty wizards currently there could speak a little English. He could manage a little French, and thanks to the grimoires they also had Latin in common. They managed. The locals in the village gave them a wide berth and only two of the wizards with a fluent command of Italian went to shop for supplies. The story around the village was that they were some kind of weird monks living in a cloistered community. The wizards saw no reason to awaken the potential wrath of the local priest by denying this.

This image was further supported, should any local prying eyes pay a visit, by the fact that all the novice wizards wore drab brown robes, while the masters wore various colours. Stefan had his own room in a wooden hut and a small table for his books and study. Contact with the outside world, while not banned, was not encouraged.

I'm home, finally somewhere I belong.

While the living was comfortable, the schedule was daunting. The first year of study required a broad understanding of the whole subject. The curriculum was extensive and challenging, encompassing Mathemagicks, Beast Mastery, Hermetics, Quantum Physics, Cosmology, Nature Studies, Lore, Divination, Alchemy, Ceremony and even the Dark Arts.

Better the devil you know…

There followed two years of specialisation in his chosen subject, and Stefan graduated from a brown apprentice to a green wizard complete with his magickal name: 'Arcturus the Green'. Arcturus was a master of working with the earth, versed in the arts of arboreal herbalism (a branch of wortcunning – the wizardry term for herbalism), fertility (the creation of prosperity, hope, joy, delight, growth of mind, body and spirit), and healing.

There are many shades of green. His preference was for working with forest green. His specialist knowledge of trees empowered him to connect with their potential to heal, lend courage and listen to the voice and wisdom of nature. He loved to talk about them, crafting colour-filled language to explain.

'Amongst the many hues, ivy green soothes the emotions, mitigates grief, and accompanies waterside musings bathed in silence. Pale green, witnessed in the colour of new-grown grass, assists the healing process when the wounded lie with their backs to the turf and their heart to the sun'

In his pamphlets he explained: 'The term "wizard" translates as "wise one". This was the wisdom of old when villages looked to the Wise One to protect their flocks, shelter them from the excesses of storms and guard against sickness. This was in the times when they were venerated and before the working of magick was demonised.'

Once his training was complete, Stefan reluctantly left Italy to find employment on reforestation and woodland management projects. His colleagues took a prosaic view of his skills and his knowledge of the properties of trees.

Openly writing 'Green Wizard' on his application forms would, he was sure, be counterproductive and guarantee he would not be selected for an interview.

To be amongst trees, and work with them that's what mattered.

However, since the renaissance of interest in wizardry, Stefan had stepped away from conventional work to develop a main income teaching classes on magick energy and/or environmental awareness – depending on the openness of the audience.

Marguerite stood with her back to him grinding herbs to a paste, exactly as he'd first seen her at the annual World of Wortcunning Conference eleven years earlier. The conference was appropriately set in the imposing medieval Clam Castle halfway between Vienna and Salzburg in Austria, which opens as an hotel in the summer. Their brochure extolled its virtues:

'Visitors at the modern Clam may explore the lovely patio, built in Renaissance architectural style, the herb room, the Gothic chapel, admire the coats of arms in the hall, and then view the accommodation of the counts of Clam, where they will find original furnishings from the 18th century. Another high point in the tour of the palace is the dining room walls, decorated with hand-painted Austrian tea sets.'

Totally magnificent surroundings. I remember seeing Marguerite walking in the garden. She was stunning. Those green eyes and black hair. I'd never seen anyone like her.

The timing was significant, the fourth anniversary of his mother's death.

After all those years hiding who I was from the rest of the family. Working in woodlands telling everyone I was just a forester. And then, with Marguerite I found an empathy and understanding I'd never encountered before. I was mesmerised. Good grief, I'd scarcely come into contact with women, never mind a woman I could talk to about being a wizard.

Stefan reflected how amazed he had been that she was interested in him.

Yes, it seemed like fate had put us together. She said she was so pleased that I could understand some of her herbal craft. And she liked the way I'd go off to walk amongst the trees to think. Enigmatic, she called me then. Not what she calls me now!

In the fairy-tale castle, romance blossomed. They married six months later.

Marry in haste, repent at leisure, is what they say; an axiom sadly true in their case, he reflected. With their shared interests they seemed a perfect match. However, each brought a very different experience of emotional need and attachment to the union.

It was fine until we moved in together. And even then, it worked for a year or so. We just had such different upbringings and completely different expectations. She was always arranging family parties. All those meals. And it wasn't just for a couple of hours; we'd have to stay for the whole weekend. Never-ending conversations, I couldn't even go for a walk on my own. They'd always want to come with me. They thought it was odd wanting to be on your own.

In business they were a perfect partnership. Medicinal uses for herbs and trees. In the early stages of heady romance, this *togetherness* was acceptable. They worked together, and lived together. Stefan, who had spent most of his life in solitude, needed hectares of personal space. Marguerite thrived on being part of a family. As the marriage progressed Stefan felt strangled. This was emotional claustrophobia in the extreme. The more he absented himself in search of solitude, the harder Marguerite tried to contain him at home. Now eleven years later, Stefan stared at his chosen partner and wondered:

What was I thinking?

A question, which applied equally to this weekend's romance with Cheryl as it did to his precipitous marriage.

Once the initial euphoria of his night with Cheryl had worn off, his thoughts circled like trapped cats. Increasingly agitated and instinctively knowing that something would have to be done.

Marguerite called him from the kitchen.

'Stefan! Can you help me carry this demijohn?'

A 'please' would have been nice.

'Stefan, what is the matter with you? Can't you see I need you to help me carry this jar? It's heavy.'

Nothing like a dose of reality to burst a bubble.

He continued his deliberations as he carried the newly-fermenting herbs to the darkness of the pantry to continue their work. He placed them on the slate shelf.

On the one hand, he felt he deserved some happiness. And he wasn't finding it at home. In addition to finding Cheryl irresistibly attractive, he had genuinely felt a strong connection to her. Something beyond that; a deep intuitive connection, as if they'd know each other for years. *Another lifetime, maybe?*

On the other, his conscience punctured his ego with a reminder that she only lived a few miles away. He was bound to see her again, possibly with Marguerite in tow. The thought of the outcome should this state of affairs come to pass sat in his guts like a sour meal.

Marguerite would milk it for all it's worth. Our business interests are tied together in the healing centre. It's jointly owned and it's our home. If she finds out about Cheryl she'll divorce me and she will probably take most of the house and the business. I'm trapped unless she decides to call it a day, or finds someone else.

His head and his heart fought it out. He had watched his friend Mark struggle through a divorce. How much better it would have been if they'd gone their separate ways first. In the end, Stefan, knew what he must do. And it saddened him deeply.

I can't face seeing her. Anyway, we might end up back in bed. Impersonal as it is, I'll just have to phone her.

'Stefan! What *are* you doing in the pantry? You've been ages. There's another one here I need carrying!'

And the sooner, the better.

CHAPTER TWENTY-SIX

Number Unknown? Cheryl's heart raced from regular to sprint speed.

'Hello, Cheryl James speaking,' intoned in her best professional voice.

The deep resonance of his voice: 'Cheryl. Hi, it's Stefan,' melted her down to schoolgirl again.

He's phoned! All the memories of past rejections were suddenly null and void. Relegated to the wastebasket of life lessons no longer required.

This time she, Cheryl, had met the man of her dreams, had thrown caution to the winds to be in his arms, and: *He's phoned!*

A warm feeling of joy flooded through her. Nevertheless, she tried to sound in control.

Be cool.

'Hi, Stefan. It's great to hear your voice and not my accountant's. He's due to ring today. How are you?'

She heard him take a deep breath.

'I'm okay, thanks. You?'

Only okay? Cheryl's psyche heard the faint and distant tinkling of an alarm bell.

'I'm really great! In fact, I've just booked myself a holiday to my favourite city in the world, Florence. It's so inspiring,' she hazarded an addition 'and romantic.'

'That's great. Really great. I'm glad you have something to look forward to.' His tone became flat and monotone. The calm before the storm.

The alarm bells suddenly rang closer. Before Cheryl could reply, Stefan hurried on. 'Yes, you see, I'm afraid I have something to tell you. I wish it wasn't like this, but it is.'

A sense of foreboding banished her former warmth, surrounding her with a clammy chill. She didn't want him to speak any more.

No! Nothing bad. I don't want to hear he doesn't want me.

'There's no easy way to say this, and I can't offer any proper explanation for myself, or my behaviour – I can't see you anymore.'

No! This can't happen. It was so perfect. It can't be. This can't be happening.

Cheryl's stifled sob filled the gap.

'I feel I've behaved very badly, but I have to tell you I'm married.'

Stefan's words felt like a punch to her stomach. She felt sick.

'Why? Why have you done this?' The question was as much directed to herself as to Stefan.

'I am so sorry. I ... I know it sounds like a cliché, but we're not happy, and I have been watching you in the park for months, imagining, hoping you might be free. And then we met and I just couldn't resist the impulse to be with you. And I was so happy for those few hours. And now, I realise I mustn't see you again, even if I wanted to. Which I do,' he added lamely.

Cheryl's shaking index finger pressed the red phone symbol on her mobile to end the call. She had neither voice nor wish to continue the conversation. Emotional pain scored through her, far worse than anything she had experienced during her divorce. She'd chosen to be free then.

Not like this. It didn't hurt like this. My chest hurts. This can't be happening. I can't bear it. Oh god! I can't breathe!

Her head swam. Cheryl's short intakes of breath turned into hyperventilation. She felt the jar of the laminate as her knees buckled and hit the floor. Heat seared her hands as she grasped the radiator for support.

I can't breathe. I can't breathe. Oh God, just let me die, then. I don't care. Just let it end. No more of this pain.

Lack of oxygen was choking her consciousness. Sound became an echo, her eyes lost focus and the room began to spin. Images pixelated. Cheryl had only ever fainted once; this, she knew, was the precursor. If she hit the floor who would find her, and when? Somewhere amongst her panic, a stronger inner voice took command.

Cheryl. Use your hands. Use your reiki.

Her survival instinct kicked in. She let go of the radiator and placed her hands on her chest, over her heart and focused on the word *reiki* will all her remaining will. The tightening in her chest relented a little. She took a deep shuddering breath, and then another. Despite their clamminess, loving warmth flowed from her palms into her heart. The boa constrictor of despair loosened its grip and allowed a torrent of healing sobs to flow.

It's not fair. Why me? Why couldn't I have the man I love? Why did I let myself fall into this? It's not fair!

A period of recrimination, raging against the universe, and heartbroken sobbing seemed to last an hour. In fact, it was only ten minutes later that Cheryl pulled herself up off the floor and shakily reached for her phone to call Sheila.

CHAPTER TWENTY-SEVEN

Stefan found himself listening to the disconnect tone as Cheryl terminated the call. A jay shrieked as it flew from left to right, from beech to oak to join its mate.

Jay? What's does it mean when a jay appears?

Stefan's mind groped for the answer. In his fragile emotional state, he was having trouble recalling the definition from the book of Animal Spirit Guides.

Deceit. Beware of deceit, and don't be afraid of being strong and standing up for your opinions. Jay. Deceit. Perfect! He thought sourly, leaning back against his favourite coastal redwood tree in the nature reserve. The reserve was his place of solace and solitary escape. He knew every path, twist, turn, nook and cranny. He had sought out the support of the huge Wellingtonia with its teddy bear shaggy russet bark. Sitting at the base between two protruding roots, hugged by its presence, Stefan had steeled himself to make the call. After weighing up the possible ways of broaching the subject, he had come to the conclusion that the only course of action was to jump right in and tell the truth.

Now his feelings jostled for priority: relief it was done got a nano second before being cast to the back of the queue. Self-loathing vied with self-pity.

It could have been so good. I can still remember her eyes, and the feeling of joy at being with her. Being in love, sharing the love. All I wanted was to hold her and share that magic. And why not? Two people who wanted to be together. She was just as keen to be with me. Yeah, Stefan, but she's not married. Who are you kidding? All you've done is cause unnecessary suffering.

Stefan replayed the brief conversation. Her words echoed accusingly:

Why? Why have you done this?

Why, indeed? How did I ever imagine I could have continued with it? Got away with it? I know some people do. For years! But I can't think how they can live with themselves and the deceit.

Still weighed down by lethargy, his back against the redwood, hoping forlornly that the world would change and he'd wake up to find it was all an unpleasant dream, Stefan released a deep sigh. It made space for the next round of emotions. Disappointment, injustice, heartache, entrapment, wound themselves into a knot in his guts and rose up into his chest to cause physical pain. The voice of self-flagellation took up the whip. *You've only got yourself to blame.* Stefan felt that being able to cry might help, but nothing came.

Okay, just get up. Go back home, and get on with it. It's done and over. And she'll certainly never want to see you again. What did you expect?

The vision of his house, that was also his business, came into his mind. A rambling Victorian house on a square footing, creating a large square drawing room with full length bay windows looking onto the rose gardens and the maze of dwarf box hedges, which delineated the herb garden behind. His room was the adjacent former dining room, with its imposing open fireplace and similar outlook onto the rose garden. Just across the mosaic-tiled hallway, Marguerite's domain was the kitchen. Sandwiched between the two, Stefan often closed the dark oak door to his sanctuary and that was certainly where he was minded to go right now.

I hope she's not at home. I don't think I could stand a row with Marguerite today. I'm not sure I'd keep my temper. I might just tell her to go to hell and damn the consequences.

He took the long way through the valley and the yew groves, reaching up to touch the spiky soft leaves.

Poison and healing all in one beautiful tree. I think I'll be spending a lot of time down here. I can't go back to the park, that's for sure. I might bump into Cheryl.

Her name brought fresh anguish to his pain. The thought of inertia, being stuck in his present situation, loveless and trapped by intertwined business and home, brought his feet to a halt. He stood, shoulders drooping, trying to accept and balance his life choices. Resignation enveloped him as he started walking towards home again.

It was a relief to see Marguerite's car was not on the thin gravel drive. His own green estate car was parked out on the street. He slipped into the house and across the hallway into his room, shut the door and turned on the computer.

Maybe doing some work on the class I'm teaching will keep my mind focused and off her.

He opened the file marked: *Hues of Green* and began to group the classifications and colour gradients. After an hour of lacklustre and intermittent typing, not feeling he had achieved very much, he heard the front door open and then Marguerite knocked on his door. For a second he thought of feigning absence, but unusually, she opened it.

'Oh, you are home. I looked for you earlier. Have you been out on one of your walks?'

'Yes.'

Stefan thought she looked unusually flushed, and not her customary cool and collected self.

'I've just been round to see Mark.' she enthused. 'I really love going round there. He's so warm and outgoing. So helpful.'

Unlike me. 'Yes, he's a great guy. He's always been like that. Ever since I've known him.' *He's one of my oldest friends. From long before I met you.*

'We've been talking some more about working together with his reiki and my herbs. You know, he really inspires me and helps me believe the workshop will be a great success. He's just great!'

I used to do that. You used to do that to me.

A pause while she waited for a reply or affirmation.

Why are you telling me this? You don't usually bother to include me in your schedule. Why are you so insistent telling me about seeing Mark? Rubbing it in, what you think of me?

'Well, good. I'm glad it's going well.'

'So am I!' Marguerite threw back at him as she swept out of his room into the hall. Stefan could hear her humming on the way to the kitchen. He felt a strange unease to add to his pain.

What's she up to, muscling in on my friendship with Mark? Something has certainly made her day. Maybe she's enjoying winding me up? Perhaps she wants me to turn green with jealousy? Well, sorry, Mrs Wolfe, that's one green I don't do.

CHAPTER TWENTY-EIGHT

Cheryl was beginning to feel that Sheila should have a place in one of her cupboards where she could hide or hang out.

I'm round here so often I feel like one of the fixtures or fittings. I hope her husband doesn't mind. I'm round here every day. He never looks annoyed. He just smiles and goes out somewhere. He's a kind man.

It was the truth and not a semantic exaggeration. Cheryl had been a daily visitor ever since she had headed for the comfort of hearth and Sheila's home as soon as she put the phone down on Stefan. Sheila had been waiting with freshly brewed coffee and a nip of brandy, secretly relieved she didn't have to break the news to her friend. Mopping up and healing were her familiar territory and strength. A sleepless night, debating how to tell Cheryl about Stefan had taken its toll. Sheila felt drained and had boosted herself with some reiki in the interval between Cheryl's call and her arrival at the back door.

'I'm so sorry, love,' Sheila shook her head. 'You deserve so much better. Did he explain why?'

'No. I don't think I gave him much chance. I just hung up. I didn't want to hear anything else. Whatever it was, it wasn't going to be anything I wanted to hear.' Cheryl burst into tears again and allowed Sheila to take her hand. Eventually, Cheryl's memory recalled Sheila's visit to Mark.

'I don't suppose you found out anything from Mark, did you?'

Sheila hesitated. She had decided not to divulge what she had discovered unless directly called upon to do so.

'Well, actually, yes. I did find out a little. I asked Mark and he had a leaflet about the workshop they are doing together. He mentioned that Stefan is married to a herbalist, called Marguerite.'

'So you knew before I called?'

'Yes, darling. I was going to come round today and find a way to tell you. God knows what I was going to say. In all honesty, I'm glad he had the decency to do the deed himself.'

'Actually, I'm glad he did, too. It would have been awful for you if you'd had to do it. And then, if he'd called as well that would just have been worse. It's easier just to sit here and talk it through.'

The scenario repeated itself every day. Sheila sat at the table and listened and passed tissues as required. Sometimes morning, other times afternoon, depending on Cheryl's work shifts. Work was a useful distraction. Her announcing shifts were live, and that meant singular concentration.

If I can get through a divorce, I can get through this Cheryl encouraged herself. *And I've got Italy to look forward to.*

Each day, in the fortnight before her departure to Italy, cosseted by Sheila's kindness and caring shoulder to cry on, Cheryl grew calmer and stronger. Sheila made sure they shared a short reiki session. Sheila would work on her, sending healing to her heart.

'The heart chakra colour is green.' Sheila reminded Cheryl. 'So when you're working, imagine or intend that you are creating a shining green light in that area.'

Then, Sheila asked Cheryl to work on her.

'It's important for you to use your reiki as well as receive. When you use it, and it runs through you, you receive a healing, too. Every time you use it, your connection gets stronger and stronger, and that is important for you right now. Make sure you use it on yourself, first thing in the morning and last thing at night.'

'Nights certainly are a problem. Even moving to sleep next door in Tom's room, so I don't have to be in the bed where we made love, hasn't helped. At least reiki makes me feel a bit more rested even if I don't sleep. I'll have to move back in there tomorrow, though, Tom's coming home for the weekend. And then, just one more week until I go to Italy. Roll on Italy; I'll be so glad to get way from everything.'

'Are you going running today? Exercise is good, too.'

'Already been. I went out early this morning. I've been driving over to the common. I can't face being in the park or anywhere near Soloman's. I might bump into him.'

'Good plan. When's Tom home?'

'Tomorrow. He's catching the train with a suitcase full of washing, no doubt.'

Sheila smiled. 'Well, that's what kids are for. Parenting and loving. It will be good to have him home. Give you a different focus.'

'Yes, it will. He's such a caring boy. I'm looking forward to it. Okay, got to go and move myself back into my own room. Thank you for being here. Give me a hug

Cheryl had managed to maintain a semblance of calm over the following weekend while Tom was home from his course on botanical art. At least, she thought she had, until Tom gave up being tactful and asked outright if there was something wrong with her.

'Oh God, do I look awful?'

'Yes, Mum. What's up? Is it something I've done? I haven't wiped paint up the walls anywhere as far as I know.'

Cheryl was touched by his innocent concern.

'No, Tom. Nothing like that. It's nothing you've done.'

'So, are you going to tell me? Is it a big secret? Has something happened to Zoë? I always thought I'd know if something happened to her.'

'No, Tom. It's not a secret. And it's not awful. Well, not for you or Zoë. It's just a man I met, and now we're not seeing each other anymore and I'm feeling a bit upset, that's all.'

'Oh.'

Tom's surprise that she might be seeing someone, despite being *old* made Cheryl smile through her melancholy. Before she could reply, Tom decided talking about his mother's love life was too unsavoury and diverted the conversation onto safer, more conventional ground.

'I've brought some of my latest drawings home if you'd like to see them.' Cheryl always asked to see his work and he hoped this offer would cheer her up.

'We've got a new bloke teaching us this term. I'm really enjoying his classes. He's been getting us to study leaves and tree bark and mosses and stuff. Anything that's green. He's got this whole grading system called *Hues of Green.* He's a really cool guy. He says green is healing colour.' Tom continued hoping he was being helpful. His mother looked a bit out of it.

'Tell you what, how about I try the colour healing on you? I can test it out.'

'Well, alright. It can't hurt,' Cheryl didn't hold out much hope that it would achieve much, but she warmed to Tom's enthusiasm and if it would help him with his course she would willingly give it a try.

Tom came back from his room with his notebook and a selection of coloured cards.

'Colour therapy is not just about making you feel good. Colour therapy aids us both mentally and physiologically and colours can be used in many different ways. Studies have shown that when colour is introduced to the human system it causes cellular and hormonal changes thus bringing the cells into synchronisation or balance with the colour.' He read from his notes.

'Green is the first aid colour to heal and balance body and mind. Blue acts much the same as green. However it is more exhilarating and aids freedom of communication and artistic endeavours.'

'So I'm going to try both of those on you. Just sit and look at these cards and then close your eyes and either imagine you are breathing them in, or they are shining on you. I know it sounds crazy mum, but lots of people say it works.'

'Tom, lots of things sound crazy. I'm keeping an open mind.'

So Cheryl closed her eyes and opened her mind.

Well, I can't see any green, but I'll just intend it's there. Maybe that will work.

'Are you getting anything, mum?'

'A bit. Give me some more time.'

Let's see. What do I associate with green? Jealousy. No! That won't do. Grass. Hmm, that feels better. Heart chakra, Sheila said. Okay, let's put some green there. I think I read it's something to do with Archangel Raphael, the healer. Hmm. Actually, that feels quite nice. Blue makes me think of sadness, that's no good! A nice lake, perhaps.

'Mum?'

'I think it is working, Tom. I do feel calmer. It's like I'm in an oasis somewhere.'

'Oh great. Can I use that in my course notes?'

'Of course, darling.' Cheryl opened her eyes to find Tom watching her intently.

He has a depth to him that Zoë doesn't. Even though they're twins, they're very different.

'Did I tell you I'm going to Italy next week?'

'Cool. Are you and Sheila going on holiday or something?'

'No. I think Sheila will be quite glad to have some time to herself. I've been round there quite a lot recently. I've practically moved in. No, I'm going on my own. On a writing course.'

'Great. What are you planning to write about?'
'Angels.'
'Angels? Seriously? Real ones?'
'Well, Tom, some people think they're real. And I have to say I've had some strange coincidences happen since I started my research.'
'Like what?'
'Oh, just little things, like parking spaces appearing when I ask for them. And little white feathers keep appearing.'
'They're just bird feathers, mum.'
'Yes, but quite often I'm nowhere near trees, and one even turned up on the car seat the other day. I don't know. It's like your colours, Tom, something to keep an open mind about.'
'Okay' Tom nodded, his mouth formed a sceptical curve. 'So whereabouts in Italy?'
'Florence. Do you remember we went there years ago?'
'I remember hating having to walk miles round those art galleries. Strange, I'd really enjoy that, now.'
'I'll send you some postcards of the most famous paintings.'
'Awesome. Thanks, mum.'

CHAPTER TWENTY-NINE

Sheila helped Cheryl unload her case from the car and together they tracked down an airport trolley to wheel it to Gatwick departures. The holiday was a godsend, Sheila decided; her heart was full of empathy for her friend.

God, you look awful, Sheila thought to herself. *And who could blame you. Let's hope you meet some nice people on this trip.*

'Shall we get some breakfast? A coffee and pain au chocolat?'

Sheila chose Cheryl's favourite in the hope that it would bring a little light into the gloomy morning.

Cheryl shook her head. Too tired to bother to utter. She had hardly slept, again. Her appetite had vanished, as had seven pounds in weight in the two weeks since Stefan had phoned.

'One way to stick to a diet. At least my favourite clothes will fit,' she'd wryly remarked to Sheila who'd come over to help her pack.

Trying to put a brave face on. Good for you. Progress.

Sheila herded Cheryl through check-in and hugged her a fond farewell just before security.

'Oh sweetheart, take care. Just throw yourself into the course. Let all those emotions pour out onto the paper. I know it will feel too soon for me to say this, but, you never know who you might meet.'

In Pursuit of Perfect Timing

Cheryl managed a watery-eyed smile, hugged Sheila and headed off through the security gate.

*

Come on, girl. Chin up. Can't be crying in front of everyone, Cheryl lectured herself. *You're from a long line of tough women. Keep calm and carry on.*

Screening over and shoes back on, and once airside with time for idle thoughts, Cheryl decided to distract herself with some duty-free shopping.

Security had permitted her to keep her laptop with her as hand luggage, but she was far too tired to tackle any writing. Her book, *Perfect Timing*, was now fully outlined and even had an opening chapter. If she could only concentrate during the course, she might get it fleshed out and finished.

I think I deserve some perfume, or maybe a liqueur? What's Italian? Sambuca? Maybe, but you need to be able to drop a coffee bean on top and set light to it. Perhaps they won't allow that in my room. I might set off all the smoke alarms. A vision of everyone on the course – classmates and strangers – standing outside, discussing which *idiot* had caused the evacuation, flashed into her mind. *No, definitely not worth the risk. Amaretto? Too sweet. I'll just browse for something different to try.*

Looking up from the lines of Limoncello, it was the long black coat which first caught her eye. Cheryl had always found something very compelling about a man in a long black coat. Something 'Darcyesque'. She had long been a fan of Jane Austen's *Pride and Prejudice*. Grey hair flicked over the back of the collar and the coat billowed slightly with the motion of walking when the man turned the corner of the aisle.

Cheryl's stomach lurched. Her sharp intake of breath was not expired. Her eyes fixed on Stefan.

Stefan seemed equally stunned. Cheryl's every instinct urged her to walk away. And yet, like some heroine from a romantic novel, she found she couldn't move from the spot. It seemed ridiculous and imperative simultaneously.

For Christ's Sake just turn round and go! Now!

Somehow the neurons weren't firing, telling her limbs to move. Stefan looked down, and then he took a step forward, hesitated, raised his eyes and walked towards her, Cheryl sensed regretful longing. She knew she looked rough. Maybe he felt remorse from the knowledge it was his fault. *So he damn well should!* Perhaps it was the light, but Cheryl thought his slate-grey eyes lacked their sparkle. Pools of sorrow. Her soul howled at the universe: *this is wrong – we should be together!*

'Hello.' His mouth formed an embarrassed attempt at a smile. Greeted with continuing silence, he found himself babbling on.

'I'm just catching a flight.' He motioned towards the departure board.

The absurdity of the statement hung in the air.

'I'm going on a course. Some research on the trees I'm writing about.'

Cheryl nodded dumbly.

Is it my imagination, or does he look like he hasn't slept, either?

His next statement was interrupted by a final call for boarding.

'Um, that's my flight they're calling, to Bologna—' He drew breath as if to say something more. His mouth closed again.

What? What does he want to say? I want to hear it is all a mistake, that he loves me.

His lips moved again. 'I'm so sorry,' is all that came out.

With a shake of his head, Stefan turned and exited the shop leaving Cheryl engulfed in misery. Her new habit of conversing with the universe kicked in automatically.

Oh bloody wonderful! That's all I needed. I try to get away, to heal, and you send him right back to me. What kind of cosmic joke is that?

Standing in the middle of duty free, tears rolled down her face. People glanced out of the corner of their eyes and tried not to notice. Cheryl tried to wipe them away with the heel of her hand and searched for a tissue in her bag.

Thank God I'm wearing waterproof mascara otherwise I'd look like a fucking panda. Rage flared up through her heartache. She felt like picking up a bottle and smashing it on the floor. She found her feet and marched forcefully out of the shop before she had time to reach to the shelf.

Mercifully, there was no sight of Stefan in the bustling departure lounge. Cheryl walked round until she found a seat and slumped down onto its hard unforgiving surface. Fifteen minutes passed as she gripped and wrung her hands, trying deep breathing, mentally saying mantras and anything else she could think of to calm down. She put her palms flat on her thighs and tried reiki.

I can't put them over my chest; I'll look like a complete lunatic.

Eventually she managed to regain control and marched back into the duty free shop, emerging with a bottle of Cognac, lid twisted off and a large slug of it inside her.

*

'We are now boarding passengers in rows fifty to one hundred,' the ground staff at departure gate sixty-nine announced. Stefan remained seated, slumped forward resting his forearms on his thighs, hands clamped together. The flesh showed white with the pressure. It would be a while before his number was called. *What are the chances of that happening? Bloody hell, what a shock! It was wonderful to see her again, but she looked so rough. Pinched and drawn, and she had dark circles under her eyes. I suppose she hasn't been sleeping any better than me. I keep waking up thinking about her and that's it for the night. At least I've been able to move into the spare room. Marguerite seemed quite pleased when I said I wasn't sleeping and didn't want to keep her awake. What the hell was I thinking getting into this mess?*

Stefan straightened up and fingered his ticket in his inside pocket hoping to divert his thoughts to his forthcoming trip, but his subconscious wasn't going to let him get away with that.

I think Mark knows something's up, too. Marguerite's been going round there at least once a week for their workshop. It gets her out of the house, but last time I was round there myself, he was asking me whether something was wrong. More wrong than usual, I suppose he meant. He knows things are never good these days.

'Attention, please. We are now boarding rows one hundred to one hundred and fifty.'

Stefan rose and joined the queue to walk down the bridge onto his flight.

Oh shit! Let's face it, I'm in love. I'm married and I'm trapped. There's got to be a way out. Damn! At least I can divert my energy this week focussing on research and writing. I always feel good in Italy.

CHAPTER THIRTY

Firenze said the sign above the airport building. Cheryl's flight to Florence had been a blur. *Flight* indeed! She had intended to flee the pain of her failed romance with Stefan, and what had happened? He'd been there at the airport!

So much for getting away from it all! La vita non è giusta. No, life's not fair, but it sounds better in Italian. Cheryl sighed. At least her language crash course was bearing fruit. The course was in a villa complex, in the grounds of an old farmhouse some miles outside the city of Florence. The itinerary promised free time for excursions. She leaned her head against the taxi window as they lurched, swerved and gesticulated through the lunchtime traffic, an Italian taxi driver – master of his craft.

'Vaffan*culo!*' his middle finger adding emphasis and his voice shouting over the shrieking horn of an offended Florentine driver who he'd just cut off at the lights. They didn't put *that* phrase in her language CD. The meaning was clear enough. She could happily apply it to Stefan right now.

Ah, Florence hasn't changed. But I have. The last time I was here, I was married with a family. And now, look at me. I have my freedom, and all I want is to be in a relationship with a married man. The irony of the situation brought back that all too familiar weight of sorrow that had afflicted her ever since her phone call with Stefan. Even more disappointing was the fact that she had allowed this to happen; to trust that throwing herself into the arms of an attractive stranger would end in a fairy tale romance. But the worst realisation of all was that she still wanted him. Falling in love had robbed her of objectivity and balance; it had elevated her to ecstasy and then sucked every ounce of joy away.

Stone walls do not a prison make,
Nor iron bars a cage;
Minds innocent and quiet take
That for an hermitage;
If I have freedom in my love
And in my soul am free,
Angels alone, that soar above,
Enjoy such liberty.

Richard Lovelace's *To Althea, From Prison* had been one of her favourite metaphysical poems since university. The tears fell, never mind that she was sitting in open view in the back of a taxi. The taxi driver caught sight of them in his rear view mirror and nodded sympathetically as only an Italian can on witnessing the pain of love.

Why can't real life work out like the movies?

It was a pathetic thought, Cheryl knew. And before the airport encounter, she had made good progress, working through her distress, analysing what had happened bit by bit.

You're attached to the idea of romance, not the man, she reasoned. *You don't even know him.*

Now that she had chosen to write a book about calling on angels to help, it seemed a good opportunity to road-test her own advice.

She had leafed through her books and research notes to find out which one they recommended to call upon in times like this. Archangel Raphael, the heart healer, Uriel, healer of emotions, Raguel, healer of relationships. So she sat and asked whoever was out there to put their arms, or wings around her. And she did feel comforted. Novice as she was in this spiritual work, Cheryl sensed a presence. Total unconditional love like a warm cloak being thrown around her.

She concentrated on sending forgiveness to Stefan.

Forgive the person, not the deed. And what's that other phrase I read? Oh yes. Holding resentment is akin to drinking poison and expecting the other person to die. Good advice, courtesy of the Buddha, allegedly.

Cheryl kept working her step programme back to peace and happiness. It was tough. Some days it felt pointless, a road to nowhere.

But I'm not giving up. Sooner or later, something will have to shift. I can't feel like this forever.

Next, she had tried writing a letter and pouring her heart, and her anger, into it with complete abandon, and then burning it. That was said to be cathartic. As each layer of the onion peeled back, it became clearer how much baggage she was still carrying from her past. And she had expected one man to wave his wand, (the irony of his being a wizard was not lost at this point), and whisk her into a life of romance and happiness. Finally, at the centre:

What I felt for him, that extraordinary outpouring of love when I lay in his arms, it wasn't for him. It was for me! I was intoxicated by the feeling that I had attracted this man. I was good enough. Attractive enough. Self-love by proxy.

All the life coaches and guru books she had read emphasised love has to start with you. If you don't love yourself and go out into the world expecting someone else to fill that void for you, all you attract is another needy partner who expects you to heal their wounds.

And we wonder why we screw things up!

Yes, that was the truth of it. But still, she hurt.

You just feel humiliated and you're angry with yourself – she tried a stern self-lecture.

The vision of Stefan in the airport returned, and Cheryl's heartache with it.

Damn you! Go to hell!

CHAPTER THIRTY-ONE

There are several ways of getting to Florence. The easiest is to fly direct from London to *Aeroporto Amerigo Vespucci*. But equally, there are excellent rail links to the city from Pisa, and, Bologna. It had never occurred to Cheryl that Stefan's writing course might be in the same Tuscan villa as her own.

Oh for crying out loud! What the hell is going on? Wasn't it bad enough he was at the airport? What am I going to do? I'm not sure I can stay here now. But how would I get home? Maybe I could move out into a hotel or something? Shit! Why am I letting him ruin my chance to write this book? He can go home!

Cheryl stood with her bags deliberating and debating the choices open to her. If she chose to stay, she realised she'd have to walk up to reception sooner or later and stop hiding behind a pillar.

Maybe I can check in for tonight and stay in my room while I decide. I've been here for ages – he must have checked in and gone to his room by now.

However, fate was apparently having fun today. She stepped out right in front of him. A round of apologies preceded a silence. Stefan took the lead:

'God, this is so awkward. I … I would like the chance to try to explain, if you could bear it. Could I buy you a drink by the pool?'

Cheryl dropped her case down between them and studied its handle with deep concentration. If she was going to walk her talk about forgiveness and moving on, she'd better agree. Besides, she wanted to stay on her course and she couldn't avoid him all week, so it would break the ice and hopefully the rest of the week would be easier. She felt a sickening in her stomach as she replied: 'Okay, I'll be down in half an hour.'

The next thirty minutes in her room felt like waiting to see the headmistress on the day she had been caught painting the genitals of the school statue, a replica of Auguste Rodin's *The Age of Bronze* in the central quadrangle. Someone had dared her in return for a ticket to an elusive sell-out concert. If she'd thought it through, she might have realised she'd been set up. The offer came from her arch rival in the class, and the tip off to the formidable deputy head probably came from the same source. During the half hour outside the head's office, where she was the subject of much sniggering from passing pupils, Cheryl had felt sick from the fear of facing the head and her mother, and more so from the knowledge that she had been so desperate to get what she desired, she'd pushed aside all caution and negated the risks. And there she sat, facing the consequences. Now, sitting on her bed, wondering if it was worth the effort of changing from her flight clothes, she wished she'd learned the lesson first time around.

I certainly don't want to look like I've changed for him. In fact, I don't even have to go, if I don't want to. I could just stay here. At least, I have a choice. But then, there's the rest of the week. Oh, let's just get it over with. And if I'm going, I want to be down there first, and not have to walk up to him.

Cheryl chose to head for the far side of the pool, under the cover of the oleander bushes. Not wishing to be beholden to Stefan in any way, she ordered a gin and tonic, which turned up just as he appeared at the far end of the terrace.

'Hi.'

'Hi.'

'I'm sorry, I appear to be late. I was going to buy you a drink.'

'No, it's fine. I prefer it this way.'

'May I sit here, on the wall?'

'Sure.' Cheryl agreed and wondered whether it put her at a disadvantage to be seated slightly lower on the sun lounger. *Too late now.*

'So, where to begin? I realise I owe you an explanation. I'm not sure how helpful it will be, but I can assure you it will be the truth.'

Cheryl listened without comment as he explained that he and his wife, Marguerite, were in business together, but for years things hadn't been good between them.

'And that weekend, well, it isn't a good time for me. It's the day my mother died. That's no excuse for my behaviour, I know. I guess I was searching for love. If I'm honest, I'd been watching you for weeks and thinking that there must be a lucky man somewhere who shared your life. And then I looked into your eyes in that café, and I just wanted to be with you. To take a chance of happiness when it seemed to be offered.' He shook his head. 'I'm so sorry. Selfish, destructive behaviour. But, I have to say, in total honesty you are the most wonderful thing to happen to me in years.'

Cheryl recoiled.

'No, no. I'm not making a pass at you again. I don't want to hurt you anymore. I just wanted you to know that you *are* wonderful, and ... you deserve better, and, well, I hope we can manage to be around each other this week without it being too awkward.'

'Well, thank you for explaining. I suppose... well, it's not as if I gave you the chance to explain at the time. It was all so fast and intense. You don't wear a ring, and I didn't ask. I suppose I wanted the fairy tale.'

Somehow, being in his presence softened the pain. Cheryl still felt the lure of his energy, but she could put it on a realistic footing. Maybe this week would be a way to put it to bed? *No, that's not the phrase I need! For Christ's sake, get a grip!*

Cheryl downed her gin and tonic in one. 'Well, I'm glad we've managed to have this meeting. If you'll excuse me, I'm feeling rather tired and I'd like to get an early night.'

'Are you not having dinner?'

'No. I'm not really hungry. So I'll say goodnight.'

Stefan rose from the wall. 'Well, goodnight, then. Thank you for listening.'

He watched her negotiate the tables of laughing groups and for once felt the deep cut of his isolation.

*

Cheryl was one of the first down to breakfast the next morning, hoping that her favourite panettoncino with coffee would buoy her up after another night of sporadic sleep. As more people started to drift in, she went to explore the view from the terrace. The villa was built into the side of a hill to make the most of the vista.

Magnificent! Rolling hills, undulating subtle shades of green, spiked with landmark cypress and black pine. Nothing like it in the world. It's magical!

The air was already warm creating its distinctive olfactory palette of olives, sunflowers and red earth. Cheryl breathed it in and stood soothing her soul with the Tuscan landscape until she became aware people were leaving and it was time to find her classroom.

The rooms of the old villa had been commandeered as classrooms. Cheryl strolled down the wide hallway under the gaze of oil portraits of former inhabitants, inspecting the white card signs on the doors. Eventually, she arrived at what was once the drawing room, preserve of a wealthy contessa, and which now opened its carved olive-wood door to Cheryl and her group of novice writers. An ornate passaro inlaid dining table graced the centre, with an outlook over the grounds. Cheryl found herself a place between an American woman and a Swedish man and gave herself entirely to the advice and guidance of their course tutors.

Just as she had supposed, constructing and writing a book was a far cry from composing short promotional scripts. Cheryl spent her first day planning an overview of what she was trying to say and transcribing her intentions onto a flow chart to lead her through the process of actually creating her oracle.

The numbering of the pages was baffling. Seven days in a week, corresponding to seven archangels. Twelve months in the year, with each one allocated to the guiding care of an angel. Twelve hours in the morning and twelve hours in the evening. So far, so good.

But how am I going to make thirty-one days fit? Or thirty, for some months. And February! This section of the book is going to be much fatter than the ones surrounding it.

Cheryl solved the dilemma with nought to three classifying the angels of the *decadays:* tenth, twentieth and thirtieth. And nought to nine as the units.

That should work! The thickest part of the book would be twelve days. So for Tuesday, 12th January at eleven it's going to look like this:

Top section of the book: Tuesday ~ Archangel Camael
First section of the book: 1 ~ Archangel Michael
Second section of the book: 2 ~ Archangel Metatron
Third section of the book: January ~ Archangel Gabriel
Fourth section of the book: 11:00 ~ Archangel Raphael

So, if I want to know who to call for help at eleven in the morning on Tuesday 12th January – it's Camael, Michael, Metatron, Gabriel and Raphael. Wow! Just turn the sections of the book until I have the angels for that time of day. Perfect Timing. It actually works!

At the outset of the class, everyone had five minutes to explain why they were there and what they hoped to achieve. Cheryl had been concerned how she might be perceived in writing about angels. As expected, some of her group assumed that it was a work of fiction. Once appraised of the idea that she was seriously suggesting they talk to angels, a fissure divided the pros and cons. Two made it plain they wanted nothing to do with her, by ostentatiously choosing to walk away from any table where she was dining to sit elsewhere.

Well, he's a devout Catholic who considers talking to Jesus is the only permitted route to salvation. And she's an atheist. At least I've united them in something! It's been so long since I started to look into all this metaphysical stuff, I'd forgotten how alien some of it sounds. It seems another lifetime ago.

Cheryl sat, inhaling the aroma of her fresh Italian coffee before she sipped. It was the mid-morning coffee break, and half way through the week. Cheryl allowed the memories and comparisons to roll in, through and over her with the scented Tuscan breeze.

I hardly recognise myself sometimes. I'm essentially the same person, but I'm more open. Is that the word? No, aware. Goodness, I was so closeted, so fixed in my own little track before. It's not that I've changed my ethos or beliefs; I've taken the blinkers off. I was like a racehorse with blinkers, charging ahead, striving for the next hurdle, to get to that winning post and never stopping to look at what I was passing by. I was missing the magic, the little things that give colour and texture to life. And what is totally bizarre is that it is so obvious when you stop and enjoy the present moment.

The hot coffee touched her lips and made her jump.

Ouch! There's a good reminder to be in the present moment. Just drink your coffee, Cheryl, and enjoy the flavour and the view.

Cheryl let the snippets of conversation floating in the air flow through her consciousness.

'... yes, self-publishing is the answer—'

'No way! It costs a fortune. I'm going to send my manuscript to every publisher I can find …'

Hmm … I'd prefer to focus on writing the best I can first. Not much good sending out something second rate and then regretting if it does get published and you realise you could have done so much better. Or is that every writer's lament?

She cupped her mug in her hands, staring through the vapours at the shimmering green and gold of bucolic Florentine landscape.

I wonder if anyone will want to use my book? There are lots of very successful angel experts. Will anyone trust me?

Cheryl took a final sip as people started to filter back to their rooms.

Well, Archangel Gabriel, you are in charge of messages and communication. You'd better nudge me in the right direction.

She walked to the tray on the table to pile her cup on the others for return to the kitchens. Strains of music from the radio wafted through the open hatch. She recognised the rendition of 'Paperback Writer'. The lyrics anthemically marched behind her, the length of the spacious corridor, until she turned into her classroom, the volume fading beyond recognition. *Clinging wife, indeed! Very funny, Gabriel. Enough!*

*

As the week went on, Cheryl and Stefan worked their way through their separate classes, occasionally, in the same coffee group, but intentionally never alone.

At least it's cleared the air, and given me a kind of closure, she reasoned. *I have been able to concentrate on my writing.*

Only in unguarded moments, did she wistfully turn back the clock to that wonderful weekend, and wish things were different.

On the penultimate day, everyone had free time while the tutors evaluated the students' writing, so Cheryl headed for a day of sightseeing and shopping; she wanted to buy some of the wonderful calligraphy pens and parchment paper for which Florence is famous. Of course, as promised, she planned to end her day watching the sunset from the top of the Basilica di Santa Maria del Fiore. She hadn't *planned* to spend it with Stefan. But there he was, silhouetted on the balcony.

'Beautiful, isn't it?' His hand arched to the sun.

'Yes, breath-taking. Just like it was last time I was here. I made a vow I'd come back someday'.

'May I?' Stefan risked putting his left arm round her shoulder.

Cheryl didn't move away.

I shouldn't be doing this, but it feels right, so what's the harm?

Stefan voiced her thoughts.

'Look, I know we can't be more than this, but just for this one moment, let's share this memory and this peace, together.'

It did feel wonderful. *Il Duomo* had worked its magic again. They gazed out over the city as the moon rose and the bells rang.

*

That same moon also illuminated the figures on the flokati rug as it beamed down through the glass of the wooden conservatory roof. Marguerite inclined her head onto Mark's shoulder as he put a comforting arm around her. Her dark hair fell down his back like a thick glossy cloak, caressing his spine.

'Are you sure you know what you're doing?' he queried.

'Oh yes! I've been a long time in the emotional wilderness. For once, Mark, I am absolutely certain what I want.'

CHAPTER THIRTY-TWO

Back from Italy, her book was almost complete. In order to construct *Perfect Timing* she had to evaluate all the reasons why people feel vulnerable and might choose to consult any form of oracle: be they angel cards, tarot, or self-help manual. Next came the mammoth task of collating her research on which angels had an affinity with which days, months and dates. And finally, she married this with the qualities with which they are known to be associated, and thus, arrived at a conclusion as to what message they might bring to that page. Cheryl felt it had been like trying to assemble a giant jigsaw puzzle without the aid of the picture on the front of the box. But it was done, finally. And it *felt* right. Ready to send out. A new chapter in her life.

'Excellent! Now all I need is a literary agent.' Cheryl knew, as an unknown writer, she might have to brave quite a few rejections, or lack of acknowledgement at all. *My synopsis is going to have to be a winner. They made that very clear on the course. But I'm not completely divorced from the media business. I do have some connections I could try.* It was time to brave calling old colleagues, many of whom she hadn't spoken to since the public spectacle of her divorce. How much credibility did she have left in that world? *Let's hope they remember the favours I did some of them, when they needed some business networking.* Cheryl's luck was in.

One of them recommended her to an agent, who agreed to read her book.

'... and therefore, we are happy to inform you that we would like to submit your manuscript to two publishers who specialise in the metaphysical genre,' Cheryl read in the reply. She remembered how much her hands had been shaking as she read the letter, which arrived six weeks after her submission. They had sent her manuscript onward to the publisher a month ago, and she didn't expect a reply for at least another month, if at all.

Fingers crossed. C'mon angels, if you want to help, this is the moment. Cheryl sat by a little white tea-light of invocation, which she had lit when she received the news from the agent. *Archangel Gabriel is the messenger, and I think I'd better include Sandalphon who is supposed to look after musicians and writers.* She let the candle burn out. *Mustn't blow it out,* was something she'd read during her research, *that blows away the magic.* Cheryl was determined to do things *by the book.* The idiom made her smile. *How appropriate!*

Having done all she could to ensure success, she could only wait. And with the impetus of writing no longer upon her, all the other quandaries from her life flooded into the void. The estate agent's brochure sat on the kitchen table. The English Channel, that grey 'sleeve' of water, which the French, therefore, call La Manche, and which hosts the busiest shipping lane in the world between the White Cliffs of Dover and Calais, looked cheerfully blue in the photograph.

Must have been a summer's day when that was taken! Cheryl thought.

But there it was on the estate agent's website, purporting to be the vista from Ash Tree Cottage in Whitstable, Kent. *Do I want to view it? How am I going to feel moving away from London, starting over in a new town? I do love it there, but it would be a huge step.*

Although, she would never consciously have chosen to meet Stefan again, she had to admit it had served a purpose. Now she could walk freely around her neighbourhood without fearing she might bump into him. The rent on Trefall Avenue was eating into her capital. She wanted her own home again. Now, it wouldn't feel like running away, it would be just moving on.

Not that it will matter if I meet him now. It will still be awkward, but at least I won't feel devastated. We got through that.

No, the only way to look at that episode in her life was as a lesson. She had desperately wanted to feel attractive, to experience passion. And now she knew more about the potential to attract people and situations into her life, good or bad, when they come from a powerful heartfelt desire, she understood what had happened. Her desire for acceptance had met his desire for escape, and: Bingo!

So, if I can do that once, I can do it again, she supposed. *But next time, I won't expect them to make me feel better about myself. Next time? It's good I'm thinking about a next time!*

How was it that some people got the lesson instinctively, and others, people like her, had to go through so much pain to wake up? Vacantly spending years living their life through others, striving to be what they thought was expected of them.

Her friend, Sheila, seemed to have been born with that awareness. Was that because she figured it all out in another lifetime? Cheryl wasn't sure if this was just one life of many. It certainly wasn't beyond the bounds of possibility – just part of a meandering conversation she and Sheila were having one morning when her friend came over for tea and toast, smothered with damson jam. Sheila's home- made, of course.

'So how did you pitch the book?' Sheila queried. 'Is it for fun, or are you aiming it at the self-help market?

'A bit of both, I hope. I just found that there were times when I felt really lost and I could have used some guidance, but I wasn't sure who to ask. I can't be the only one. Besides, you can't permanently carry a small library round in your handbag on the off chance that's the day you put your foot down one of life's major potholes and need some instant help.'

Sheila was glad to see Cheryl's sense of humour had bounced back.

A very good sign of healing, she thought to herself. She knew Cheryl well enough to know it was genuine and not a brave face. So she felt she might open the subject of Italy again.

'So, are you over the Stefan thing? I still think the synchronicity of being on the same course was remarkable.'

'You know, Sheila, I spent a long time thinking I never would be. That it would hurt forever. I still have the odd twinge of longing, and hurt. But I am beginning to accept that I pulled it in. I mean, I poured so much energy into wanting him, what did I expect? I never even paused to think that he might be attached, or worse, married. I just have to accept it was bad timing. Or maybe, it was perfect timing. Maybe, it's what I needed to move me on.'

'Hm. That's sounds like a good title for a book, to me,' Sheila quipped.

'Ow!' Cheryl winced as Melchior leapt from her lap with a twist of feline claws, startled by the clatter and thud of post being pushed through the letter box and landing on the parquet floor in the hall.

'It's from the agent!' Cheryl squealed looking at the post stamp on the envelope. 'Gosh! That's much quicker than I thought. They can take months.'

'I'll make tea while you read it. We'll need some whatever it says.' Sheila thought she should give Cheryl some space.

The look on Cheryl's face said it wasn't good news.

'Dear Ms James ... thank you for your ... blah, blah, blah. Unfortunately, the publisher didn't think your book *Perfect Timing* was commercially viable. The unusual layout of layered pages and the colour graphics required would make the cost of publishing prohibitive ...'

Sheila shot Cheryl a sympathetic look.

'Wait a minute! ... however, they *are* prepared to discuss developing it for the electronic market as a reference booklet to accompany a mobile phone application. Oh my God, Sheila I don't even own one of those smart phones. I scarcely know what an app is. How on earth am I going to do that?'

'Maybe you don't have to. They have specialists who do that kind of thing. All they want is your idea. Cheryl, you've done it! Talk to them! Have you got anything stronger than tea? We need to celebrate!'

'There a bottle of bubbly in the fridge! Is it too early in the day?'

'Who cares? It's not every day you become a published author! Where do you keep the glasses?'

The cork came out with a very satisfactory *pop* and the fizz bubbled over into the pink-tinged flutes. Cheryl searched out some candles and lit them in gratitude to Gabriel and Sandalphon.

'I wonder if they'll mind us drinking this early?'

'Shouldn't think so. It's not as if we a couple of regular old soaks. And we have got something to celebrate. Here's to you, angels, thank you.'

'Cheers!'

'Congratulations!'

After two glasses much giggling ensued.

CHAPTER THIRTY-THREE

The grey walls of the classroom at Goldmarks College, London echoed the mood of the rain clamouring for attention on the large sash windows. Wet student footprints marked the doorway, and the smell of damp clothes, and slightly unwashed student floated through the air.

'So, has anybody had a chance to complete any fieldwork?' Stefan asked his group of five boys and two girls once they had lounged into the chairs and taken out their files.

No one spoke for a while, each casing out the others. Eventually, Tom offered.

'Yeah, actually, I did a bit a couple of weeks ago.'

'That's great, Tom. So tell me more about it, if it's not private. Who did you use as a test subject and what were you hoping to achieve?'

'Mum. I tried it on Mum.'

'Okay, well, *I* can't call her Mum, is it all right if you share her name with us?'

'Sure.' Tom shrugged. 'She's Cheryl. Cheryl James.'

Christ! I've been teaching her son.

'So, Tom, er ... tell me a little more about it.'

'Well, it's just she was looking awful. You know, really tired and upset. I think she'd been crying.'

Stefan's gut tightened. 'You don't have to share if it's personal.'

'No, I'm sure she'd be cool with it. She'd been seeing some bloke, that's all, and it hadn't worked out. So I tried the meadow green and the azure blue on her. I asked her to close her eyes and imagine them shining on her. And then I asked her whether she felt any change.'

'I see. And did you document you findings?'

Tom handed over a printed page from his file. 'It's just notes at the moment. I'm writing it up in full on the laptop.'

'Good.' He was glad to see the name of *the bloke* wasn't mentioned. 'Well, I'm glad it effected an improvement,' Stefan commented having appraised the outlook at the bottom.

'Yeah, well it did okay, but I reckon the prospect of having lunch with the guy from her publishers is cheering her up more than that did. She was actually smiling again, more like her old self when she got off the phone,' Tom quipped and winked at his friend in the next seat.

Disappointment and approval twisted through Stefan. *Of course, she's moving on. Good. I'm pleased for her. God, I miss her.* Stefan felt the nagging pangs of loss and resignation for the rest of the hour as he took his students through his next discourse on the *Hues of Green*.

'Right, I'll see you all in two weeks. Please write up your notes and leave them in my pigeon hole for marking. Thank you.'

They mumbled their replies and shambled out to the refectory for lunch leaving Stefan to his thoughts.

What the hell am I going to do? I can't go on living like this. I've never been one for counselling, but they've got someone here at the college, perhaps I should go and talk things through. It's got to be better than trying to carry on. And Marguerite's been acting very strangely. Ever since I came back from Italy she's been smug. As if she knows something I don't. A cat that's got the cream.

He closed his laptop and collected his papers at the sound of approaching footsteps. The next class was due in the room.

I wonder whether Mark has any insights? She's been round there regularly. And he knows all about divorce. I'm meeting him for a coffee this evening. Maybe it's time to open up and ask for advice.

*

Stefan waited until the waitress delivered the drinks to the table where he sat with Mark, and then continued:

'You see the thing is, I'd rather get everything out into the open. Tell her how I feel. That I want a divorce. I don't like living a lie. But if I do, our lives are so entwined. Both the businesses run out of the house. I can't afford to buy her out. And I don't think she can buy it, either, even if she asks her family for help. So we'd have to sell.'

Mark studied Stefan carefully as if weighing his reply, intuitively searching within his friend. His long fingers gripped and relaxed and then tapped on the table edge with uncharacteristic agitation. 'I know it's a terrible chasm to be staring over, but once the inevitable has been faced, there's a strange catharsis, as if the fear of it is worse than the actual event. That's how it was for me, anyway,' Mark shared.

'I hope so. I'm really close to calling it a day. Just out of interest, did you get a sense that anything was going on?'

'Ah, well. I did, actually. That day you came round and seemed in a really good mood. I hadn't seen you so relaxed in a long time. And there was joy back in your eyes. I hadn't seen that in ages. I did wonder. And then Sheila was asking about you on behalf of a friend. That really piqued my interest, I must admit.'

'You didn't say anything.'

'Not my business. I thought you'd share when you wanted to.'

'So, you've been seeing Marguerite a lot lately, do you think she knows something's going on?'

Marks fingers ceased their tapping and stilled, pushing into the tabletop. 'If I'm honest, yes, I'm pretty sure she does.'

'Oh?'

Stefan became aware of Mark's extreme stillness.

'I feel it's probably the moment to confess that she came round to see me while you were away in Italy and we had a fairly deep heart-to-heart.'

Stefan's body also stilled and stopped breathing. 'And?'

'She's not at all happy, either. Pretty obvious really. Neither of you are. I think you need to call a truce and sit down and talk it through.'

An instinct that had been hiding came to the surface of Stefan's mind. He let the breath go. *They're more than friends. They haven't just been working on the workshop. That's why she's been so happy – and so smug. Bloody hell! Here I am, beating myself up over one night with*

Cheryl, and Marguerite has been seeing my best friend, right under my nose and laughing at me! 'Yes,' he said, 'I think we do need to talk. Before we do, there's something I need to be sure about. Mark, I have to ask you something. We been friends a long time, and I know you'll give me a straight answer.'

Mark looked down to the tabletop and then back up steadily meeting his friend's gaze. He was ready.

'I can see that you get on very well with Marguerite. Are you two more than just good friends?'

'Stefan, we are just still friends. Close friends. We were working together and there was nothing more in it, until that week you were away. Marguerite came round to see me, and she shared how unhappy she was, and I gave her a hug, and it just carried on from there. We haven't fully taken it further, yet. But we want to; we have deep feelings for each other. I couldn't countenance anything more until you and I had spoken. We've been friends for too long. I just couldn't do that. I'm sorry, I was hoping to find a way to tell you earlier, but until tonight, we haven't really spent any time together. And now it's said, I'm glad that you know. I don't like deceit, either. Especially not with you.'

'I see.' Stefan let the full picture settle in his mind. 'That certainly changes things. I have to admit, it's a shock. But in a bizarre way, I'm glad. It makes it easier.'

He could see the tension relax from Mark's torso, and his fingers lessen their pressure on the table top.

Yes, I'm sure I'd be tense if I'd been in his situation. How strange, I should be angry and all I feel is relief and release. It's like being let out of prison.

CHAPTER THIRTY-FOUR

Gazing down on her new smartphone and its instruction booklet, Cheryl reflected that the meeting with the publisher had gone better than she could ever have imagined. Initially apprehensive, she could see their point as soon as they explained the application. The phone already knew what time, day and month it was. All they had to do was take her information and write it in a form of code that the chip in the phone could access. The perfect combination of technology and guided information. And better still, as far as anyone knew, no one else had yet done it. *Perfect Timing*, indeed!

In fact, the meeting had gone so well that Terence, the editor they had assigned to help Cheryl hone and polish the details, had taken her out to lunch. Covent Garden would always be Cheryl's preferred location in London with its eclectic mix of artisans and commerce. Soho came a close second, but it couldn't compete with some antipasti, a glass of Italian red and the performance of the comic opera quartet who regularly busked in the sunken courtyard outside The Crusting Pipe.

This is lovely. It's how life should be. Cheryl reflected. Terence was a confident man, relaxed in his milieu, and making the effort to be charming and complimentary.

I wonder if he's like this with all the female clients or whether he is making an effort for me? Anyway, it is nice to feel appreciated. Just for this moment, I can savour being successful and feeling attractive again. Without any rose-tinted glasses! Although, he is quite attractive. Thinning on top a little, but very nice eyes. And he knows how to create a look of office sophistication without looking like a salesman or a banker. Stop it, Cheryl! He's just your editor. Although, the fact I'm even thinking about it means I must be moving on. Good. Very good.

After their lunch, Terence had offered to help Cheryl choose a new phone.

'You can't be the author of an app and not have a phone to use it!' he teased.

She slid her antiquated old mobile into her bag, *to keep as a spare for emergencies,* and left the store with an expensive carrier bag and a state of the art smartphone. Her one-hour meeting had extended into lunch followed by an hour of shopping. Terence was certainly generous with his time. When it came to the parting of their ways Cheryl was going for a handshake, but he leaned forward and kissed her on the cheek.

'So, goodbye for now. I'll be in touch as soon as I know the next stage is complete. Perhaps, we could do lunch again?'

'Yes, that would be lovely. And thank you for all your advice and today's lunch. I really enjoyed it.'

'My pleasure.'

Cheryl watched him negotiate a path through the street audience watching some jugglers and wondered again whether he was being naturally polite or whether she should read more into his offer.

An hour later, sitting at her kitchen table with her new phone and wondering who would know how to help her work it, Cheryl allowed herself the luxury of projecting her wishes into her future.

So many new beginnings. A new life. A new branch of my career. A new phone number. So what about Ash Tree Cottage? Am I going to make an offer to buy it?

Ash Tree Cottage was in a side road above a golf course affording distant sea views, in a fashionable seaside town on the Kent coast. On her day off, Cheryl had driven down to meet the estate agent and viewed her potential new home. Living by the sea had always been on Cheryl's wish list, but never near the top of possibilities – until now.

The trouble with most English seaside towns is they've been ruined and have lost the charm they once had. And, even though I sound like a snob, they tend to lack sophistication – except Brighton, and that's a city, not a town.

Cheryl had found Whitstable many years before it gained a reputation as the weekend haunt of trendy Londoners. It was often showcased in glossy magazines and Sunday supplements.

'Whitstable has remained true to its roots as a quaint fishing village with 19th century cottages and colourful beach huts. The fishing industry thrives, and the town is particularly famed for its oysters. The annual oyster festival is a must for lovers of seafood,' the reporter had written in one such article.

The other bonus, Cheryl remembered, was the lack of any road running alongside the beach, which further added to the atmosphere of authenticity and history, and made it a favourite with the thriving artistic community.

Although the locals were not entirely enamoured of the 'Down From Londons', *or* 'DFLs', as they christened the intruders, they enjoyed prosperity from an income that was the envy of other resorts.

And I was one of the DFLs. We often used to take the children there for a day out and an ice cream on the pebble beach. On a clear day you could see the outline of the Essex coast on the far side of the Thames estuary. Zoë used to think it was the coast of France.

She smiled at the memory, and sighed away the nostalgia for her family life.

And now, there is nothing to stop me living there, or anywhere I choose. That's a rather frightening thought. All those years of yearning for freedom, and now I have exactly what I wished for, I'm faced with a blank canvas and I have to decide what to paint on it. Can I see myself living in a cottage by the sea? On my own? Well, not quite alone – I'd have the cats.

Cheryl decided she had two ways of tackling the possibilities. The first was her old default, to list the pros and cons:

- Tom and Zoë have flown the nest.
- I love Whitstable.
- This place is only rented and I do want a home of my own.
- Sheila will always come to stay.
- I won't be likely to bump into Stefan.

Cheryl's list was weighted on the positive, with no negatives that really mattered. She did still think about Stefan, and it irritated and saddened her in equal measure that she couldn't entirely let it go. Out of sight, out of mind she hoped. Furthermore, the physical and mental energy she would have to expend in moving house and building friendships in a new community would leave precious little time for idle regret.

So much for logic. Okay, plan B: what about sitting and asking my angels? After all, it is thanks to their influence and the sale of Perfect Timing that I am in a position to consider moving to a gorgeous little cottage by the sea.

Cheryl rummaged about in the kitchen drawer until she found a white candle and some matches. She had read, somewhere that you were supposed to use different-coloured candles to ask specific questions.

I've no idea what colour I'm supposed to use for this, but white has all the colours of the spectrum in it, so let's hope that will do.

Cheryl cleared the kitchen table. Clearing clutter was also deemed to be very important. She put the picture of Ash Tree Cottage in the middle, lit the candle, placed it in a glass crème brûlée dish for safety, and placed it over the image. She took a deep breath, sighed and dropped her shoulders to let all the tension go and tried to clear her mind of anything but her question.

I don't know about angelic, this feels a little witchy! Not unlike casting a spell – perhaps I should try an incantation? That's what you get for mixing with a wizard. Cheryl smiled at herself. *Well, at least you can reminisce with a drop of humour.* Even so, regret had a dig at her ribs before she cleared the landscape of her feelings and tried again to focus.

So, let's see ... I visualise myself surrounded by a protective bubble of white light, like my candle, and I am asking my guardian angel, and anyone else who would like to help me, find the perfect place to live to come into my space ...

Cheryl sat in the stillness and waited. She was aware of feeling calm, but nothing else.

You're going to have to help me with this, she advised her unseen mentors, *how do I get the answer?*

A thought came into her mind.

That's odd. It's an idea, but somehow it doesn't feel as if it came from me. It's like someone just popped it into my mind. Okay, I'll try it. I'll try imagining staying in London, and then, I'll try to feel what it's like being in Ash Tree Cottage.

Cheryl placed herself in neutral, just sitting and breathing. Then she imagined living in London, in her present house, walking the same streets, meeting the people she was used to seeing.

Doesn't feel bad. It feels familiar, a little staid, like a favourite jumper that's gone a bit saggy and has bobbles.

Next, she imagined sitting in Ash Tree Cottage and stepping out to walk down to the beach. The strength of her feelings caught her unawares.

Oh my goodness! My heart's swelling, my chest feels as if it's expanded and I can almost smell the sea air and hear the seagulls. The pebbles are crunching under my feet and I'm throwing my arms open to the sky with joy. Oh, wow!

Cheryl opened her eyes and looked into the candle.

So that's how you work. Interesting. Well, thank you, I think I've got my answer. All I need now is the courage to follow my heart.

The flame suddenly grew tall and flickered although Cheryl knew there was no source of a breeze. *Thank you.*

*

Yes! The estate agent confirmed her offer had been accepted. The lawyers were all doing their stuff, and she had a completion and moving date for mid to late July. That left the problem of where to live from the end of June. The rent on her current house ran monthly. She knew Sheila would offer to have her. She also knew there wasn't enough room in Sheila's compact and already cluttered house for an itinerant and their belongings. And then, as if someone above were orchestrating events, Joanna e-mailed and invited Cheryl to stay with her in France.

'Of course it's alright!' Joanna assured her when Cheryl called to say she needed somewhere for three weeks. 'We've got acres of room in this old place, and we'd love to have you.'

'All of you? Are you sure Christine doesn't mind me moving into your life. It's three weeks not just a weekend. You've only just set up home together.'

'Cheryl, stop it. She's dying to meet you.'

'Well, okay. I'd love to come and stay until I can move into Ash Tree Cottage.'

With the decision made, Cheryl guiltily settled Merlin and Melchior into the most comfortable cattery she could find. Their reproachful eyes stared at her through the mesh.

'It's only for three weeks, guys. Please don't look at me like that. You'll love the seaside. It has mice and great big noisy seagulls.' Not sure they were convinced, Cheryl walked firmly to the car. It felt like taking the twins to nursery school for the first time. Once she was out of sight, the nursery school staff had assured her that Tom and Zoë had settled happily down to play. Cheryl had wept all the way to work feeling like the Wicked Witch of the West. She started the car and drove away from the imagined wrath of the felines. Destination Whitstable via Bellefontaine in Normandy.

CHAPTER THIRTY-FIVE

Stefan waited until his wife had finished bottling her latest batch of herbal potions so there would be no excuses.

'Marguerite, I think we need to talk.'

His voice had a timbre and authority which demanded her attention. For once she didn't dismiss him, but turned from the table to face him.

'Well, this is unusual – we don't seem to do much of that these days.' *Did she have sense of what was coming?* Although Stefan didn't know how since Mark was sworn to secrecy.

'Let's sit down. Do you want tea?'

'Yes, that would be nice, thank you.'

Marguerite watched as Stefan followed the ritual of warming the pot, measuring the leaves, pouring the boiling water and bringing the cups to the table while it brewed. Tea wasn't the only thing brewing. The storm broke.

'I was talking to Mark last night; I asked his advice about something and the conversation took an unexpected turn.'

'Ah, I see.'

'Do you want to tell me about it?'

'Well, that depends what this conversation was about. I might not be on the right track.' Marguerite wasn't going to hang herself until she knew the game was up.

'He said that you have been getting on very well while you've been working together, and that while I was away in Italy, the friendship developed into something more intimate.'

Marguerite squared her shoulders.

'Yes. Yes, that is true. Stefan, we haven't been happy, or even compatible for some time. You know that. And I have felt an attraction to Mark growing over this last year. I'm sorry; I don't like infidelity or deceit. I'd rather we'd had this conversation a long time ago.'

'Yes, so do I, Marguerite, so do I. It might have saved us both a lot of angst.'

'You don't seem as upset as I thought you might be.' Marguerite's intuition kicked in. She inclined her head to the left before enquiring, 'Have you been seeing someone else? It wouldn't surprise me. You haven't been near me in years, so it makes sense you might be going somewhere else.'

'Well, I haven't been *going somewhere else*, as you put it. There was just one occasion, and that was it. I ended it – because I'm married,' Stefan added pointedly.

'Oh. I'm still not surprised. There had to be someone.'

'If it makes you feel, better yes there was. So we're equal.'

'Were you in love with her?'

'Yes.'

'Does she live round here? Do I know her?'

'No.'

'Well, I'm glad of that. I don't like the idea that I've been talking to someone who was having an affair with my husband. That's just too insulting.'

'And you don't think getting together with my best friend is a problem?'

Marguerite had the good grace not to initiate a row; she knew she was the more culpable if recriminations started to fly.

'I'm sorry, Stefan. It wasn't by choice. It just happened. Let's just focus on how we're going to move forward. Do you want a divorce? I don't want a fight. I shouldn't think you do, either.'

'Yes, I think a divorce is the only answer. We both know that. But what are we going to do about this house and the businesses?'

Marguerite raised herself up in her chair. She had run this scenario in her head daily. She knew what she wanted to manipulate, what her dream solution would be, but would Stefan go for it?

'Actually, when I think about it,' she tried nonchalantly, 'there is a very easy solution. My business is totally tied to this house because of the herb garden. It would take me years to establish that again somewhere else. Of course, you could buy me out, but as far as I'm aware you can't afford that.'

'No, I can't.' Stefan knew that look. He knew she had a scheme already hatched.

'Why doesn't Mark move in here, and you have his house?'

'What? Does Mark know you're proposing this?' Stefan wondered whether the betrayal of friendship and trust had cut deeper than he knew. Had they planned this together?

'No! No, of course he doesn't – yet. But it does seem to solve the problem, doesn't it?'

Game, set and match! I hope Mark knows what he's taking on with you.

'So, do you agree it might work? After all, he lives by that wood, and he has that wooden conservatory that you like to spend so much time in when you're round there. You have always said you felt at home there.'

Although he disliked Marguerite's machinations and game playing, he had to admit, it might be a satisfactory way out for everyone. 'Yes, I admit, I do like his place. But I am not going to be the one to suggest this. If you're so close to him, you can go and broach the subject.'

'Fine, I will. By the way, are you ever going to pour that tea? It will be completely stewed soon.'

'No, thanks. I'll leave you to it. I'm going out for a walk to the nature reserve.'

CHAPTER THIRTY-SIX

Cheryl slowly negotiated the exit ramp from the cross-channel ferry to Dover. It had been a choice between that or a fast rail trip on Le Shuttle. In the end, economic considerations made the choice. And the ninety minutes on the ferry would give her some emotional respite and time to reflect. Thirty-five minutes on the shuttle would hardly leave time for coffee and a muffin. The crossing had been smooth and looking back at the iconic White Cliffs of Dover, Cheryl felt as if she were leaving her old life behind in addition to her country.

I wonder how I'll feel seeing Joanna in her new situation? And what if Christine doesn't like me being there? Okay, stop that right now! You are projecting negative expectations when you have absolutely no foundation for them. In fact, quite the opposite; Joanna said Christine was looking forward to meeting me. So, stop it. That's an old habit you can do without.

Cheryl pulled herself up from leaning on the ship's rail and took a photo on her phone.

There! Goodbye to the old, and hello to the new me. New home, new life, a blank canvas to paint whatever I like. Every time I look at this picture of the white cliffs, it will remind me to keep my focus positive.

The journey from the port of Calais to Bellefontaine was more of a challenge than Cheryl had expected. After all her years globetrotting with television crews, she had assumed it would be fairly easy. Two hundred and two miles running parallel to the coast on major roads – she even had the toll money ready. All went well until she got to Rouen, where one wrong turn pitched her in the direction of Paris instead of Bellefontaine.

Drat! All the times I've wanted to go to Paris, but this isn't one of them!

No time for that now. I need to get back on the right road.

The detour added half an hour onto her journey, so Cheryl found herself approaching the gîte some four hours after she had driven off the ferry. The road was lined with trees.

Some kind of cypress? Where is Tom when I need him? He'd know. And Stefan. Damn and blast, get out of my head, man!

The sign for *Chez Nous* nestled in the foliage growing through the wooden fencing which flanked the drive. It was a hand-painted sign with apple blossom and a pair of intertwined turtledoves. Cheryl overshot it the first time, and had to reverse. As she manoeuvred her car into the drive a mixture of apprehension, relief and fatigue overcame her.

Well, I'm here. My home for a while.

As her wheels crunched over the gravel in front of the big stone house, the wide rustic wooden door creaked open on its giant iron hinges and Joanna strode out to greet her, arms outstretched and beaming.

My goodness! She is changed. I've never seen her so demonstrative.

'Darling! You've made it in, and in good time. I am so pleased to see you.' Cheryl was enveloped in Joanna's hug.

'So good to see you, too! It feels wonderful to be here. Another step on my road.'

'Leave the bags in the car and come on in. Everyone's waiting to meet you. They wanted us to have the first few minutes out here to ourselves. Come on!'

Joanna put her arm round Cheryl and guided her through the cavernous doorway into a thin small stone hallway running laterally from left to right. An apple-wood table housed a vase of summer flowers and a basket full of keys. Turning right, Joanna pushed open the wooden door at the end and led the way into the kind of old farmhouse kitchen that would do any rustic film set proud. The ceiling was vaulted like a small church, with diamond-leaded windows either side. Herbs and drying lavender hung from hooks on an iron rack to the left, and apples filled the baskets stacked in tiers on the right. At the far end a double-oven range in bright red and silver livery had the kettle steaming on one of the rings, and the centre of the room was filled with a rectangular dining table of banqueting proportions. Christine stood at the far end, between the table and the range; when Joanna and Cheryl entered, she came round to greet them.

'Cheryl.' She opened her arms. 'Joanna has always spoken so fondly of you. I am so glad to meet you at last. Welcome to *Chez Nous*.'

Cheryl felt the strength of her embrace. Although tall, to match Joanna, Christine was lithe and sinewy. Her dark hair was still cropped at the nape of her neck, and this time Cheryl saw her face with its strong features: dark eyes; black eyebrows and broad cheekbones above a generous mouth.

Striking. Yes, that's what I'd say if I had to describe her. Her eyes command that you look back at her. And a very warm feeling. She feels like someone who is very genuine and honest. Someone who'd tell you what they think without any rancour.

'Christine, it is so good to meet you, too. Thank you for inviting me. It is great to be here. This place is amazing.'

Christine laughed. 'Yes, it was a great find, we love it. Come and sit down – what can I get you? Tea? Coffee? Some apple juice, perhaps?' She gestured towards the baskets of fruit.

'Actually, apple juice would be wonderful. I feel I need something refreshing after being in the car all that time.'

Christine busied herself turning the taps on a barrel of juice besides the baskets, while Joanna reached up into the wooden cupboards to get glasses. At the far end of the wall a small door, only a few feet high, shaped into an ecclesiastical point to match the vaulted ceiling, began to open. Cheryl stared at it as it inched open. She had assumed it was another cupboard, but clearly something was pushing it from the outside. A small tousled head of curls poked through.

'*Maman*, is she here yet?'

'Open your eyes and look, *ma cherie*.'

The tousled head tipped up and Cheryl found herself being scrutinised by a pair of curious hazel eyes.

'Are you the lady from England?'

'I am. Are you the little girl from France?'

Leanne giggled, crawled through the doorway and straightened up.

'Oh, well now you're here, I brought you this. I made it.' Leanne took her right hand from behind her back and proffered a straw doll with a little cloth hat towards Cheryl. 'It's a corn dolly. It's to make you welcome and you should put it by your bed to ward off evil spirits' she added with the knowledgeable confidence of a seven year old who has seen it all.

'Well, thank you, Leanne. I will make sure I do that. And it is very nice to meet you.'

Leanne smiled.

'Can I go back out to play now, *maman*?'

'Don't you want any juice?'

'No thanks.'

'Okay. Be back for dinner.'

Leanne nodded and disappeared back through her little doorway into the garden. Christine smiled as Cheryl watched her daughter vanish through it.

'Sweet, isn't it? We have no idea what it was originally for, but Leanne loves it. It's her private and secret entrance.'

'Fabulous. And she is really gorgeous. What a beautiful character.'

'Takes after her mother.' Joanna threw in. She and Christine touched hands. 'Cheryl, I am so happy here. I didn't know life could be like this.'

'You've got to tell me all about it and all about coming here.' Cheryl countered.

'I will, over dinner. Promise. Let's get you moved in first and you probably need a rest.'

Cheryl agreed she would like a nap. Together she and Joanna moved her bags into the back bedroom overlooking the orchard and the fields beyond.

You could write a book just about this, Cheryl mused looking out of the window. *I can't wait to hear the full story tonight.*

*

Dinner was a delicious but simple affair. Freshly tossed salad with a crusty baguette, served alongside aromatic ratatouille. The remnants lay on the table as Cheryl finished telling her story of how she had forsaken her old life, fallen in love with a stranger, followed her heart and, finally, her journey to Florence, her foray into publishing and hopeful steps to healing and moving on.

'And I thought *my* journey was an upheaval. Cheryl, you could write a book about that!'

'I'm not sure who'd read it.'

'You couldn't make it up! Celebrity scandal – a wizard!'

'Yes, I suppose it is a bit bizarre.'

'Unless you'd told me, I would never have believed there were real wizards. Did you see him do anything magical?'

'Outside the bedroom, you mean?'

'Cheryl!' Joanna was laughing at this unaccustomed frankness from her customarily reserved friend.

'No. I didn't know him long enough for that. Although, I did lots of googling while I was waiting for him to phone, and it seems wizards really do exist. I managed to find some pages on his teaching and some blogs he's written. It came across as a mix between a herbalist and healer with magical intention, if that makes any sense. There was a time when I would have dismissed it all as nonsense. But since I've been working with energies, I have to allow that intent is quite powerful. A form of magic. I did plenty of intending to wish him into my life, after all.'

'And are you really over him? It sounds a tough act for someone else to follow.'

'I'm trying, Joanna, I'm trying. The editor in London seems to be more than professionally friendly. He took the time to help me buy my phone, and I've just had an email to ask if I like opera. Apparently, he has some free tickets to Covent Garden and wants to know if I'll go with him. I've got to go back for a meeting with him in about ten days.

'So, what's he like? Has he got potential, or is he just a diversion?'

'Oh, I don't know. He's very personable, and polite and generous.'

'Sounds more like an uncle than a love interest to me.'

'Yes, you're probably right. But at least it's a start.'

'Do you still have strong feelings for the wizard?'

'I'd like to say no, but if I'm honest, I don't think I'm there, yet. I've still got a sinking feeling in the pit of my stomach when I think about him. A longing for what might have been. It seems deeply unfair that it was so good, we wanted to be together and we couldn't. I look at you and Christine and wonder why I couldn't have that happiness? You did get your fairytale ending.'

Christine, who had been allowing Joanna and Cheryl to explore the conversation up to this point without interruption reached over and took Joanna's hand.

'We are very lucky, we know that. And it was against the odds. But we never gave up believing in our love. It may not be universally so for everyone, but I think that love is strong and I hope it will always find a way. Some people may say that's a cliché; I happen to believe it's true. A form of magic, if you like.'

Cheryl was touched by the sincerity of the moment and not sure she could reply without her voice shaking. All her hopes of magic with Stefan surged back to the surface.

So, not over him, then.

Sensing her friend's impasse, Joanna took up the conversation.

'I think what I came to understand was the importance of not living a lie. I existed with Richard. Sure it looked okay from the outside. We were comfortable, both following good careers, but there was no true caring, no sharing of dreams, desires. I think we had both *settled* for each other. With hindsight, I married Richard because it seemed the best offer I was going to get. And Richard chose me because I suited his image of a successful wife who could entertain his clients and allow him to come and go without the trappings of children and obligation. A fashionable accessory. We were married and yet autonomous. But there was no depth to it. No intimacy in the fullest sense of the word. And then I met Christine, and I understood for the first time what it should really feel like. What it is to truly love, unconditionally.'

Cheryl recovered her voice. 'Yes, I understand that. When I was with Stefan, I felt truly exposed. Emotionally vulnerable, allowing someone inside the shell and having the courage to let them see how you really feel, who you are. A kind of surrender. I had a connection to Ross, a contract, but it didn't feel like that.

No connection of the soul.' Christine squeezed her hand in empathy and released it.

'How did Richard take it? Did he ever understand?' Cheryl asked.

Joanna shook her head ruefully. 'No, sadly, I don't think he ever grasped it. He took it very personally. And some would say why not? After all, his wife was leaving him for another woman. If he'd loved me, that might have some validity. But he didn't. It was all about status, image and loss of face.'

Christine stood up to get dessert. Sliced apples with camembert cheese and tiny savoury muffins.

'And yet, Cheryl, you have reinvented yourself.' Christine steered the conversation away from the raking over of failed relationships. 'You have kept your career and created a new one as an author. It is a wonderful achievement to have negotiated that amongst all the change flowing around you. You are amazing. That must feel so uplifting?'

'Yes, it does. To tell the truth, I am rather surprised. So many people write and never get published. I feel I've been watched over.'

'So tell me about the angels?' Joanna prompted. 'You never used to talk about them before.'

Cheryl poured herself another glass of Merlot and slid a runny slice of camembert onto her plate. They were eating *paysan* style, which in France means one plate, cleansed between courses with bread.

'I found them after I did my reiki.'

'Ah, you are a reiki master, too?' Christine asked.

'Oh, no. Just a reiki one at the moment. I will take it further once the move is over, perhaps. Do you know about reiki?'

'Christine is a master.' Joanna answered for her.

Why am I not surprised? She has that same calm presence that Sheila emanates.

'Well, then you understand how it feels when you discover universal energy. You just know there is more to life than we see. And one night, at a reiki share, I met an angel lady. She kept talking about how connecting to them could change your life, and I thought it was worth a try. Do you work with them, too?'

Christine inclined her head from side to side and shrugged. 'I don't know. I assume I do. I was raised as a Catholic and we were always in church, so I would think so. But I've never made a particular study of it. How do you know they are there? Have you seen one?'

'I wish! No, I don't see them. Although, I think some people do. I just talk to them – mostly in my head, and a couple of times out loud. Then, I wait to see what happens. The angel lady said the most common sign is feathers, and I've got lots of those. And sometimes I find little coins. Maybe they were always there, and now I'm just attuned to notice them. Whatever the truth, I certainly see plenty of them. And quite often if I'm thinking about something, I hear a snippet of conversation or a line from a song on the radio that is very relevant. Again, I know sceptics would say it's coincidence or wishful thinking, but I don't care. It has really helped me over the past months. I find it comforting, as if someone is really watching over me.'

'So you've written a book about this?'

'Sort of – it's more of an oracle. Once I'd started to talk to them, I found they have specific attributes, a kind of speciality subject: Archangel Michael does protection; Raphael heals; Gabriel deals with communication and children; that kind of thing. There are so many, and it was so complicated to remember, I thought perhaps other people had the same problem and having a way to know which angel to call on might help. That's when I discovered they are also affiliated to certain days or months. I just woke up one night with the idea and the title – *Perfect Timing* – in my head.'

'Fabulous!' Christine raised her glass for a toast. 'Here's to health, wealth and happiness and success for us all! Which angel do we call for that?'

'Um ... Chamuel, I think. He finds us what we need. Cheers!'

All three glasses clinked in unison and universal celebration.

What a magical evening. Cheryl's heart sighed. *I will be happy, I know I will. I just have to believe with all my heart, just as Christine and Joanna did.*

CHAPTER THIRTY-SEVEN

The scent of the yew trees, a distinctive aroma of resin with a piquant overtone, wafted down over Stefan as he walked into the grove. It was an ancient place where the yews clung onto the side of a precipitous rocky slope and formed a circle around the base. One had long fallen in a storm and new shoots had grown upward from the prone trunk, forming a barrier along the bottom of the enclave. New life springing up from the old. It was one of Stefan's favourite places; a sanctuary to think things through, off the beaten track of the nature reserve, only accessed by a single-file track which traversed the hillside. He was rarely disturbed. He had headed straight there after the denouement with Marguerite, and daily since.

He thought back over the first meeting with Mark.

It went well, all things considered. It was a little awkward at first, which in itself is strange. Finding out about him and Marguerite should have been the worst, and yet, all I felt then was relief and release.

Stefan remembered the caution in their conversation, not knowing whether Marguerite had broached the subject of swapping houses.

She hadn't, and didn't do so for a week. It transpired she had been consulting a lawyer as to the feasibility of such a transaction. Stefan had waited for Mark to make the first move. He was relieved to find that Mark was as surprised as he had been by the manoeuvre.

At least I don't feel as if they are ganging up on me. Marguerite may have planned it, but Mark wasn't part of the plotting.

The first time he had seen them together was, he had to admit, a challenge. He was visiting Mark when Marguerite called round. She appeared to be equally ill at ease on finding him present. Mark became the go-between.

Yes, he was very calm and handled it well. He definitely walked his talk about keeping calm, detaching from the emotional charge and honouring the friendship with each of us without giving precedence to either. It is going to be strange while the exchange happens, moving belongings and cutting ties to the past. I wonder how we will feel the first time we visit each other and really engage with seeing some else living in our former home? Stefan reached up for the comforting touch of a feathery yew branch. *Well, yew tree, my healing friend, I'm going to need all your help and strength in the coming weeks. You're going to be seeing a lot of me in your grove.*

And then, there was the dilemma of Cheryl: to run to her immediately, or to wait until all was settled and he was officially a free man? Stefan sat under the yew bower daily, and thought about Cheryl. He allowed his hopes to shoot up to the sky.

I'll call round to her house. She'll open the door and I'll explain that I'm free. No, maybe I'll have to write to her first, or she won't open the door to me. Then, I could phone and arrange a good time to come round so that we won't be interrupted and I can say everything I've wanted to say. I can let all my feelings out.

Stefan sighed and released his longings to the birdsong and the skies above. He decided, eventually, to wait until all was settled.

'Many a slip twixt cup and lip' the proverb cautioned. *I can't risk contacting her and then have something go wrong or find that Marguerite has thrown in some new condition for getting divorced. She'll never trust me again if that happens. No, I'll have to be completely free before I make contact.*

Those had been Stefan's musings and his decision until the final weekend before the end of term. He approached Goldsmark College with a youthful stride. His renewed physical vigour reminded him what an emotional weight he had been carrying. He also knew he would be teaching Tom in his morning seminar and wondered if he might risk fishing for a little information.

The day was bright and moderately warm. The classroom had swapped its aroma of damp sweatshirts for that of sunscreen, and the students now wore T-shirts. They were already sprawled in the hard backed wooden seats with integral raised writing desks, exchanging banter and demob happy. Stefan knew better than to try and engage them in serious work.

'Good morning you lot!' he lobbied at them.

'Hiya.' they chorused back.

'Right, we've only got this session to wrap things up before the summer break, so I'm not going to hang about. If you have finished your assignments please hand them to me now. If not, I expect them in my pigeon hole by the end of the week.'

Groans and mumbles of assent greeted this instruction and two folders were passed forward.

'Have you enjoyed the colour work this term?' he canvassed them.

More monosyllabic mumbles with a positive note.

'Good. Well, I hope it is something you will continue to be aware of, and continue to develop in your lives. Anyone doing anything different or interesting this summer?' Stefan tried not to look directly at Tom.

'I'm going travelling to India with a couple of girls!' the class Romeo boasted.

Cheers and hoots of derision followed.

'Great light in India.' Stefan assured him.

'He won't be looking at the light if he's with those two girls!' someone quipped from the side. More laughter. Stefan chose his moment.

'How about you, Tom? Anything interesting on the horizon?'

'Nah. I'm spending it with my Dad and my twin sister, 'cos Mum's moving house. She's decided she wants to live in a cottage and be a writer,' his face expressed teenage disbelief, eyes flicked to the ceiling.

Oh God! She's moving.

'That sounds nice. Somewhere exotic?'

'Nah, it's in Kent.'

Stefan dare not try harder.

How am I going to find out where she's gone?

As soon as he could dismiss the class, Stefan paced the quadrangle trying to work out what to do.

I can't wait until I'm divorced now; I'll have to find her or I could lose her forever. No good writing if she's moving – although she might have a postal redirect service. Maybe I should just go round there? No, a text. I'll try sending a text asking if we can meet.

Stefan spent three anxious days waiting for a reply to his text. When nothing came, he deliberated whether this was because she didn't want to reply, or whether she hadn't received it.

I'll just have to risk calling.

He rehearsed what he might say; how he might start the conversation so that she wouldn't hang up on him. All in vain because his five attempts at calling went straight to voice mail.

Maybe she's screening her calls? I'll just have to risk going round there.

He tried several times, morning, afternoon and evening across three days. No one appeared to be at home. Eventually he put a handwritten note through the door and still there was silence. He'd tried all weekend and after his last day at college he found himself back again, pacing Trefall Avenue, wondering if he was being deliberately ignored. Out of ideas and frustrated, he watched a small white Fiat draw up outside, and a couple walk up to the door, and then let themselves in with a key. Their puzzled faces greeted Stefan when he rang.

The woman spoke: 'I'm sorry, do you have an appointment?'

'No. I ... er ... I was looking for Mrs James?'

The woman's estate-agency clipboard caught his eye.

'Mrs James doesn't live here anymore. I'm just showing people round, that's why I thought you might have an appointment.' She explained. 'Mrs James moved out at the end of the month.'

Stefan looked crestfallen: 'Do you have a forwarding address for her?'

'I'm sorry, I don't. And even if I did, I'm afraid I wouldn't be permitted to tell you. I believe she's gone abroad.'

Abroad? Tom said she was moving to Kent?

'Well, thank you. Sorry to have bothered you.'

Stefan found himself back on the pavement scrabbling for the next course of action.

I can't contact Tom; college is finished for the summer. Why has she gone abroad? Italy? Maybe she's gone back to Italy. Tom said something about writing. It's all I can think of. Who would know?

On his mobile, he clicked on contacts and started to search.

CHAPTER THIRTY-EIGHT

Contacts. Add contacts. Search contacts. Cheryl looked from the manual to the smartphone – it was all so different to her old mobile. She still had her old handset, complete with original sim card and number, packed somewhere in the storage boxes back in London: *just in case I can't get on with this smartphone thing.* She had been undecided about whether to transfer her number to the new phone. In the end, she opted for a clean slate and new beginning. *Anyone I want to hear from has the new number.*

'Want some help?' Christine had turned out to be something of an expert.

Cheryl handed the phone over with the instruction:

'Okay, step by step, so I can see what you do and, maybe, I'll learn by Wednesday.'

Wednesday 16th July was the day she had to be back in London for the next meeting with her publisher. *My publisher!* The words set off fireworks of celebration in her heart and mind, followed by a jolt of anxiety. *And that also includes Terence. What am I going to say to Terence? Am I going on a date to the opera?*

'There,' Christine handed it back. 'All updated.'

'Thank you so much – you're so patient.'

The techno-savvy Christine had installed a high-speed landline so that Joanna could do voice-overs without having to make frequent trips back to England. Cheryl realised that she could do the same from her Whitstable cottage. It was relatively easy to commute to London for shifts. But more expensive.

But I'm not doing so many shifts these days, so that's okay. And I wonder if I can write something else? Something with a seaside theme? A novel, perhaps? That would be a good challenge. Something to focus on. Maybe I could run the idea past Terence? And if he is going to be my editor in the future, perhaps I should be cautious about getting too involved with him? It might turn really awkward. I'll go to the opera and see what happens. If he seems to want to be more than friendly I can gently put the brakes on. Yes, that's a plan. I'll just see what happens, it's no good jumping to conclusions about what he wants. One step at a time, Cheryl.

Cheryl weighed up her options sitting in the old comfortable chair in the front room of the gîte. A room with shelves of books on everything from cooking to 'Aga saga' novels. A room to lounge in and allow the days and nights to unfold at their own pace. After spending time in these tranquil surroundings Cheryl felt it was going to be quite a shock to the system, returning to the hectic pace of London. She was looking forward to catching up with Sheila again. Sheila had offered to be a forwarding address for her post, and there was, apparently, quite a bundle waiting for her.

To avoid a long drive back to Calais, Joanna and Christine had both advised her to catch the ferry from Caen to Portsmouth and then take the train up to London.

'Is it easy to park at Caen?' Cheryl had enquired, remembering the complex roads she'd encountered en route to Bellefontaine. Her diversion round Rouen was still fresh in her mind.

'Oh, don't worry about that, we can drop you there. It isn't far and it'll be a good excuse for some shopping!' Christine assured her.

So the journey was organised. Cheryl only had to pack hand luggage for the trip, not the carload she had brought over with her. That was easily done, leaving her time to lounge about and daydream to her heart's content until she had to leave after lunch the next day. She had to promise Leanne that she would take her protective corn dolly with her, though. They shared a goodbye hug before Leanne went to bed that night; she had school early in the morning and wouldn't be around when Cheryl set off.

Hugging Leanne made Cheryl think of her own children. She was pleased Ross had offered to host them for the summer. All the uncertainty and disruption of moving would have meant they had very little rest over their summer holidays. She calculated she would be in Ash Tree Cottage before the autumn term began, so they could come down for a visit once she was settled with the cats. Their initial reaction when she told them about buying the cottage had been bewilderment and mild irritation.

'What do you want to move down there for?' Zoë had quizzed. 'When we went there as kids it was really boring. Not like London.'

'Well, Zoë, it's quite busy, actually. There are lots of artists and musicians and crafts people when you look. And you know, I'm quite looking forward to slowing down a bit. I've done my years of rushing around, and I can always catch the train to London whenever I want to see people. I'm rather hoping they'll want to come down to see me, too.'

'Suppose.' Zoë grudgingly acknowledged.

'What about you, Tom?' As usual he had kept his own counsel.

'I guess it's okay. I can't remember much about it except the stone beach and some sailing boats. Not much to look at, no trees or anything.'

'No, it isn't very green, I'll grant you that. But it does have a charm of its own. Lots of colourful fishing huts and curious little houses. And the harbour has a really thriving craft market at weekends. I think you'd enjoy that. Just come and stay and see how you feel.'

'He won't come down unless he can bring *Charlotte.*' Zoë opined with heavy emphasis on the name.

'Shut up, Zoë.'

'Oh, is Charlotte someone I should know about?' Cheryl asked, already ahead of the question. *He's got a girlfriend.*

'Not especially.' Tom replied guardedly.

'Not what I heard,' Zoë countered 'they go round like they're joined at the hip is what Alex told me.'

'Well, I like her.' Tom admitted looking rather bashful.

'Well, if you're happy I'm very pleased, Tom. Please feel free to bring her with you if you would like to. What about you, Zoë? Is there anyone you'd like to bring?'

Zoë shrugged. 'No, not really. I have been going out a bit with this guy, but he's down in Southampton, and it's not that great. We just hang out sometimes. He's not anyone I'm going to bring home for you to meet, Mum.'

'Well, the same applies. You are very welcome alone or with a friend. Doesn't have to be a boy, you know.'

Zoë smiled. Tom had settled back into his comfortable slouch.

I think, once they get used to it, they'll quite like having a seaside retreat. And if they want to keep in touch with their London friends they can always stay with Ross. It'll be fine. Yes. I'm quite looking forward to tomorrow, and staying with Sheila will be the perfect place to catch up with all the news.

CHAPTER THIRTY-NINE

Standing on the pavement in Trefall Avenue outside Cheryl's last known address, Stefan called Mark so see if he was available for a coffee. Mark, as it happened, was out and about himself and about to go past Soloman's.

'See you there in fifteen minutes, then.' Stefan hung up and headed for his car.

'I hope I can park at this time of day.'

Luck was on his side and a space materialised as if by magic on the opposite side of the road by the park, just as he drove up. Looking at the path in the park reminded Stefan of Cheryl's jogging figure. Mark was waiting in one of the booths.

'Hi, sorry I didn't get you anything. I wasn't sure whether you're on the caffeine or not this week.' Mark knew caffeine was Stefan's *bête noir*. Something he loved, but needed to avoid from time to time.

'No problem, mate. I'll just get myself something. Back in a mo.'

Stefan returned with a liquorice tea and sat opposite Mark. He wondered if Mark had been round to see Marguerite while he'd been out. It still felt strange and he wished the move would happen sooner, *so we can get it all over and done with.*

'So, you said you needed help to find some information?' Mark kicked off the conversation.

'Yes, you see there was someone I was very attracted to. Truth be told, we had a quick fling and then I stopped it because I was married.'

'I did wonder. Are we talking about that friend of Sheila's you mentioned a while back?'

'Yes, I am. Her name is Cheryl James.'

'Of course. Sheila introduced her to me and I did her reiki attunement.'

'The odd thing is, I found out I was teaching her son Tom at Goldsmark and he happened to mention that she was moving. I wasn't going to make contact at all until … well, you know, until all our arrangements have been sorted out and I'm a free man. But when he said she was leaving, I went round to her house and the estate agent said she had gone abroad. And now it seems like I've lost her, that if I don't find her soon it will be too late.'

'Ah, I see. And you want me to find out where she's gone?'

'I was hoping, as you know her that you'd know.'

'Sorry, mate. I haven't seen her for a while. I didn't even know she'd moved, although that would explain why she hasn't been at the last couple of reiki shares. I could ask Sheila if you like. They have been friends for even longer than us, I think. The chances are she'll know where Cheryl is. Do you want me to try?'

'Yes, please, that would be great.'

'How soon do you need to know? I could call her. Or, I think she's coming round at the weekend. That might be easier, face to face. I can't make any promises, though. Sheila might not be prepared to tell me.'

'OK, whatever you think would work best. You're right – Sheila may be cautious giving out the information. After all, if they're so close, Sheila will know all about me! I doubt that my reappearance will be very welcome after the way I behaved.'

'Leave it with me. I'll see what I can come up with.'

CHAPTER FORTY

One vanity case, and a small holdall. Is that what my life has shrunk to? Cheryl smiled when she thought of all the paraphernalia and clutter she used to marshal and co-ordinate in the family villa. The only things she'd kept were currently in store and waiting for a trip to the seaside. It seemed years ago, but was, in fact only eighteen months.

Goodness, if I'd been able to see what was coming back then, I'd have been horrified: a scandal, public humiliation, and a divorce; moving home; falling in love and getting it so wrong. It would have been so good if it could all have just fallen into place. If I'd fallen for a man who was a free agent. There are a lot of fallens in there – I'm a fallen woman!

Joanna had expressed pretty much the same idea over lunch. Although not quite so wantonly.

'Any regrets?' she asked, staring into Cheryl's eyes for truth.

'No. Absolutely not. My life is so different right now; I hardly recognise myself at times. But I'm so much more ... I feel so free. And bizarrely, even though I've let go of so much, I feel I have more control over what I bring into my life now. Does that make any sense?'

'Well, I'm not sure I'd have put it quite like that, but yes, I know what you mean,' Joanna acknowledged. 'My life is my own, perhaps? Have you decided what you're going to do about this amorous new publisher? It is him you're meeting for lunch, isn't it?'

Cheryl shrugged. 'Yes, and I'm quite looking forward to it. He certainly makes the effort to be charming and interested. I'll just give it a chance and see if he grows on me. Although, if he *is* going to me my publisher, it might be a bit awkward, mixing business and pleasure. I don't know, even if it goes nowhere, I'll have taken a step forward towards a new beginning. I'm almost getting used to having this blank canvas in front of me. It's never happened before. I've always had family and other obligations to consider. I was thinking yesterday that when I was at school, I was always aiming at exams and trying to please my parents and teachers. Same thing at university. Then came trying for a job, aiming to get promotion. And when a family got added, that was it. Every spare moment accounted for. Now it's just me, I can do what I like and it's a little scary sometimes. I can create whatever I want, but if it looks a mess, I'll only have myself to blame!'

Joanna laughed. 'I've done it the other round. Now *I've* got all the delights of fitting into family life, and I wouldn't have my painting, my Picasso, any other way! Maybe we need the contrast to make us see the worth of our choices.'

'Yes, you have your Picasso.' Cheryl expanded the conceit. 'Mine is more like a half-finished Monet. Lots of colour washes but not much definition yet. It's fun, though. Moving is going to be a big step. You *will* come and visit me in Whitstable? All of you? Promise?'

They promised.

And so, after the dishes were cleared, the household went its own way and Cheryl, with nothing further to do before her departure for London, swung lazily in the hammock between the apple trees.

'You've got to have apple trees in Normandy,' Christine had remarked. 'It is the home of Calvados.'

Although Cheryl didn't know it, Christine had slipped a small bottle of the famous Normandy apple liqueur in the holdall.

Cheryl let her thoughts drift back to their lunchtime conversation. Did she have any regrets?

Would she do the same again, given the chance? Even Stefan?

Yes, I would. She decided. *I know I got hurt. I know I attracted him by putting all my focus on him. But I was in love with him. I loved him. I loved me. I loved the feeling. Total exhilaration. And if it turned to the other extreme, well, that was just part of it. Even if I never get the chance to do that again, I'm glad I experienced it.* And so Cheryl and her musings swung back and forth in the dappled shade with the fragrance of apple wafting around her.

Maybe I should spend more time alone? Swing left. *Maybe if I'd woken up and addressed the problems at home and got divorced earlier, things might have been different.* Drift right. *Maybe I'll meet someone else I'll feel that strongly about?* Sway back .*I wouldn't have appreciated where I am now, if I'd tried to live this life when I was younger. Timing. It's all a matter of timing.* Inertia.

The final thought prompted her to look at her watch.

Two thirty. Time to go. I'd better say my goodbyes.

CHAPTER FORTY-ONE

'Yes, Stefan Wolfe. Yes, that *is* correct.'

Stefan was used to all the jokes about Steppenwolf.

'Born to be wild, eh, Sir?'

Do I look like a rock band? Still, he mused, *imagine if I had Arcturus on my passport.*

'Do you have any other luggage with you today, Sir?'

'No, just hand luggage.'

While waiting to board the flight Stefan fingered his ticket impatiently. 1045 BA0334 Wednesday, 16th July. He wondered what kind of reception he might get, but he knew he had to try.

Ninety minutes later, Stefan's plan of travelling light with only hand luggage worked. He breezed through customs and headed for the car hire desk. Navigating the polished floors, the forest of steel and stone pillars, hanging arrival screens and direction markers, he felt anxious. This man-made environment, sparsely endowed with plastic ferns and artificial fig trees, presented an alien yet necessary rite of passage to the outside world and his mission. His slate-grey eyes, dry in the air conditioning, squinted and scanned for the appropriate counter. Once located, he was dismayed to see the queue snaking out into the main thoroughfare. He ran his fingers through his hair and down the nape of his neck. Nothing for it, but to line up at the rear and wait.

After fifteen minutes he had only moved up one place. He shifted his weight to the other foot. This was madness! He didn't even know what he was going to say. What if, after all this, she wouldn't see him, or speak to him? His jaw clenched, and his shoulders rose before he let out a sigh and straightened up. The queue inched forward. He glanced up at the clock. *Christ! I've been in this queue for half an hour. It's almost one.*

Finally, he took possession of the keys. The car was basic and didn't have sat nav. Neither did Stefan own one. Halfway through the flight he had remembered that Mark did, but it was too late now to regret his failure to borrow it.

CHAPTER FORTY-TWO

Cheryl plopped out of the hammock onto the grass, sauntering her way back up the path where she could call to the open upstairs window.

'Joanna? Joanna, I need to make a move.'

'OK, darling. I'll be down in a sec,' Joanna's reply drifted through the gap. 'Cheryl, I think I can see the farm delivery at the gate. Be a love and collect the vegetable boxes.'

Cheryl strolled up the path, past the small apple orchard and round the cypress hedge, carrying her holdall to leave at the gate ready for her departure. The vegetable boxes were there, neatly stacked, and just beyond a small car was parked. As she gazed at it, backlit by sunlight, she was aware of the engine turning off.

That's not a very good place to park she noted, watching the man silhouetted inside fumbling for his things and opening the door. Something seemed to have startled him and he stood staring, apparently in her direction. It was hard to tell looking into the sun.

'Cheryl! Thank God!'

She knew that voice!

It couldn't be? I'm going mad.

She squinted into the light, watching the figure walking towards her, and as he came under the shade of the tallest cypress there was no mistake. *Oh my God!*

'Stefan! What are *you* doing *here*?'

'I've come to find you!'

What? What does he think he is doing? No, no, no! I'm not getting involved again. It's been so hard working my way back to some kind of equilibrium. And how has he found me?

'Stefan, I don't know what you're doing here, but I don't—'

'Cheryl!' his words rode over her protest. 'Stop! Just hear me out before you say anything.'

Her right foot drew back as he stepped forward, placing his hands on either side of her shoulders. They felt hot, and she sensed a tremor. He was bracing her to hear whatever plea he was about to make. His presence charged through her like a solar flare.

She stiffened against it. 'How did you find me?' No surrender. She'd been fooled by his mesmerising power before.

'Through Mark. I'm afraid he told Sheila a small white lie to get the address. She was very protective of you. She's a good friend.'

Cheryl stood motionless still trying to marshal her thoughts. *He's been using Mark and Sheila to track me down? Just when I'm starting afresh!* Her stomach lurched, as much in distaste, as in hope. *Why?*

'Cheryl, I have been texting you and calling you, but I couldn't get a reply. I assumed you were screening the calls and didn't want to talk. I can't say I blame you.'

'I have a new phone. The old one is packed, somewhere in London.'

'So you've never received my texts, or messages, then?'

'No, and I'm quite glad,' Cheryl allowed the animosity to flow out of her mouth. 'I've come here to relax and get a new perspective on my life. It's been really cathartic and I've had space to think about what I want and where I'm going. In fact, I am just about to leave. I'm due in London for a meeting with my publisher,' she added with a softened emphasis on the word *publisher,* allowing the implication of a more intimate relationship to linger in the air.

She registered a loosening of his grip on either side of her shoulders. The rebuff had hit home. Then his fingers re-engaged and his arms closed like a gentle vice. 'Cheryl,' he pleaded, 'I wouldn't have come all this way, to find you, if things were still the same. I wouldn't be that unkind – to either of us. So much has happened since I left you in Italy. It's over. I'm getting divorced. I'm going to be a free man. Free to love you – as you deserve.'

Holy shit! Just when you think you have a grip on life, when all the facts are sorted! Can I trust him? Can I trust myself to let go, again? Is this really the fairytale ending I dreamed of so often? Her thoughts addressed the higher realms, whoever they were today. *Please don't let this be some cruel joke.*

His eyes were steady and intense, and yet pleading. Her glance dropped to the pine needles on the ground beneath them. She couldn't look up. If she did, a decision might be made. She felt herself starting to tremble. He must feel it too, he was pulling her closer.

'Cheryl, I can't stop thinking about you. I never could. I stayed away because I thought it was the decent thing to do. You invade my waking thoughts, and what little sleep I get between wanting things to change. It really is true. While we were in Italy, my wife, Marguerite, was making a play for Mark.'

The shock of this news jerked her head up to look into his face.

'Mark? – reiki master, Mark?'

'Yes! They have been very close for a long time, and it all changed while I was away. He was waiting for me to return so we could talk it through. She doesn't care what I do so long as she gets a divorce and is free to go her own way. I wasn't going to come and find you until it was all settled, and then I went to your house and found you'd moved. Cheryl, I was frantic – I thought I'd lost you. I felt if I didn't come and find you, you might meet someone else and I would be too late. And it seems I might be. This publisher ...'

She couldn't bear it. Cheryl turned her head to look into the chaotic criss-cross leaves of the cypress hoping to find a refuge to think, her mind befuddled. Everything around her was changing. Joanna and Christine. Now Mark with Stefan's wife. *If they could reach for happiness why not me?* Could authenticity mean being brave enough to reach for what felt real? She was used to disappointment. Could she trust him? Could she trust her judgement?

'I'm just leaving, for London,' she repeated unnecessarily, buying time, allowing her heart and her head to come into some sort of harmonic agreement.

'Well, thank God I got here in time, then. Cheryl, I've said what I came to say. Is it too late? Have you given up on me and found someone else? I know we don't know each other very well, but I'm quite clear I want to be with you with all my heart. This is no ordinary attraction I feel.'

A whisper of a breeze ruffled through the trees, the only sound between them. Cheryl's thoughts were spinning almost too fast to catch hold of them. Her heart was hammering as hard as it had the first night they met. Her gaze dropped, her eyes tried to focus on the reality of her cases and the ground her feet could feel beneath them. Everything else seemed surreal.

It is real. I'm not imagining this. It's like a film scene. I am standing in this idyll, amongst the apple blossom looking into the eyes of the man I've fantasized about for months – the man who broke my heart and shattered my dreams. This man, I'm standing in his arms, the man I loved and who now says we can be together. He wants us to be together. Do I want us to be together? If I'm painting this picture, writing this story, what do I want? I'm totally free to choose – marrying Ross was sort of inevitable, not really a choice. This feels like freefall. I have never been so free, or so scared. Angels, help! I'm so scared.

A wave of heat flushed through her, even as the breeze chilled her skin, goose bumps raising the hair on her arms. *Angel bumps she'd heard them called.*

She could no longer feel the heat of his right hand on her shoulder; it was against her left cheek now, gently guiding her to look and engage with him.

'Cheryl? Say something. Please! Am I too late?

Cheryl shook her head with a bemused smile. She looked into the soul-mirror of his eyes, searching for her answer and found her truth. 'Another few minutes and we would have missed each other. Again. Stefan, you *do remember* what the book, I was writing in Italy, was called, don't you?'

'Yes, *Perfect Timing*. And I remember this, too.'

Stefan's other hand rose to cup her face. She allowed herself to be drawn slowly closer, holding her eyes with his until the last moment when their lips touched, their eyes closed and their hearts and souls connected.

The decision was made. *Thank you, and bless you.* Cheryl mentally offered to whichever of her angelic team was on the case. Her heart opened and she allowed the love to flow between them. *For once I can say with all my heart, I love you. It's safe. It's real. I love you.*

They stood caressing each other's face, until the sound of footsteps approaching along the gravel drive prompted them apart. Cheryl took his hand and they walked back towards the house, into their future. Neither of them could explain whence the three white feathers appeared, nor when they arrived. But they were sure that they weren't there a moment ago.

In Pursuit of Perfect Timing

Acknowledgements

Not until you try to write a book, do you realise how many people will walk alongside you with advice, input and support. Thanks are owed to all my friends who have endured listening to me talk about the process for years. Jemma Forte, thank you for inviting me to all your book launches and inspiring me to keep going. In particular, I owe gratitude to Mark Husson who offered the platform that started it all; C.A. Brooks for her advice; to Maggie Hammond whose writing course and editorial review helped turn a muddle into a story; to Claire Woodward for further editorial development reading; and to Miles Allen for advice and preparing it for publishing; to Claire Wicks for proofreading; to Leonie Bunch for the cover design. And most of all to you for choosing to purchase and read the result.

Made in the USA
Lexington, KY
20 October 2015